REVENGE OF THE SEQUEL

# DIMENSION WHY 2

## REVENGE OF THE SEQUEL

## JOHN CUSICK

HARPER
An Imprint of HarperCollins Publishers

Library of Congress Control Number: 2021938243
ISBN 978-0-06-293761-2

Typography by Chris Kwon
21 22 23 24 25   PC/LSCH   10 9 8 7 6 5 4 3 2 1
❖
First Edition

This book is dedicated to its first reader,
Ms. Molly C. of Brooklyn,
as well as to its most recent.
(That'd be you.)

"There's something very familiar about all this."
   —**Biff Tannen,** *Back to the Future Part II*

"Let's do this one more time."
   —**Nicki Minaj, "Starships"**

## A Brief Note on Sequels

**THE SINGLE BESTSELLING BOOK** in the galaxy is, of course, *ShadowMancer Wars*, the 100-percent-true story of how the space wizard known as the ShadowMancer tried to erase everyone in the universe and was thwarted by a plucky young space cadet, Skylar Powerstance, who sacrificed herself to save the galaxy.

This is not that book.

This is not even the sequel to that book.

This is the sequel to a book called *DIMENSION WHY: How to Save the Universe Without Really Trying.*

It's been said by many wise philosophers that sequels are never as good as the original. It's also been theorized that the universe itself is but the continuation of some other, earlier form of existence, and that the Creators of the Universe are merely trying to get it right the second time around.

Many agree that if this is the case, the universe is probably due for a reboot.

## LISTEN.

It began a long time ago, in a small pocket of our galaxy not often visited by outsiders.

Orbiting a medium-sized yellow sun was a medium-sized blue-and-green planet. It was a perfectly average planet, with a handful of nice continents and some pretty buttes if you knew where to look. The only remarkable thing about this planet was this: it was shockingly overpopulated. In fact, there wasn't a square foot of the place that didn't have at least three people trying to stand on it.

One of these life-forms was a young girl named Sandy. She lived in a modest house with her mother and father and a dog named Pogo. Also living in the modest house were seven other families, bringing the total population of this two-bedroom home to about thirty-two people, plus one not very bright dog.

Sandy had not spent a single moment alone her entire life. In fact, her species didn't even have a word for loneliness.

Neither did it have a word for solitude, privacy, or elbow room.

"What about outer space?" Sandy asked her mother at dinner one night. At least, she was pretty sure it was her mother. All she could really make out through the crowd was a familiar bouncing ponytail.

"What about it?" her mother asked, gingerly removing someone's elbow from her plate.

"Maybe if we went to outer space, there would be more room," said Sandy.

"More room?" asked one half of the two sets of twins who lived in the first-floor bathroom. "Why would you need more room?"

"Sometimes," said Sandy, as someone politely lifted her above their head so they could squeeze by before gingerly setting her back down, "I feel like I want to be . . . like I want to be . . ." Sandy searched for the word, but the one she wanted didn't exist in her language. "Not . . . around people . . . so much . . . all the time."

"What a ridiculous thing to say," said her mother.

Sandy wanted to continue the conversation, but just then the doorbell rang, announcing twenty-five neighbors who'd popped in just to say hello.

That night in bed, between the elderly couple who slept on her right and the three toddlers who bunked on her left, Sandy lay awake, dreaming of a place where there was no one but her. A big open and dark place, without light or noise. *Well, maybe Pogo could come, too*, she thought. Pogo was curled up at the edge of the bed, affectionately chewing on a sock.

Sandy turned to look out the window. The first star of the night was visible, sticking like a glittering burr to the black hide of night. She closed her eyes and made a wish.

And the star exploded.

Or at least it appeared to. There was a flash of light, immense and hauntingly silent, and for a moment Sandy's street was so brightly illuminated it might have been midday. Then the light was gone, and the star was where it had been, but something new had arrived in the night sky.

Sandy untangled herself from the knot of arms and knees, threw on a bathrobe, and dashed downstairs and out into the street, Pogo bounding after her.

The street was dark, but Sandy could make out the lumpy forms of people slumbering on porches, in yards, and in their vehicles. The air was filled with the ambient sound of dozens upon dozens of snorers. Other than that, things were quiet and dark. The thing that had come out of the blinding light in the sky arced gracefully above the rooftops. At first it was impossible to tell the size of it, or quite how far away it was, but as the object drew near, Sandy saw that it was long and thin, like a steel rod. Both ends glowed with a fearsome yellow light, but close-up, it was actually quite small.

It buzzed her street, slipped behind the tree line, then reemerged, zagging through the air like something out of control—which it was. The strange object tumbled end over end, and then fell gracelessly to the ground, as if a baton twirler had tossed it into the air, forgotten about it, and gone for coffee.

The object bounced once, and then came to rest in the street, its strange lights dimming and finally going out.

Sandy was awestruck.

Pogo whimpered, also awestruck, though the thing that had awed him was a pinecone.

Sandy approached the strange little baton, but just as she did, a compartment opened in its side. A little green man, no taller than a thumbtack, hobbled out. The tiny man looked up at Sandy, but his large gray eyes didn't seem to see her. Instead, with a gasp the alien collapsed onto the concrete . . . and dissolved into nothing.

Sandy stared for a long time. Pogo, who had gotten himself lost in a nearby bush, stuck his head out into the street and whimpered once more for good measure. The sound seemed to wake Sandy from a dream. She crouched and dared herself to touch the little baton-like spacecraft. It was cool. She wrapped her hand around it. She picked it up. It was light. As she held it, the lights on both ends began to glow once more, and Sandy felt a charge thrill up her arm and into her brain.

It was, she knew instantly, a magic wand.

And though Sandy herself could not see it, this was the moment her eyes, which had been a pretty hazel with green flecks, turned a brilliant white.

"I want to be . . . *alone*," she said, as if the wand had taught her the word she needed.

An arc of white-yellow light crackled from one end of Sandy's wand. There was a horrible flash, and when Sandy's eyes adjusted to the darkness once more, something had changed. At first, she couldn't tell what was different, only that the air had grown somehow . . . *smoother*.

Then she realized what it was. The night was no longer filled with the sound of snores.

The lumps of sleeping bodies had vanished, without ceremony, without sound. It was as if they had never been there in the first place.

This, then, was *silence*. This, then, was *solitude*.

Sandy loved it.

She turned now to Pogo, who tilted his head and barked at her.

An arc of white-yellow light crackled from Sandy's wand. The wind gusted, lights flashed, and where Pogo had been trembling now stood a beautiful, enormous, golden dragon. The beast stretched its long neck, regarded its new scales, which shone in the moonlight, and flexed its mighty wings.

Then it regarded its master and whimpered expectantly.

With still, deliberate movements, Sandy climbed onto the dragon's back.

"Come, steed," she said. Her voice was hollow—still her own, yet ancient, as if some unknowable power had seeped into her blood, into her bones. She sat astride the great golden dragon in her bathrobe and surveyed the neighborhood before her: the houses, the trees, the pop-up tents and empty sleeping bags littering the lawns.

Then Sandy turned her eyes to the sky and the billion stars glittering there.

"Them next," said the girl, for she was no longer quite Sandy.

And with that the dragon began to beat its massive wings and together they climbed into the sky.

The name of this planet, whatever it had been before the space wizard found her wand, is now lost to history. Today, everyone in the civilized galaxy knows it as Ombre Prime, the Dead World, home of the ShadowMancer.

# PART 1

## THE LAST DAYS OF FLIGHTY SHINY THING UNIVERSITY

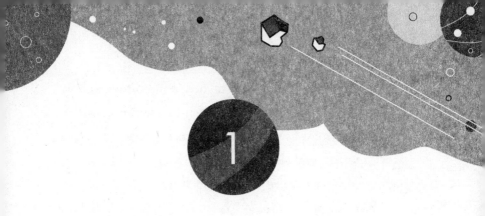

**DEEP IN THE EASTERN** arm of the Milky Way, a hyper-gate turned in space. Its great metallic ring, three hundred miles in diameter, rotated slowly in the dark, aglow with tiny lights. Then, with a great flash and ripple of quantum sauce, a vessel emerged from its depths.

It wasn't a large vessel—only fifty meters from prow to tail fin—with the words *Econo-Shuttle* written across the side. As the shuttle banked, something small, dark, and boxy could be seen clinging to its underside: a second ship stowing away on the belly of the larger craft. Jets *whooshed*, couplings disengaged, and the two ships sailed off in opposite directions. The Econo-Shuttle made for a nearby refueling station and the smaller craft for a small blue planet hanging like a jewel in the Venulian night.

The ship was a Volvo Rescue Wagon. The world was Venus Beta, planet of the cats.

On board the Rescue Wagon sat a girl who was a long way from home. Her name was Lola Ray, and since takeoff her brow had been furrowed, stitched, and knitted, and was on its way to being positively French-braided in consternation. The reason was this: Lola had recently learned that her father, mother, and sisters were quite possibly still alive and trapped in a place called Dimension Why.

"*Don't eat my heart, baby,*" her traveling companion sang along to the radio. "*I was saving it in that jarrrrr. . . . You might think I wasn't gonna eat it / But that don't mean that you can treat it . . . that wayyyyy. . . .*"

The boy, who was now performing a very clumsy but enthusiastic drum solo on the steering wheel, was none other than Phineas Fogg, kid trillionaire and heir to the Fogg-Bolus Hypergate and Baked Beans Corporation. His brow was smooth as a fresh-minted million-dollar bill.

"I know you're worried about your family," Phin said, "but this is totally a solvable problem! Professor Donut knows everything about parallel worlds and pocket dimensions. If anyone can tell us how to find Dimension Why, it's him."

Lola looked out at the wash of stars, and at the blue dot of Venus Beta growing larger in their frontal view screen. "And what if he doesn't know?"

"We'll find someone who does," said Phin. "Well, I mean, *I* probably will. You'll just sit there and ask what's going on all the time."

Lola considered punching him, and then decided he was probably right. Phin was almost always right. And even when he wasn't, he was always certain.

"Fine," she said, and then after a moment, "turn up the music."

"*Everybody garglepooch!*" Phin sang as the next song came on. "*Garglepooch, garglepooch . . . !*"

Lola allowed herself a small grin. With Phin, it was impossible not to always have at least a little bit of fun.

"*Everybody garglepooch!*" she joined in. She had never heard the song, but it was one of those ultracatchy pop tunes that, after hearing the chorus once, one can pretty much just sing along.

"*Garglepooch! Garglepooch! Everybody gonna go garglepooch!*" they sang together, both unaware that in old Venulian, the term *garglepooch* means "explode and die horribly in a fiery cataclysm, to be incinerated so exhaustively even your dreams are burned."

But then, who pays attention to the lyrics?

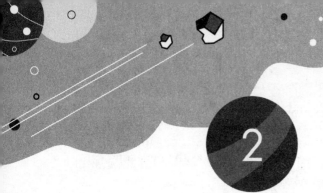

**IT WAS DAWN ON** the planet of the cats.

The sun had just begun to rise, and the Nip fields were glistening with dew. In the Cardboard Mountains, spangle fish were leaping upstream, scales glinting, dorsal bells jingling. Feather fruit swung from the feather fruit trees, and the Rebirds sang their morning song, eager for a big day of flying around, being caught and killed, and then reanimating a dozen times before bed. It was paradise—assuming, of course, you were a cat.

The spires of Flighty Shiny Thing University shone. First-year students hurried along the parapets, their tails twitching in anticipation of another day of higher cat learning. Soon the lecture halls would be filled with students of every stripe and spot, ready to hear the latest research into the nutritional value of mice, the existential necessity of hairballs, and to debate the eternal cat question—*What Was That Noise Outside?*

Standing in one of the highest windows in one of the tallest towers, Professor Donut tapped his cane, his orange fur bristling in anticipation. Behind him, a mottled tabby wrung his paws and considered clearing his throat. Instead, after waiting what he judged to be the most respectful amount of time, he spoke.

"Uh, Professor Donut?"

"What is it, Assistant Professor Tinkle Poops?"

"Uh." Assistant Professor Tinkle Poops decided to clear his throat after all. "I'm sorry to interrupt your morning staring-at-the-wall meditation, but the Academic Committee meeting started ten minutes ago, and we were supposed to be—"

"Assistant Professor Tinkle Poops," said Professor Donut with the kind of grim seriousness only a highly educated cat can manage, "what am I doing right now?"

The tabby wrung his paws some more, then smoothed down his left ear, which had a habit of folding over itself when its owner fidgeted. Professor Donut was one of the most brilliant minds in the galaxy, a pioneer in the Cute Sciences, and a respected member of the university faculty. He also had a habit of missing meetings and ignoring the chancellor's messages, which were often relayed to Assistant Professor Tinkle Poops, accompanied by promises of where Assistant Professor Tinkle Poops could stick his academic future if Professor Donut didn't start showing up to things on time.

"Um," said Tinkle Poops, hoping to make this conversation

go as quickly as possible. "You're . . . staring out the window, Professor?"

"Correct," said Professor Donut. "So it's not my staring-at-the-*wall* meditation you're interrupting, is it?"

"Oh, uh . . ."

"I'm looking out the window," said Professor Donut, "because I heard a noise out there."

"Hmm," said Assistant Professor Tinkle Poops, unsure if this was some kind of intellectual metaphor, or if the professor had literally heard something out the window.

"Do you know what I heard?" the professor asked.

"No, Professor."

For the first time, Professor Donut turned to regard his assistant. "I heard the approach of friends," he said with a wise smile.

This made Tinkle Poops feel not a bit better. Professor Donut kept some strange company. For instance, he'd just returned to teaching after a ten-year sabbatical, which he had spent hanging out with a time traveler, a child trillionaire, and a fungal brain the size of a planet. Whoever was coming to see Professor Donut, Tinkle Poops was not sure he wanted to split a spangle fish with them.

"Look," said Professor Donut, gesturing with his cane. "They're coming."

Assistant Professor Tinkle Poops looked where Professor Donut pointed. The perfect sky was clear except for a single object. Something large was flying toward them very quickly. It looked less like a spaceship and more like an enormous shaggy beast.

"*That* is your friend?"

"*Those* are my friends," said Professor Donut.

"What?" said Assistant Professor Tinkle Poops. "Behind the mastodon?"

"No," said Professor Donut. "*Inside it.*"

The Majulook SuperFake cloaking device is one of the most unique methods of spaceship camouflage in the civilized galaxy. It's less reliable than the Wareja-Go Total Invisibility Sheath, and easier to disable than the ultrasecure Never-saw-M SuperCloak 9000. But what it does offer, which those systems do not, is a shuffle button.

As Phin and Lola's Volvo Rescue Wagon came in for a landing, their cloaking device shuffled through a few old favorites, making the ship appear to be, in this order: a mastodon, a box of frozen steaks, an armored battle cruiser, a drinks trolley, a handbag, a 1970s New York City yellow-checked taxicab, and a plate of sliced pears.

A crowd had gathered in the courtyard where the Rescue Wagon was coming in for a landing. Outside ships did not often visit their remote and secluded university, especially ships this strange.

"I like how it challenges your assumptions of what a

spaceship is," said one cat in a pair of small round spectacles.

"Mmm." Another nodded sagely and sipped her skinny latte. "It has a real *otherness*."

The Wagon lowered itself dustily to the flagstones, settling at last on its true form: a small and boxy escape pod that someone had outfitted with a racing stripe and a pair of adorable fuzzy ears stuck to the roof.

A hush descended as the engines died.

Professor Donut emerged from the crowd, hobbling a bit with his cane, and approached the vessel with arms flung wide.

"Kids!"

The ship's door opened, and two intrepid young explorers emerged. To pretty much everyone, they were the biggest celebrities in the whole wide universe, the Child of Space and the Child of Time, heroes both who helped save reality from being permanently unraveled. But to Professor Donut they were Phin and Lola, and he accepted their hugs and rubbed his big furry face on their tummies.

"Oh!" said Lola, noticing the crowd gathered around them. "That is a lot of cats. Hello. Hi."

Lola was in a state. She was clutching to her chest a small metallic lockbox, of a kind commonly found on twenty-first-century Earth, but to Lola it was the most precious object in the universe. First, it had belonged to her father, the inventor Dr. Alfonso Ray. Second, it had her name stenciled on the side and a message to her tucked inside—a message that had waited, unfading, for Lola to find it a thousand years hence.

"I received your communiqué," the professor now said with grim seriousness. "A message from Lola's father, you say?"

"I'm certain it's from him," said Lola. "Believe me, this box is the only thing keeping me from freaking out about all these cats wearing waistcoats and bomber jackets."

"*That one's got a little Hacky Sack!*" Phin hissed gleefully.

"*I know!*" Lola whispered, and tried to collect herself.

Phineas Fogg was also in a state, one of near-delirious excitement. Up until a few months ago he'd spent most of his life in his parents' astronomically priced and catastrophically under-insured penthouse, waiting for the day he could step out his front door and explore the universe. And it was Lola Ray who had made that happen. In the weeks that followed, she'd nearly gotten him blown up, vaporized, arrested, and tossed into a dying star, but today was a new day, a fresh adventure, and he couldn't wait for the chance to do it all again.

"Let me see it," said Professor Donut, gesturing to the lockbox.

Lola glanced at Phin, who nodded, before gingerly open-ing the lid and showing the professor what was inside.

"What is the meaning of this?" came a commanding voice

from the edge of the courtyard.

The crowd, which was already hushed, seemed to stop breathing.

The cat who had come forward was important—and not just in the way that every cat thinks she's important. This cat would have had gravitas no matter what her species—she would have made a compelling and intimidating water bug. She stood taller than the others, and wore a long flowing robe and sash, befitting her station. Her muzzle was flecked with gray, and though one eye was cloudy, the other was sharp and yellow as a detention slip.

"Chancellor Mittens," said Professor Donut, "allow me to introduce my friends . . ."

"Hello, there!" said Phin in the tone of a boy who is quite sure everyone in the galaxy is delighted to meet him. "Pleasure to meet you. As official ambassadors of Earth, let me just say that you are indeed *adorable*, and—"

"I know who you are," the chancellor snapped. Phin did a double take, and then backed away slowly, like a party clown who's just realized he's burst into the wrong birthday party.

"Ah," he said. "Hm."

"Professor Donut," the chancellor continued. "Are you aware we had an Academic Committee meeting this morning?"

"Why yes," said Professor Donut. "I'm sorry I wasn't able to make it."

"Professor Donut," Chancellor Mittens pressed on. "Are you also aware that you have missed . . ." The professor gestured to a second, smaller cat. "How many Academic Committee meetings was it, Provost Buttercup?"

"Two thousand, four hundred, and forty-three Academic Committee meetings, Chancellor."

Phin let out a long, low whistle. Lola elbowed him.

"I," said Professor Donut, bringing himself up to full height, which was less than half Phin's and Lola's, "have tenure."

"What you have," growled the chancellor, "is a probationary hearing tomorrow at eight a.m. sharp." With this pronouncement she turned her gaze on the travelers. "And you."

"Us?" said Lola, who had a problem with authority, in that she felt terrible whenever it wasn't happy with her. "I mean, *us*, Your, um . . . Chancellorship?"

"We aren't accustomed to visitors here. This is a place for cats to study in peace." The chancellor's whiskers twitched. "I trust there won't be any trouble from you two."

Phin opened his mouth to speak, and Lola stopped him, knowing that Phin also had a problem with authority, in that he made it break out in hives.

"You'll have no trouble from us," Lola said. "We just need Professor Donut's help, then we'll be on our way."

The chancellor appraised Lola, as if wondering what she

might look like left on someone's back porch. "Very well."

With that, the Academic Committee, including the chancellor and the provost, turned to leave.

"Come," said Professor Donut. "A moment to lose," he added, "is what we haven't."

As the crowd began to disperse and Professor Donut led the children toward the courtyard's exit, a small cat in an adorable blue uniform tugged on Phin's cuff.

"Excuse me, sir," he said, "but I'm afraid this is a no-parking zone. You'll have to move your plate of sliced pears . . . er, your ship."

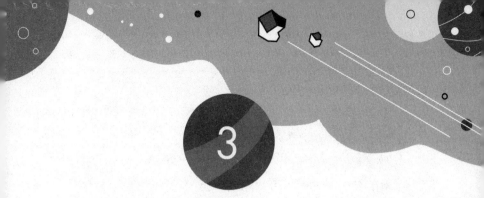

3

". . . AND THAT WAS 'Everybody Garglepooch' by Toady and the RocketButts, right here on WVEN, Venulian Radio, the Mix!

"I'm Flag Jackson. Coming up to the top of the hour and the news: Absolutely nothing interesting happened today. The Warlords of Crim have called a temporary cease-fire for the Festival of St. Blubflub. Our galaxy's new privatized health care service continues to run smoothly with no emergencies to handle. In entertainment, production continues on A Hero's Tale, the miniseries chronicling the Battle of Singularity City. All the actors in it are getting along famously and not dating or breaking up with one another at all. Keep up the great work, guys!

"Oops! Here's a bit of news that might interest our more literary listeners: after a thousand years at the top of the charts, ShadowMancer Wars has slipped to number two on the Galactic Gazette's Bestselling Books list, supplanted by Grango Hardtossel's Food Synthesizer Meals for One: How to Eat Without Experiencing Any Pleasure at All. Way to go, Grango!

*"After the break we'll be kicking things off with our Top 100 countdown of the best Arachnopod love songs. Be our ten thousandth caller and you'll get a visit from WVEN's own Phyllis the Party Rhino! And now, here's Hannah Starfoot with an important message about Gold's Medicated Tentacle Cream. Made for tentacles, by tentacles. Stay tuned!"*

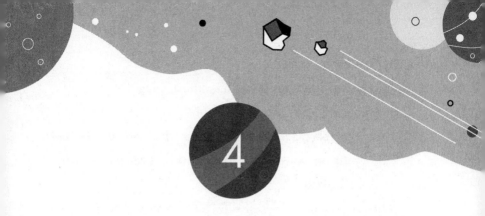

**THERE IS A BRANCH** of intellectual study known as the Cute Sciences. It explores the theory that cuteness—like gravity and electromagnetism—is a fundamental force of the universe. Research has shown that cute spacecrafts have a greater statistical likelihood of getting where they're going, and that hang gliders wearing bunny costumes have a much greater chance of surviving an encounter with the ground.

Professor Donut was an expert in the Cute Sciences, and boy did his lab show it.

Set on a high floor, overlooking the valley, the room itself was long and narrow, arrayed with workstations that bubbled, steamed, rang, and hummed with his experiments. A picture of a piglet in a bow tie was hooked to electrodes, and a toy hamburger phone lay half dissected on a table. There were also several large display screens. What they were for Lola couldn't imagine, but someone had hot-glued crepe fur and googly eyes to them, so that they resembled big, flat Muppets.

"Children," said Professor Donut, having finished his arrangements. "The box, please."

Gingerly, Lola placed on the counter what had become, to her, the most precious object in the world. Professor Donut opened the lockbox's heavy lid.

There were two objects inside. First, a note. This is what it said:

> Dear Lola Girl,
> I'm so sorry for what's happened to you. I fear something may have gone terribly wrong and it's all my fault.
> If you get this note, whenever you get it, your mother and sisters and I will be waiting for you.
> Find us in Dimension Why.
> Love, Dad

Included with the note was a Twinkie, still fresh as the day it was sealed in its cellophane wrapping nearly eleven centuries ago.

"Oh, actually," said Lola, clearing her throat. "If you don't need the Twinkie, I'd sort of like to keep it. You know, as a . . . oh," she added, as the professor set the Twinkie aside, not in the trash bin as Lola'd expected, but on an important-looking little pedestal with blinking lights up the front.

"Oh," Lola said again, as Professor Donut unceremoniously clapped the lockbox shut and shoved it off the workstation. "Oh," Lola said a third time as the lockbox landed with a dull thud in the trash bin. She added a final "oh," just for good measure, as the little trash bin stood up on tiny robotic legs, hobbled over to the incinerator, and jumped in.

"It's the Twinkie, children," said the professor, tapping a button on the little pedestal with the blinking lights up the front. In a flash a translucent dome enveloped the little snack cake. The containment field's surface was oily, like a soap bubble, but seemed solid as glass. "This Twinkie holds the key!"

"But . . . it's just a Twinkie," said Lola. "My dad used to leave them in my lunch box, even after Momma said we had to cut back on sugar."

"Ah," said Professor Donut. "But it is also one of the few materials your father *knew* he could leave you that would not expire or decompose for *centuries*. It's the perfect means to preserve the historical record." He ran a paw over the containment field's shimmering surface in a kind of awe. "Well, surely you see it, don't you?"

"What?" said Phin. "Behind the Twinkie?"

"*On* the Twinkie!" said Professor Donut. "Look closer!"

Phin and Lola brought their noses to the containment field's edge. They looked. They looked closer. They scrunched up their faces in ways that didn't help them see any better, but that let Professor Donut know they were really looking hard now.

Through it all, the Twinkie persisted in its Twinkiness.

"Is this like the thing where you unfocus your eyes and a 3D image appears?" said Lola.

"Here," said Professor Donut, and punched a few buttons on the containment unit's base.

On the screens hanging above them, an image of the Twinkie appeared. Professor Donut pressed a few more buttons and the image focused, then zoomed in until the yellow skin of the snack cake took up the entire display. Up close, the flesh looked like a satellite view of some barren desert planet, its cakey crenulations like the ridges and bluffs of a rocky yellow wasteland. But there was something else, shadows in the crinkles, almost like . . .

"Is that writing?" said Lola.

There were squiggles. Squiggles covering the whole of the Twinkie, just barely darker than the rest. Phin and Lola had failed to notice them for several reasons. First, the writing, if that's what it was, was so faint it was nearly invisible. Second, if it was in fact "writing," it was in a language neither of them had ever seen before. And finally: Who looks that closely at a Twinkie?

Phin went, "Hm."

"They're burns," said Professor Donut. "Very, very light ones. Your father could have inscribed them with a 3D laser array and a simple computational algorithm. The heat from the laser would color the Twinkie without compromising the cellophane seal. The technology would have been available to him in your time."

"What are you saying?" said Lola. "My father wrote me a message on this Twinkie?"

"It could be a message," said Phin, tapping his chin. "It could be something else."

"Like a picture?" said Lola, her pulse quickening. "Or maybe . . . a *map*?"

"A map," said Professor Donut with awe, ". . . to Dimension Why."

Lola thought, if this were a television show, right then would have been the perfect time for a dramatic stab of music. But since it wasn't, the only sound was the whir of Professor Donut's instruments.

He flicked a few more buttons and suddenly the image of the Twinkie distorted, stretching and straightening out like a globe flattened into a two-dimensional plane. Her father's writing had been highlighted in green, but Lola could no more understand it now than a moment ago. Numerals, dashes, and decimals seemed to topple over each other in the mind-boggling cacophony of mathematics.

"It *is* an equation!" said Phin.

Lola shook her head. "But why would Papa send me math?"

"If your father left a note to find him in Dimension Why, it only follows he would leave you a *way* to find him," said Professor Donut. "It is my contention that before us are the *coordinates* of Dimension Why. You were right, Lola, it is a map. A *mathematical* map to the space between spaces."

"How do we read it?" Lola said.

"*We* do nothing," said Professor Donut. He smiled at Lola. "Not to worry. Your father's work is profound, but I should be able to decipher it. This will only take a moment."

With this pronouncement, Professor Donut wandered off to a nearby workstation to make tea. Lola took the opportunity to tug on Phin's sleeve.

"What is it?" she asked.

Phin had been unusually quiet since sending the Rescue Wagon back into orbit to wait for them. He was doing the thing he sometimes did: frowning, staring hard at stuff for a bit, then letting his eyes trace around the room, as if following their own train of thought. It was a train Lola wasn't sure she wanted to hop on.

"This is good," he said.

"I know," she whispered, trying to contain the excitement in her voice. "I think this might actually be working."

"Oh, sorry," said Phin. "Did I say good? I meant incredibly, terrifyingly bad." He boggled his eyes at her. "Do you want me to tell you why?"

"I suppose so . . . ," said Lola. "But keep smiling so it sounds less horrible."

Phin's grin stretched to an unnatural width. "*Well*. If the professor's right, that makes this Twinkie the most dangerous object in the universe—"

"Actually," said Lola, cutting him off, "don't do it with the smile. That's worse."

"Right," said Phin. "Well. What we have here is a harmless little snack cake that might very well offer a doorway to another dimension. Who knows what kind of power Dimension Why holds, or what kind of beings live there? Plus, opening this door could grant the wrong person the ability to move freely through time, potentially changing the course of history or the fabric of reality itself! It's basically Pandora's . . . well, Twinkie." Phin's eyes widened in terrible wonder. "A weapon of mass confection."

Lola thought about things, and how they had a habit of going catastrophically wrong. She was about to say something about this when Phin took her hand, which she hadn't realized she'd been clenching. She squeezed back.

Professor Donut returned with his tea. "I'm afraid Phineas is quite right. This Twinkie can now be considered an object of universal significance and," he added, letting the steam collect around his whiskers dramatically, "peril."

They were quiet for a moment. Then Lola said, "Well, at

least no one knows about it but us three."

Before anyone could agree that yes, it was an awfully good thing that no one else knew about the cosmic significance of Lola's snack cake, there came a blinding flash of light. At first, Lola thought the sun had gone supernova, but there was no blast. Only the flash, and the utter silence accompanying it. One minute, Phin, and Lola, and Professor Donut were just standing there, looking reverently at the Twinkie in question, and the next, Phin, and Lola, and Professor Donut were just standing there, blinking, standing next to an enormous gold dragon with a small child dressed in her bathrobe riding on its back.

"I shall have it," came a voice that was at once young and incredibly old.

Before anyone could say anything or even so much as gawp, a second blinding flash left them all blinking and rubbing the glare from their eyes. When they could see again, the containment field was empty, and the Twinkie was, of course, gone. So were the dragon and the girl.

"Well, that was—" said Phin, and it's a shame the planet exploded right then, because what he was going to say was super clever and would have been the perfect funny note to end the chapter on.

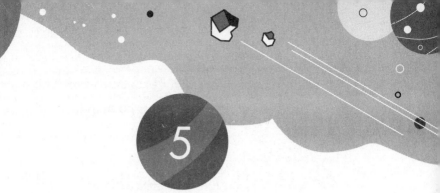

5

**THERE'S AN OLD ADAGE** that asks: If a planet explodes, and there's no one around to hear it, does it even make a sound? This is widely considered to be a stupid question for an adage to ask, since the answer is obviously *no*. There is no sound in the vacuum of space, and therefore exploding planets are, as any good astrophysicist will tell you, silent but deadly.

Those who *have* been near a planet when it explodes say that astrophysicists are a bunch of out-of-touch nerds. You can absolutely hear it when a whole planet goes up like a dynamite piñata just a few million miles from where you're having lunch. Just you try it and see.

In fact, in a galaxy as large as ours, with over two hundred billion stars, each with its own system of local orbiting bodies, planets are exploding practically all the time. But that doesn't mean no one cares, or that no one takes notice.

There was darkness. And then, in the darkness, was Phin.

"Lola?"

He had no lips to speak, no lungs to push air past his nonexistent vocal cords, and so there was no sound.

"Hello?"

Darkness and silence answered.

Phin considered he might be dead. He figured in all likelihood he was dead, and that this was the afterlife. And so far at least, being dead was boring.

"Hellooo . . . ," he tried again. "Hellooooo. Hello, hello, hello . . . ," he went on, determined to continue until someone, somewhere, told him to stop, that he was being annoying. And amazingly, this seemed to work. After his forty-fifth or forty-sixth *hello*, something answered. The words resolved themselves in Phin's mind as clear and unbidden as a sudden flash of memory—and they were not his own.

This is what they said:

*"Do not be alarmed. You are not dead."*

"Oh," said-thought Phin, and if he'd had hands, he would have folded them behind his head if he'd had one of those too. "Well, that's all right, then."

*"You are currently experiencing"*—the words filled his mind—*"corporeal difficulties."*

Phin blinked, an especially absurd thing to do in the dark, without eyes or eyelids, but he did it anyway. He cleared his throat, which was also unnecessary since he didn't have a throat. "I'm sorry. *What?*"

*"All of our representatives are currently assisting other cus-*
*tomers. Please be patient."*

Though he had no skin, and there was no breeze to chill
him, Phin felt himself go cold.

*"This near-death experience,"* came the words, *"may be*
*monitored for quality assurance."*

This was followed by soothing music.

Phin told himself not to panic. This was exactly the sort of
situation in which panicking was inadvisable. Panicking could
lead to hyperventilation, hypertension, and hyper-screaming,
all of which are very bad for the lungs, veins, and throat.
Then Phin suddenly remembered he no longer had any of
these, and so went right ahead and panicked.

*"All of our representatives are currently assisting other cus-*
*tomers,"* the words repeated. *"Screaming won't help."*

"Let me out of here!" Phin bellowed, or rather didn't bel-
low. "Do you have any idea who I am?"

This statement usually got *some* kind of reaction, even if
it was only a sneer and a "No. Am I supposed to?" And this
was Phin's favorite sort of response, because it meant he got
to explain what a fabulously important person he was.

The words, or whoever was beaming them into his mind,
had no response to this.

But then an idea seized him, an idea so radical, wacky, and
daft it could actually work. "Lola!" He would try doing what

Lola would do. He would try being polite. "Um, hello," he said in his most Lola-like tone. "How are you, disembodied-words person? That's great. I'd love to hear all about your hopes and dreams. I hope you're having a nice day."

Nothing.

"Listen," said-thought Phin, "I don't mean to trouble any-body, since y'all seem pretty busy." *Y'all* was not a word Phin had ever used, and if he'd had a throat it would have stuck in it. "But if you don't mind, I'd like to go home now."

The soothing music, which Phin now recognized as an instrumental version of the Sagittarian national anthem, played on repeat for forty-five unnerving minutes while Phin waited, patiently, politely, for something to happen.

"I WANT TO SPEAK TO YOUR SUPERVISOR!" he bellowed at last, and at last, the music stopped.

There was a dial tone, and then, the sound of a phone ringing.

There was a click, and at last, someone spoke to Phin. Not with words popping into his brain, but with an actual voice. And a familiar one at that.

"Phineas Fogg? I thought that energy signature looked familiar," the voice said in a friendly and professional patter. "Sorry about the wait. After that cat planet exploded, we've got a *lot* of cat consciousnesses to sift through here. Sit tight. I'll move you to the top of the queue so we can talk properly."

"Is that—" Phin started, but before he could finish, the

nothing around him began to shrink, sucking in on itself like water down a drain. Suddenly, Phin could feel his skin, and could feel cool air on it, and could feel that same cool air rushing into his nostrils, down his throat, and into his lungs. He could smell the fresh scent of pine.

Then he opened his eyes and saw a familiar green blob hovering before him.

Phin blinked. "Mr. Jeremy?" His voice was hoarse, but it was his own, and it felt good to speak words out loud again.

"It's still *Miss*, actually," said the blob as it resolved itself into a face, feminine and green. "But we're on a first-name basis, I think."

"Gretta," said Phin, recognizing the former head of the Temporal Transit Authority. "You look amazing . . . ," he added before passing out.

". . . in white," Phin said three hours later when he regained consciousness.

The room he found himself in was large, cavernous, and clinical. The air smelled of fresh paint and something else—something antiseptic and artificially scented with pine. Somewhere nearby he could hear footsteps and voices, but his ward was empty and quiet save for an electronic thrum and beep. Everywhere Phin looked was white. The bed he lay in was white. The linen was white. The privacy curtain, the floors, the walls, the ceiling, and the equipment monitoring his vitals were all white—except for the small, round, red badges that were the intergalactic symbol of medical aid.

Phin was in a hospital.

He felt weird. Weak, sure, but also brand-new, as if his body had just been vaporized down to its very atoms and then painstakingly reassembled molecule by molecule—which was, of course, exactly what had happened. Everything seemed to be in the right place, but not quite working as it should.

He blinked. He tried to sit up. These were clearly two bad ideas, right in a row, and he eased back onto his pillow and shut his eyes. After a lot of internal debate, he opened his eyes again and noticed for the first time a call button on his bed. He pressed it.

After a moment the doorway to Phin's ward slid open with a pneumatic hiss. A nurse entered. Phin knew it was a nurse from the crisp white nurse's uniform he wore.

"Hello," the nurse said, then waved, then dropped the pen he had been holding in his waving hand, bent down to retrieve it, knocked his forehead on a gurney, and toppled onto his back.

"Of course," groaned Phin.

The creature that was struggling to its feet was a Bog Mutant. Bog Mutants were person-shaped, gelatinous, and possessed a tremendous work ethic. Grown like mushrooms, Bog Mutants performed most of the odd jobs throughout the galaxy. They were sweet by nature, and performed their tasks with relish, which were the kinds of admirable qualities one tried very hard not to ignore when faced with how monumentally stupid they were.

"My name's Jeremy!" said the Bog Mutant. All Bog Mutants were named Jeremy. "What's yours?"

"Look—" started Phin, which was his first mistake.

"Ah, Mr. Look! We're so pleased to have you on board." The Bog Mutant took out a small notepad and added "Mr. Look" to the list of patients he'd introduced himself to today, right after Mr. Listen, Mr. Who the Devil Are You?, and Ms. What Are You Doing Get Out of Here This Is the Ladies' Room for Heaven's Sake.

"Can someone please tell me what's happened and where I am?"

"Well—" The Bog Mutant tapped the pen on his chin, and it stuck there. "First there was nothing, and then there was the Big Bang."

"What are you doing?" said Phin.

"I'm telling you what happened," said the Bog Mutant.

". . . from the beginning?" said Phin.

"Oh! In that case, before there was nothing, scientists theorize that there was another universe much like ours, which collapsed in on itself and—"

"Forget it," said Phin.

"I'll handle this patient, Jeremy," came a familiar voice from the far end of the ward.

The young woman who sauntered up to Phin's bedside wore a crisp white suit with the same intergalactic noncombatant symbol stitched on the lapel. Her skin was a lustrous green, her hair cut short in a wicked new bob. She was Gretta, the only known female Bog Mutant in existence. And it was safe to say she and Phin had some history.

"Oh hello, Gretta," said Phin with a tight smile. "Try to crash anyone into a star lately?"

"Jeremy," said Gretta to the Bog Mutant nurse. "We've got new arrivals in bay four. Why don't you go check on them?"

"Sure thing!" The Bog Mutant was relieved. He'd been trying to forget the origins of the universe as he'd been asked to do, which was a confusing process. Checking on the next ward sounded much more gratifying.

"So what's going on here?" Phin said as Gretta helped him to his feet. "The last time I saw you, you were disbanding the Temporal Transit Authority. Now you're dressing up Bog Mutants as nurses? What gives?"

"Well, they are my biological brothers, you know," said Gretta. "And they're good workers. You just need to be *very* clear with your instructions. Come this way."

She led Phin toward the ward's exit.

Phin moved on unsteady feet, still trying to make sense of his surroundings. "This looks like a medical frigate of some kind," he said, inspecting the clean white lines of the ship around him. "Where did you come across this frigate? Is it a big frigate, or more of a medium-sized frigate? Where does one purchase a frigate anyway?" Phin liked to say *frigate* and planned to work it into the conversation as often as possible. "I'd think a frigate like this—"

But he didn't finish his sentence. They'd come to the entrance to the next ward, and what Phin saw made his blinkered neurons positively gawp. The room was enormous, easily bigger than the Murder Ball Field at Singularity Stadium. It was a flurry of activity. Hundreds of nurses, Bog Mutants in starchy, poorly fitting uniforms, hurried between dozens upon dozens of transport bays, adjusting the settings, checking stats on their electronic clipboards, and attending to the cats who were blipping into existence in teleport tubes all the way across the ward. It was an immense, planet-sized rescue mission, the ship's massive computational turbines working overtime to hoover up the disintegrated inhabitants of Venus Beta and reassemble them, safe and mostly sound, on board Gretta's seriously massive rescue-and-recovery ship.

"Impressive, isn't it?" said Gretta. "The moment our ship's computer detected the explosion it began analyzing the debris for sentient energy signatures. With a bit of speedy math, we were able to reassemble most of the occupants of Venus Beta, molecule by molecule. Fourteen thousand, two hundred, and twelve cats rescued. And one Earthling kid, of course. Speaking of," she added, elbowing him. "Where's your girlfriend? I thought you two were traveling together."

"Lola's not—" said Phin, but before he could finish protesting, Lola's absence, and her current whereabouts, blipped into his awareness like a ship coming out of hyperspace into a bowl of cereal—that is to say, violently. "Um," said Phin. "I think I need to use your deep-space scanner."

**LOLA AWOKE WITH A** *f'wonk-wizzle*—which is not an alien word, but a close approximation of the sound Lola made when she woke up.

She awoke with a *f'wonk-wizzle*, stretched, wiped her nose, and felt the warm and familiar thrum of engines in midflight, as she had most mornings during her recent travels with Phin. It was a sound she'd become accustomed to, and it reminded her of the cars on the freeway that had rumbled her to sleep back in Hoboken. She didn't let her eyes open, not yet. She was the kind of person who liked to eavesdrop on the day before diving into it.

She listened as engines purred and instruments beeped and cooed. The only thing missing from this now homey and peaceful soundscape was Phin ruining it.

Lola *grunt-humphled*, which again is not an actual word exactly but a close approximation of the sound she made.

She opened her eyes. She was aboard the Rescue Wagon all right, though she couldn't remember how she'd gotten there. From the view out her window the ship appeared to be suspended in deep space above a pale, unfamiliar planet. She rubbed her temples, feeling groggy, and, now that she thought of it, slightly queasy, as if she'd just gone through a short-range teleport.

All at once Lola remembered what had happened. The girl. The dragon. The explosion. She'd been on a planet when it exploded!

Luckily, there is an old Septarian word that perfectly describes the sound Lola made just then. She *smarkleblarted*.

She had to stay calm. She decided she should find Phin, and immediately looked around the cabin interior. She could see the whole of the ship from where she sat, and being that Phin wasn't behind her, wasn't in the driver's seat, and wasn't in her lap, she concluded, *ipso facto*, he wasn't there, *period*. She knew she was alone.

"What's going on?" she shouted, but the only one listening was the ship's onboard computer, Bucky.

"Howdy there, horny toad!" came Bucky's synthesized voice through the dash-mounted speakers. "How jangle your spurs this fine morning?"

"Bucky!" said Lola. "What's going on? Where's Phin? Where's Professor Donut? How did I get here?"

"Well, lick my beets and butter my cabbage, I can't rightly say," said Bucky with his usual degree of helpfulness. "But I got a message here saying Emergency Protocol Two has been activated."

"Emergency Protocol *Two*?"

"And now I'm to play the following holographic recording. Sit back and enjoy!"

A panel slid away, revealing a small holographic projector. There came a fizzle of light, and suddenly Lola found herself sharing a cabin with an enormous, seething, hideously deformed, blind albino porpoise.

The creature was beyond horrifying. Its twin toothless mouths gaped; its horrible eyeless bulk twitched and seethed. Lola screamed.

"Oops, dang it," came Phin's prerecorded voice. "Who set the zoom on this thing?"

Suddenly, the horrible albino porpoise flew backward as if repelled by a great force. It shrank into the distance, revealing itself to be but a lump on a much larger creature with eyes and *teeth* and sort of floofy hair and . . .

It was Phin. The porpoise had been, Lola now saw, an ultramagnified image of his nose.

In its place was a holographic image of Phin, as if he were seated beside her in the cabin.

"Okay," said the holo-Phin recording. "There we go. That's better. Hi, Lola! First of all, don't freak out."

"Too late. I'm already freaking out," said Lola.

"I know you are," said Phin's prerecorded image. "Stop it."

Lola kept freaking out, but privately.

"I know you're just going to keep freaking out privately, so here's the scoop. If you're watching this, that means Emergency Protocol Two has been activated. I've synched the Rescue Wagon's short-range teleport to your energy signature. In the event of a catastrophe, the system is to transport you back to the Wagon and out of harm's way. The thing is, the Rescue Wagon's a small ship, and there's only enough energy for one emergency teleport. So if you and I were both in trouble, I hate to say it, but I'm probably dead now."

"No!" Lola screamed.

"And in honor of this sad occasion," the prerecorded Phin continued, "I've composed a remembrance reel, which I'd like you to watch in its entirety during your flight back to Earth."

The ship shunted and turned in space. As it did, music began to pipe through the dash-mounted speakers. It was the kind of melancholic, inspirational fare people like to play at funerals. The holographic Phin vanished, and in his place a series of still images began to pan slowly from right to left, and from left to right. They were pictures of Phin, all of which he'd clearly taken himself, in various touching scenarios—walking down a beach, looking manfully out at a sunrise, rescuing baby dolphins from a burning building (some of these images had been heavily edited).

"No, this is impossible," said Lola. "You can't be dead."

"*I'm totally dead*," came Phin's prerecorded voice.

"Bucky, mute recording," said Lola.

"Well, sure, my little sarsaparilla!"

"And, uh . . ." Lola tried to think like Phin. "Scan the local, um, quadrant." That sounded wrong. Were quadrants a thing? She decided to go with it. "Scan the local quadrant for Phin's energy signature. Or whatever."

"On it!" said Bucky. "Found him!" he added an instant later. "Phineas Fogg's energy signature detected just under a light-year away on a dreadnaught-class space vessel called . . . ," the computer chirped as Bucky scanned a few databases, "the SS *Calming Breath*. It's a rescue-and-recovery vessel. Looks like it scooped up Phin and the cats of Venus Beta!"

Lola collapsed in relief. She sighed, took a breath, and gathered herself. "Good," she said. "Take us there."

"I'm afraid I can't do that, little lady."

"What? Why not?"

"My control's been overridden by Emergency Protocol Two. The Rescue Wagon's autopilot will now return you to the Fogg-Bolus headquarters on Earth."

"What? I can't go to Earth!" Lola launched herself into the driver's seat, trying and failing to swat away a black-and-white image of Phin playing with some puppies in a dandelion field. "I need to find Phin and I need to find the girl who stole my Twinkie and I need to save my family!"

"Golly, I'd love to help, little lady," said Bucky, sounding genuinely apologetic. "But my circuits are as tied up as a . . ."

"Yeah, okay, I got it," said Lola.

". . . a snake-charming contortionist . . ."

"Uh-huh."

". . . in a washing machine full o' rattlers!"

"Right," said Lola. "Just . . . let me think."

And she thought.

She was alone. In space. Moreover, she was *lost* in space. Lola had no idea how to do any of this space stuff without Phin. She'd always had him by her side, and now . . .

Lola shook herself. No. Some dragon-riding jerk had stolen her Twinkie and blown up her friends. They needed her. Her family needed her. She had to work with what she had.

One thing she did have was a spaceship. That was definitely a start. The Wagon did have a steering wheel, technically. Maybe she could pilot it herself. How hard could it be? Phin certainly made it look easy.

"Bucky," she said, "I want you to turn over guidance to manual control."

Something on the control panel chirped, and the wheel before Lola came alive with blinking lights. Tenderly, she took the wheel in her hands. She could feel the ship's vibration through it. She was flying. She was actually flying a spaceship!

"Right," said Lola. "Now I'm just going to turn this slightly in the direction we came . . ." Lola nudged the wheel.

The Rescue Wagon went immediately into a death spiral.

Alarms blared. Sirens wailed. Red lights flashed like it was their job—which it was.

"Ahhhh!" Lola screamed as the g-force smashed her back into her seat. "What did I do? What did I do?"

"Can't says I know!" Bucky replied. "But we appear to be crashing into the nearest planet!"

"But I barely touched it!"

Text began to scroll across the view screen in front of Lola. This time it said, *Activating Emergency Protocol One.* The memorial slide show blinked out, and was replaced by another image of Phin, this one more or less from the waist up. Because Lola was in the driver's seat, Phin's face was now inches from hers, and it looked supremely disappointed.

"If you're seeing this message, Emergency Protocol One has been activated, because Lola is crashing the ship, probably because she tried to fly it by herself," said the holographic Phin. "Lola, if you're watching, don't feel too bad. Piloting a spaceship is all about *confidence*. And let's face it, you—"

"Phin!" Lola bellowed over the recording as the Wagon banked through space and spun madly into the atmosphere of the pale planet over which it had just been in orbit.

"Phin, if *you're* watching," the holographic Phin continued, "man, what were you thinking letting her drive? You know she can't fly! If you survive this, which you probably won't, I hope you've learned your lesson."

"What do I do?" Lola shouted, wrestling with the wheel, which bucked and spun freely beneath her hands. The cabin was now a cacophony of warning alarms and flashing red error messages. The collision sensor refused to sigh contently, and instead sighed in disgusted annoyance, as if to say, *Typical!*

"Lola, if you're asking what to do now," said Phin, "don't worry. I've programmed the ship to automatically teleport you somewhere safe. More on that in Emergency Protocol Two."

Nothing happened, except that the ship continued to crash, and Lola continued to scream.

"Unless, of course," the holographic Phin said, coming back into frame, "you've *just* used Emergency Protocol Two and the short-range teleport needs to recharge. If that's the case, then, Lola, I'm sorry," said Phin. "The only thing you can do now is crash."

And that is precisely what she did.

## 7

**THE STARSHIP** *CALMING BREATH* rocketed through space less than a light-year from where the planet Venus Beta had, until recently, existed. The local star cluster illuminated the vessel's spires and shield generators, its battle turrets and triple-barrel ion cannons. It also showed off an impressive new coat of white paint.

The *Calming Breath* had, until recently, been a dreadnaught of the Temporal Transit Authority. That was until Gretta, the TTA's director, had disbanded the organization and begun her latest venture.

"Rescue and recovery," Gretta explained to Phin, who wasn't really listening but was instead fiddling with one of the *Calming Breath*'s computer terminals. "The TTA had a fleet of six thousand ships," she went on. "I figured this was more productive than selling them off for scrap. They're positioned all over the galaxy now, scanning their local quadrants for distress signals or, in your case, massive explosions. We used our Mind Net to keep your consciousness whole while we reassembled your body. Patent pending, of course."

"Uh-huh," said Phin, and continued his furious interrogation of the ship's energy field readouts.

The bridge was truly impressive, suspended on a platform within a massive frontal dome. Bog Mutants were seated at the many terminals (which had been, until recently, battle stations) monitoring local space for distress calls. Between the displays and instruments, someone had hastily hung a few inspirational posters about wellness and the importance of low-calorie alternatives to cola. One of these was peeling away from the wall, and behind it another, older poster showed a fearsome creature, like a combination of a gremlin and a bat, climbing out of what appeared to be a very high-tech telephone booth. It read, TOGETHER WE CAN STOP THE TIME TRAVELER MENACE! SUPPORT THE TEMPORAL TRANSIT AUTHORITY.

"Also, the health care business is a *racket*," Gretta went on, surveying her kingdom over the rim of her tea. "I'm making *three times* what I earned heading the Temporal Transit Authority."

"That's truly fascinating," said Phin, "to someone, presumably."

"You now find yourself on the flagship of the best-armed medical rescue service in the galaxy. You know"—Gretta twirled a finger lazily around the rim of her mug—"an investment from your family could *triple*—"

"Aha!" said Phin, having at last found what he was looking for.

The ship's recent scans confirmed the Rescue Wagon had teleported Lola away to safety. Emergency Protocol Two should have gone into effect, autopiloting the Wagon back to Earth. The thing that was troubling Phin, however, was that none of the subsequent scans showed any sign of the Wagon at all. It was like it had just fallen out of the sky.

"I should go to Earth," he said. "I think. Make sure Lola is okay."

"I'm sure she's fine," said Gretta, sounding less chipper and more exasperated. "Besides, I thought you said you needed to find some kind of incredible snack cake?"

"I do. I am." Phin scowled at the computer terminal. He wasn't used to being uncertain, and it nagged at him like an ill-fitting turtleneck with the tags still in the collar.

"Well, if you want to go, we'll be landing in twelve hours," said Gretta. "The cats want to address the president."

For the first time Phin looked up at Gretta. "The President of the Galaxy? Why?"

Gretta shrugged. "I don't know, but I heard one of the big tabbies saying something about a 'return of the great evil' and 'the government must be warned.' Come on," she said, setting down her mug, "they're having some kind of meeting in Theater One right now. Maybe they know something about the girl who stole your Ding Dong."

"It was a Twinkie," said Phin distantly, and stroked his chin. After a moment he looked up to see Gretta had set off without him, and he hurried after her, trying to ignore the deadly turtleneck of uncertainty closing around his throat.

Surgery Theater One, like the bridge, was large, impressive, and covered by a transparent dome. Rows of seats climbed up the inclining walls, which were occupied by hundreds upon hundreds of cats rescued from Venus Beta. They had assembled here to decide just what to do next. In the center of the room was an elevated dais, and here stood the chancellor and provost of the now disintegrated Flighty Shiny Thing University, along with Professor Donut and the other department heads, from the Cute Sciences to Advanced Aviary Physics (the study of whether or not there is a bird in the yard, and if there is, where is it going, and can it be pounced on).

Phin stood near the back with Gretta and fiddled with a small pocket tablet he'd pilfered from the bridge. He'd still had no luck locating Lola or the Wagon.

Professor Donut approached them and embraced Phin. "Phineas, so glad you're all right. Any sign of your better half?"

"If you mean Lola, I'm working on it." He leaned in to whisper, "Hey, I'm hearing something about the return of an ancient evil, end of the universe . . . You know, that kind of deal. What's the scoop?"

"We'll be getting to that," said Professor Donut. "Let me know if you hear from Ms. Ray."

The murmuring settled down as the professor returned to the dais. Chancellor Mittens cleared her throat and called the caucus to order.

"Cats of Venus Beta," she said, her voice weathered but unwavering. "Good staff and crew of the *Calming Breath*, my friends . . ." She cleared her throat. "Today we have suffered a great tragedy, and though our loss of life was blessedly small"—a few cats bowed their heads to mourn the spangle fish and Rebirds—"our venerable university, indeed our *home*, is now gone."

Chancellor Mittens coughed. Someone brought her a glass of water, and she nodded gratefully before taking a sip.

"But it is not the way of cats to wallow in the wake of a catastrophe," the chancellor continued. "When we fall, we land on our feet. And when we don't, we pretend we did. We shall sit down and lick ourselves, as if we meant to do it all along."

"May you also lick yourself," the cats intoned as one, reciting the spiritual mantra of their race.

"My friends," Professor Donut said, now that it was his turn to speak. "The being that destroyed our planet is a threat to us all, of that there is no doubt. However, our enemy may be far more nefarious than we first assumed."

An image appeared on the wall-mounted screens. It

showed security footage from Professor Donut's lab, just moments before the explosion. Phin watched as a black-and-white version of himself looked on dumbly as a girl astride a golden dragon pilfered Lola's one chance at finding her family.

At the sight of the girl and her dragon, the crowd gasped.

"It cannot be!"

"But she's gone, never to return!"

"The dark one! The ShadowMancer!"

"Yes," said Professor Donut. "What we have here is, we believe, conclusive proof that the ShadowMancer has returned."

A feeling seemed to descend on the room. It drifted in, like a fog, and quickly enveloped every cat, kitten, and mutant. It was a feeling of darkness, of dread. It was a feeling of waking from a nightmare, only to discover the nightmare was real and the world you love is a dream.

Phineas Fogg stared at the image of the girl on her dragon. It hadn't occurred to him. It simply had never occurred to him, the resemblance. How could it? Who would expect to ever see, ever *be in the presence of,* the ShadowMancer herself? It was unfathomable. Like discovering that roundish kid in first grade who liked to wear fluffy red sweaters had been the planet Jupiter all along.

"She'll erase us all!" someone wailed.

Panic threatened to erupt, but Chancellor Mittens put out

a steadying paw. "My friends, we have faced this evil before. And it is true many perished. But we will face it again. And this time we have the advantage!"

"Yes," said Professor Donut to the surprised murmurs of the crowd. He referred to the footage. "The snack cake the ShadowMancer stole—you can see it here clearly in frame thirty-four—contains, we believe, the means to access an alternate dimension known as Dimension Why."

"She wishes to spread her evil across the multiverse!" someone else bellowed.

"If we know her motive, we may counter her," said the chancellor.

"But how?"

"And what about the children?" snapped Dr. Scruffles, who taught Defense Against the Dog Arts. "They brought the world destroyer to our planet. What do *they* have to say for themselves?"

There were a few enthusiastic jeers, and a few hesitant ones.

"Sounds like it's her fault the world destroyer came!" someone shouted from the gallery.

"Yeah!" shouted someone else.

"She brought the Twinkie here! She's evil! Evil!"

"Now, now," said Professor Donut, but his words were overpowered by the hissing mob.

"Professor Donut," said the chancellor, and her tone

commanded absolute silence. "I appreciate your fondness for the Earth children. But Dr. Scruffles is right. They must be questioned."

"Detain the Earth children! Perhaps they're in league with the world destroyer!"

"It could have been an act of terrorism!"

"Do they have any ties to the Canine Republic?"

"Let's hear it from him!" growled an associate professor of Hairballs, an immense and intimidating Persian whose voice boomed over the others. He leveled an accusing claw at Phin.

Suddenly all eyes were on him, and the crowd had fallen into a hungry hush.

Phin thought fast. His mouth helpfully started making words, just to give his brain a little head start.

"You know, I'd love to stick around and help you guys out," Phin said in his most commanding and confident voice. "But right now, I've either got to chase this ancient evil or find my friend or both. And no offense, but working with you guys would be a bit like herding . . . well . . . you know what I mean. So!" said Phin, "if you wouldn't mind giving me, like, a ten-second head start, I'd really appreciate it."

"Get him!" someone shouted.

"Quick!" shouted Phin to the nearest Bog Mutant. "Play some escape music!"

The Bog Mutant shrugged, pressed a button on a wall-mounted terminal, and an instant later the hit single by

Toady and the RocketButts, "Gotta Run Run Baby 'Cause You'd Never Believe What's Chasin' Me," wailed through the ship's public address system as Phineas Fogg ran, pursued by five hundred furious cats.

Phin barreled down one anonymous corridor after another. He had no idea where he was going, and the ship seemed endless.

He turned a corner and almost ran face-first into an enormous black cat.

"There he is! He's here!"

Phin doubled back, leaped through a door, did a combat roll, sort of stumbled, and then he was up and running again. Escape pods, he knew, were usually located along the belly of a ship, and he made his way down, knowing that once he got there, a decision would have to be made.

He passed a sign that read *Escape Pods This Way* over which someone had hung a smaller sign that said, *Escape Pods Decommissioned, Please Use Teleports on Level 34.* Phin ignored the latter and kept running.

He turned another corner and was faced with a long, tubular hall with ports along the walls. The ports were escape-pod entrances, and all of the pods were either jettisoned or permanently disabled. Only one port at the end stood open.

Phin dived inside it, whirled around, slammed the door shut behind him, and hit the big flashing automatic-jettison button. The blast knocked him off his feet as the escape pod shot away from the *Calming Breath* and into the darkness of deep space.

Phin was, for the moment at least, safe.

Phin's heart was pounding. He lay still for a moment and caught his breath. When he opened his eyes, there was a kitten staring into them.

"Are you the babysitter?"

Phin blinked. He sat up. He looked around.

The vessel was a standard dreadnaught-class escape pod— essentially a long, rectangular craft the size and shape of a minivan. It was a single room with a private lavatory, the door to which was now closed. The walls were austere white and lined with storage bins, filled with supplies, rebreathers, rations, and first aid kits—or rather, they were supposed to be. But someone had painted them blue with little white clouds. The floor was littered with building blocks and plastic, nontoxic toys. And instead of the cool, clinical smell of recycled air, Phin detected paste and finger paints.

"What is this?" he said with growing panic.

"It's snack time!" said the kitten. "The others are washing their hands, but I already did, because I'm always superclean. Can I help you set up?"

"No," said Phin, and scrambled to the controls. "No, no, no, no, no!"

He was staring at the view screen, which normally would

have shown him an unobscured view of space, but someone had papered over it with a bulletin. This is what it said:

*The* Calming Breath *is happy to provide complimentary day care service from 11–3. Please check with our staff.*

Phin made a noise of utter terror, dismay, and surprise. The kitten began to laugh and pointed at him.

"What's so funny?" said Phin.

"You *smarkleblarted*!" said the kitten as she began setting out the animal crackers and juice for snack time.

# PART 2

## THE HORRIBLE COST OF A MAYBE MEAL

8

"... *AND THAT WAS the Over-Mind of MegaDome Six with his new hit single, 'You Will Obey Me, You Will Obey Me, You Will Obey Me.' You're listening to WVEN, Venulian Radio, the Mix!*

"*I'm Flag Jackson. Coming up to the top of the hour and the news, the planet of Venus Beta, home to renowned center of cat learning, Flighty Shiny Thing University, exploded this morning. Eyewitnesses say the blast occurred not long after a figure bearing a striking resemblance to the ShadowMancer was seen on the planet's surface. If the report is to be believed, this is the first sighting of the infamous space wizard since her campaign of terror and subsequent mysterious disappearance over a millennium ago. Most recently, the book detailing her exploits,* ShadowMancer Wars, *has suffered declining sales, slipping down the best-seller list to the number three spot. But hey, maybe this latest tragedy will boost sales! Always look for the silver lining, that's my motto.*

"*After the break we'll continue with our Top 100 countdown of the best Arachnopod love songs. Remember, be our ten thousandth caller and win a rocking afternoon with WVEN's own Phyllis the Party Rhino! And now, here's Hannah Starfoot with an important message about Dr. Burt's Medicated Yellow Jellyfish Bite Ointment: We Swear It's Not What It Looks Like!"*

**LOLA FELT LIKE SHE'D** been hit in the face with a small mountain range, because she had been.

The Rescue Wagon had come to a smoldering rest on a craggy outcropping. The last ten minutes had been an epic crash, the sort that action movie executives and special effects teams lose sleep over. First there was the fireball descent through the upper atmosphere, then the twisting rolls through miles of jagged rock formations, a quick skid across the surface of an oily lake (which immediately caught fire and sent sheets of liquid flame pluming into the air), and at last the finale as the little ship skidded into the forest, shattering the ancient and brittle trees.

Now, half buried in the dirt and having left a mile-long gouge through the woods, the Wagon ticked, popped, smoldered, and finally settled, wisps of excess coolant and pine-scented AromaSave Ultrasoothing Scents for Every Catastrophe leaching from under the hood.

Inside, Lola coughed. The emergency impact rescue

foam burst through its special vent ports, engulfing Lola in its impact-absorbing sponge for an instant before retreating back into its containers as if satisfied that it had done its best.

Dazed, Lola checked herself for injuries. There were none on her outside, and she decided any internal injuries would just have to sort themselves out. The door was jammed shut; she had to open it with a kick. She stepped out into the wreckage of the morning and took in her surroundings. The countryside seemed to be in pretty bad shape. The forest was old and half dead, its trees gray and bare, more like dried bone than flora. The forest floor was littered with what Lola could only think of as *junk*. There were hunks of metal of unknown origin, strange semitranslucent blobs of blue and pink, great drifts of colored paper and cardboard, etched with alien writing and symbols, along with unused garments, deflated pool toys, and what looked like a refrigerator or two. All of it was piled in drifts across the landscape. Looking back the way she'd come, past the lake that was still burning much more than lakes usually do, Lola saw that the rock formations she'd just tumbled through were not rock at all, but stacks of mismatched crates and boxes hundreds of feet high. There was also a suspiciously large number of fast-food wrappers blowing around. Her first thought, as she took it all in, was *Garbage Planet*.

"*Drab droof* it all," said Lola, but no one was around to hear her incredibly rude language.

She stepped back on board and checked her ship's computer for signs of life, but the computer was kaput. In fact, the only thing on the ship that still functioned was the magnetic trailer hitch, but the hitch was without a rope, and in any case there was nothing for Lola to hitch to.

Lola sighed. Had Phin been there, she would have asked him what on Earth they were supposed to do now. But since he wasn't, there was no one to make a joke about this not being "Earth" at all.

Then, with a sudden cold shock, Lola remembered her summer reading list.

Some readers may be surprised that at this, of all times, Lola remembered she'd neglected to do her summer reading.

Now, it's true that Lola's summer reading list was, at this point, roughly a thousand years past due, but it was then that Lola remembered she'd never written her book report on *Hatchet* by Gary Paulsen. (Of course, she'd *read* the book. Lola loved reading. It was the assignments that came after that made her brain cry.) Anyway . . . Lola remembered that in *Hatchet*, the main character's prop plane crashes in the mountains, leaving him with only a hatchet to survive with. There was one scene Lola remembered in particular, where the boy tried to retrieve emergency supplies from the downed aircraft. Things like flares, rations, a first aid kit. Surely the Wagon would have a kit like that. It was a "Rescue" Wagon, after all.

After a quick search she found a small red-and-white rations kit tucked under the back seat. Inside was an instant fire starter, a promotional refrigerator magnet for the Fogg-Bolus Hypergate and Baked Beans Corporation, and two packets of something called InstaBeef! There was also a small card that read: *Rations Kit Last Inspected June 4th, 3010, Inspector Number 57B-42A. Inspector's Notes: Don't eat the InstaBeef!*

Lola would have preferred a hatchet.

Tossing the InstaBeef! aside, she slung the little kit over her shoulder by its handy strap and set off through the woods. She tried to think of what else happened in *Hatchet*. She remembered something about turtle eggs—which you were definitely supposed to eat or definitely not supposed to, and also something about a moose, which she was pretty sure you *could* eat, if you could somehow persuade the moose to follow you to a meat-processing plant. But neither moose nor meat-processing plants seemed handy, and besides, Lola was considering becoming a vegetarian.

But she *was* hungry.

She picked her way over the piles of garbage. The going was slow, it was tricky to keep her footing, but she kept an eye out for anything that might look useful, like, say, a turtle egg or, preferably, a turtle egg taco. The trouble was, everywhere she looked were potentially useful things, but she wasn't sure how she could use them. Someone had discarded an old skateboard. There was an unopened eight-pack of paper towels, and no shortage of plastic figurines—characters from some movie or show Lola had never heard of or seen. She was debating whether to collect some of the very strange (and suspiciously unused-looking) trash, when she found herself stumbling onto a narrow road. It must have been in use, since someone had cleared all the stuff off it. She followed the road until she came to a sign. The writing was in a language she couldn't understand, but Lola knew a road sign when she saw one. A symbol that might have been an arrow pointed straight ahead, and there was an image of something that looked like a temple. Maybe there were some friendly monks there who liked to make lunch for wary travelers, and who knew how to fix spaceships and would accept payment in paper towels and skateboard wheels.

She came up over a rise and looked down into the valley below. Just beyond the tree line was a small village—really just a handful of buildings and some crisscrossing streets. Some of the structures were small and squat—homes, Lola guessed. Others were larger, with blunt spires or towers. The buildings were odd, in that they seemed to be constructed from hunks of garbage. And yet, a few of the houses had golden detailing. There was lots of polished chrome, and several of the roofs seemed to sparkle as if encrusted with diamonds. One house had a picket fence that looked like it had been fashioned from the teeth of a gigantic android, and another looked as if it were fashioned out of a disused storage freighter. It was the strangest mishmash of trash and treasure. Whoever lived here, they'd built their town out of whatever was at hand, which seemed to be just about everything and anything.

From where Lola stood on the hilltop, she couldn't make out any people, but she heard what might have been voices, the thrum of a lawn mower maybe, and somewhere someone was playing music. Despite its strange appearance, it was otherwise a pleasant-seeming place.

But of course, pleasant-seeming places can still produce awful people, and Lola was about to meet two prime examples.

A rock beaned her on the forehead, and Lola fell over.

"Flan pickle Cheerios!" laughed one of her attackers. "Gorgonzola, mustard!"

"Heavy cream," said the other with less enthusiasm. "Havarti."

Lola winced and looked up. A pair of aliens loomed over her. They were big, and their bulk was only magnified by their attire. Like the houses and buildings, their clothing was cobbled together from found garbage. The first speaker, the one who was laughing, was wrapped in shower curtains. Pepper grinders hung from her belt like trophies, and her knees and elbows sported pads made of luxury seat cushions. The second one wore a kind of armor made from lunch boxes, her face partially obscured by a "helmet" fashioned from an actual steel safe with the door hanging open.

"Bumblebee chicken dinner," said the first, whom Lola pegged as the rock thrower.

"I'm sorry?" said Lola, whose default mode was politeness, even when someone threw a rock at her.

"Swiss," said the other, shaking her head. "Double-cream goat gouda."

"Please stop saying cheeses at me," said Lola, glancing around for something she could use as a weapon. Politeness didn't mean one couldn't defend oneself.

"Ah!" said the first, and punched her partner in the shoulder, pepper grinders rattling. "Garden brick pants gazebo." She held up a finger, which Lola interpreted as the universal sign for *just a sec*. She fiddled with an object hanging around her neck. It was a flat black box with a few dials on its side. The girl in the shower curtain robes adjusted the knobs, and suddenly her strange speech began to make a bit more sense.

"Yellow goose better?" she said, turning the knobs. "Or trickle bunk this?"

"I don't understand," said Lola, wondering if she should get to her feet now.

"Wait! Here we go," the girl said, honing in on the right setting. "Can you understand me now?"

"Yes!" said Lola.

"You see?" the shower curtain girl said to her friend. "I told you these translators were junk."

"Jarlsberg," growled the second, who was wearing an identical black box clipped to her belt. She adjusted it, and when she spoke again, Lola heard something other than cheeses. "There. We good?"

"I . . . ," said Lola. "I can understand you, if that's what you mean."

"Excellent!" said the first, and taking a deep breath, added, "Get off our planet, you alien scum!" and readied another rock.

"Wait!" said Lola, scrambling to her feet and shielding her face. "Stop! I'm not alien scum! I'm alien . . ." She groped for the word. "Detritus? No. A castaway! That's better. I'm an alien castaway."

"We don't know this word," said the lunch-box girl. "Did you crash here?"

"Yes! My ship crashed!" said Lola.

"Balderdash," said the first, wincing as if this hadn't been quite what she meant to say. The boxes the girls wore were some kind of local translator, Lola figured, but a local translator that was clearly not well made. "You came to steal our stuff."

"I didn't! I didn't even know you had any stuff," said Lola. "I crashed here by accident."

"She doesn't *look* like a thief," said Lunch Boxes, scratching the tip of her nose. "Thieves dress in black catsuits and dangle down on wires and all that."

"Maybe her catsuit's in her bag," said Shower Curtains. "Let's take it and burn it."

"No!" said Lola. "These are my supplies." They weren't much, but they were hers and Lola would be *droofed* if she'd let them have her little rations kit.

"I'm Mango Corona," said Shower Curtains, and furrowed her brow. "Mango Corona," she tried again. "Okay, well, I guess this thing can't translate my name, so now I'm Mango Corona."

"Hi," said the other, and gave a little wave. "Bumblebee Kitchen-House."

"Uh," said Lola. "Lola. Lola Ray."

"That's a weird name," said Mango Corona.

"I thought thieves were supposed to have cool names," said Bumblebee Kitchen-House. "Like *the Black Spider*, or *the Night Panther* or something."

"I'm not a thief," said Lola, finally, finally standing. "I'm just a kid."

"Could be she's an alien invader," said Mango, "who's come to invade the village."

"Could be she's here to invade the Golden Cathedral," said Bumblebee in a hush.

"You think?" said Mango. "In that case we should *definitely* tickle her." Again Mango winced. She smiled apologetically at Lola. "Sorry, translation issue. What's the word when you . . . ?" Here she described a horrifically sadistic and violent series of activities that made Lola's throat go dry.

"I . . . don't think there *is* a word for that," Lola said.

"Okay, well, we'll just go with *tickle*, then," said Mango. "Let's tickle her *viciously*."

Bumblebee Kitchen-House considered this. "I suppose. Better safe than sorry, no?"

"Right," said Mango. "A horrible tickling it is."

"Wait!" said Lola, but before she could protest any further, the sound of engines filled the air. Mango and Bumblebee looked up, and Lola followed suit as a giant silver ship broke over the tree line. It was unlike any ship Lola had yet seen. There were no jets or propulsion systems. Rather, the ship seemed to swim through the air like a minnow. Its face (Lola immediately thought of it as a face) was flat and noseless, its body tapering to a silvery tail that flitted through the air before inscribing a graceful arc and landing on the main street.

"Bookmobile!" shouted Mango with delight, shoving Bumblebee to the ground before taking off down the hill toward the ship.

"Hey!" Bumblebee growled, lunch-box armor clattering. "You raisin! Wait for me!"

"Uh," said Lola, as Bumblebee grabbed her hand and dragged Lola down the road after her.

Bumblebee was a good foot taller than Lola, with such long legs that Lola had to run double-time to keep from falling. They followed Mango down the road and into town, past a handful of buildings and then out into a kind of road or trench that had been cleared between the mountains of junk. The eel-like ship had come to rest halfway down the block, hovering a few feet off the ground as if it were waiting for them. Other alien creatures, all dressed in similarly eclectic attire, were rushing out of their homes, running out into the street, as they hurried toward the ship that had just landed in the center of their town.

"I thought Tuesday would never come!" said Mango, who'd reached the craft first. As they approached, panels along the side of the ship opened. The vessel was roughly the length of a school bus, and its entire flank was a kind of display case. A transparent shield retracted and shelves upon shelves extended themselves mechanically from the side of the strange ship, and on the shelves were objects Lola recognized immediately. They were books.

"A bookmobile?" said Lola as she and Bumblebee came to a staggering stop beside Mango.

"Book Möb Eel," corrected Bumblebee. "Three words."

"Oh," said Lola, ". . . of course."

The other book lovers had joined them now, and though they all towered over Lola by a good ten to eighteen inches, they were all obviously children. Running out to meet the bookmobile, or *Möb Eel* or whatever, on a sunny summer morning.

Lola was being held captive not by postapocalyptic road warriors but instead by bored preteens with nothing to do on a summer Tuesday. Lola shivered.

"Who's that?" asked one of the others, dressed in a sequined wedding gown and fighter-pilot-helmet ensemble.

"Just some alien that Mango and I found," said Bumblebee. "We're gonna tickle her later."

"Cool," said the newcomer, eyes going wide with interest.

"Do you have the latest issue of *Tender Is the Tentacle*?" Mango was asking the ship. The Möb Eel's blunt face was expressionless, but in response a mechanical arm extracted a small paperback from one of the shelves and offered it. "Bindle! If I don't finish this by Monday, Mrs. Stroop Waffle is gonna tickle me something fierce."

"Why do you always wait until the last minute?" said Bumblebee, shaking her head. "I'll take the latest issue of *Massively Weird Weekly*, please." The mechanical arm retrieved a slim periodical from its shelves and handed it to Bumblebee.

Lola caught a quick glance at the cover, swallowed, and decided to ignore what she'd seen there.

"It doesn't have any books on ship repair, does it?" she asked.

"And who's going to pay for it, you?" snapped Mango. "I've saved my money; I'm not buying your book."

"Me neither," said Bumblebee.

"Right," said Lola. "I was just asking."

"Hey!" shouted the boy in the wedding dress and fighter-pilot helmet. "*I* want *Tender Is the Tentacle*! That's mine!"

"The Shrek it is!" Mango snarled, her translator struggling with the local profanity. "I had it first!"

"Well, I'll have it last!" growled the boy in the wedding dress, brandishing a coffee mug.

"You throw that mug, you're getting a pepper grinder in the eye!" snapped Mango.

"Whoa!" said Lola, throwing herself between them. "Everyone calm down! Can't you share?"

"What's this word? Share?" said Bumblebee.

"Sharing?" said Lola. She took a deep breath. She smiled. "Sharing is a wonderful thing. It's when you have something, and another person—"

"She's teasing you, you pickle. We know what sharing is," laughed Mango. "We just don't care!" She hurled the pepper grinder at Wedding Dress Kid, and it shattered against his helmet.

Lola felt a tap on the shoulder. She turned and saw the Book Möb Eel's mechanical arm. It was holding out a book, offering it to her.

"Oh, thank you," she said. "But I don't have any money. Shekels. Whatever."

The mechanical arm extended, insistent.

"Whoa," said Bumblebee. "I've never seen it give out a free book before."

Mango and Wedding Dress had forgotten their fight and watched with open mouths.

"Why does she get a free book?" said Mango, unhooking another pepper grinder.

"Uh, thank you," said Lola, taking the old battered paperback from the Eel's robotic claw. She felt oddly touched by the gesture and held the little book to her heart. "I appreciate it."

The arm and shelves retracted back into the hulk of the Möb Eel's hull. The ship gave a little shiver, and then lifted gracefully into the air, swimming in a circle over their heads and then slowly slithering higher into the atmosphere.

Lola could have sworn its glowing eyes seemed to watch her as it departed.

"Mango!" came a voice from one of the houses. "Get your things, it's almost time to go."

"Coming, Mom!" Mango called. "Come on, Bumblebee. It's Cathedral time."

"Woo!" Bumblebee Kitchen-House pumped her fists in the air. "Golden Cathedral time!"

"What's that?" said Lola, worried they might drag her there.

"It's only the most wonderful place in the whole *world*," said Mango.

"What's there?" Lola tried again.

Bumblebee's eyes went wide with mystery and wonder. "Only literally *everything*."

"Oh man, I want to go to the cathedral," said Wedding Dress Kid, kicking a new PlayStation 4 that was lying by the side of the road.

"At the cathedral, you can find anything you want. Anything in the whole universe," said Bumblebee with a sigh. "It's the best."

Lola thought of her downed ship. This Golden Cathedral could offer a means of escape, or at least a place to make a long-distance phone call. "I want to go."

"Tough tarmac," snapped Mango. "You can't."

"The cathedral ain't free, you know," said Bumblebee.

"We don't even know who you *are*," said Mango. "You can't bring some weird off-worlder stranger to a place as sacred as the Golden Cathedral."

"Well," said Lola, swallowing. "I *am* on the cover of your magazine."

Mango and Bumblebee went still. Then slowly, Bumblebee raised her copy of *Massively Weird Weekly*. And there, on the cover, was a picture of a weary but smiling Lola Ray, arm in arm with Phineas Fogg, along with a big crowd of grinning Bog Mutants. The photo, Lola remembered, had been taken on the surface of the planetoid-sized father fungus, Mr. Jeremy, just after she and Phin had sent the Phan back to their alternate dimension.

The lead line read:

*She was a girl from the twenty-first century. He was a lonely heir to a massive fortune. Together they met some interdimensional beings. You won't believe what happened next.*

And just below:

*The Battle of Singularity City: an exclusive photo essay!*

The others looked at each other, then looked at Lola.

"You're a *celebrity*?" said Bumblebee.

"This changes everything!" said Mango. "Mom!" she called, and jogged up the road toward what was presumably her house. "Mom, a famous person is coming with us, is that okay? Say it's okay!"

"Wow," said Bumblebee, flipping through the pages. "I thought your name was Lola Ray. It says here your name is Passport." She wrinkled her nose in a way Lola found awfully judgmental for a person calling herself Bumblebee Kitchen-House.

"No, my name is Lola," said Lola. "They just got my name wrong."

"Mom says you can come!" said Mango, returning from up the lane.

"Great," said Lola, letting out a sigh and allowing herself a smile. Things had been touch and go for a minute there, but now she felt like she was getting a handle on the situation.

Together Lola, Mango, and Bumblebee made their way back to Mango's house.

"So what did the Book Möb Eel give you?" Bumblebee asked, nodding to Lola's paperback.

"Oh, I don't know," she said, examining the cover. "It's, um . . . it's . . . it's . . ."

*Her!* was the word Lola's brain was struggling to come to grips with. The cover of the little paperback was a black, starry background, with a single figure front and center—or rather, two figures. The first was a girl about Lola's age, with fiery blond hair and fiery wild eyes, holding what looked like a sparking magic wand. The second was the great golden dragon she sat astride.

Lola didn't need Bumblebee's translator to read the title, as this was the English edition. The gold raised lettering read:

*Gardyloo Books Presents,*
*The #1 Bestselling Book of All Time,*
*Based on the Incredible True Story:*

*SHADOWMANCER WARS*

## A Brief Aside About the Phrase Based on the Incredible True Story

**THE BOOK** *SHADOWMANCER WARS* is in fact based on an incredible true story. However, the writers did take some creative liberties, especially with the ending. In the book, as in all of the movie and TV adaptations that followed, the heroine, Skylar Powerstance, defeats the ShadowMancer by steering her ship, the *Heterochromia*, into the heart of the star, sacrificing herself to defeat the enemy.

In truth, the exploding star that consumed Skylar, her ship, and most of the neighboring star system missed the ShadowMancer by several light-years, due to a grave miscalculation and misread bus schedule (the details aren't important). Nevertheless, it is true that within hours of the explosion, the ShadowMancer *did* disappear. She vanished entirely from the face of the galaxy, despite being nowhere near the blast. (In fact, some reports suggest that at the time of the explosion, the ShadowMancer was somewhere near the planet called Earth.)

However, as the then editor of Gardyloo Books observed, this made for a horribly unsatisfying and confusing ending—heroes, after all, are supposed to defeat the bad guy. And so, in the book, Skylar is given credit for the destruction of the ShadowMancer, though no one really knows where the

ShadowMancer disappeared to, and why, or, for that matter, what made her come back.

To date, *ShadowMancer Wars* has sold eight to the eighteenth power copies, which means just about everyone in the galaxy has bought one. Twice.

Phineas Fogg owned two copies. The first he'd downloaded and read at the age of eight. The second had been a limited first edition, an eleventh birthday gift from his parents, which had been delivered by registered interstellar mail, as it happened, exactly three hundred and sixty-five Earth days ago.

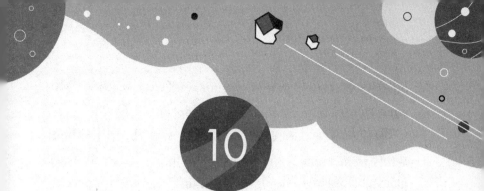

## 10

**PHIN'S ESCAPE POD, WHICH** he had begun thinking of as an Escape Van, hummed quietly through the outer reaches of the Venulian System, toward the star Venula C6-127, and its neighboring hypergate.

The atmosphere on board was tense: the low rumble of juice boxes being slurped, the crumble and snap of animal crackers crushed between incisors, the foreboding crackle of plastic wrap. It was the hushed ceasing of hostilities that typically accompanies snack time.

"All right," said Phin when he'd finished his juice box and tossed it toward the back. "Who are you people?"

The *Calming Breath* catered to a variety of species, so it was no surprise that the ship's day care sported a cross-section of alien toddlers. The three now finishing their animal crackers with Phin couldn't have been more different.

"You can call me P-Money," said the Persian kitten who'd set out the snacks. He looked to be only a year old, and clearly fancied himself the teacher's pet. The only trouble was, he'd established immediately that Phin wasn't the teacher. "My mom's a very important professor at the university!"

"His name's not really P-Money," said the girl sitting across from Phin. She was not a kitten, but looked instead like someone had given arms, legs, a face, and glasses to a baby mushroom. She was eating her animal crackers with slow, intense concentration, her face buried in a book. "His real name's Princess. But he hates it."

"I hate! That! NAME!" said P-Money, standing and beating his little fuzzy chest with his little fuzzy paws. Then, as quickly as the tantrum had begun, it passed, and P-Money went back to stalking his animal crackers.

"What about you?" Phin asked.

"I'm Bella," said the mushroom. "My big sister runs the SS *Calming Breath*."

"You mean Gretta?"

Bella turned another page and licked her lips—or would have, if she'd had any. "Yeah."

This was not in and of itself so surprising. Phin had met baby mushrooms before—they grew from the same fungal core as the Bog Mutants, making them sort-of siblings, but were awfully different. The mushroom people were smaller, and in Phin's experience, more intelligent. Until now, however, Gretta was the only female of the fungal family he'd ever met.

"And what's his deal?" Phin asked, nodding to the third child in their company.

The final member of their party was a round blue brain about the size of a basketball. It hovered a few inches off the floor and seemed to be manipulating its snacks using telekinesis.

"That's Randall," said Bella, not looking up from her book. "He's all right."

"I AM A NODE OF THE MEGA MIND COLLECTIVE. YOU WILL OBEY ME," said Randall. "LOVE AND WORSHIP ME, SLAVES!" Electricity arced from his frontal lobe, incinerating the animal crackers before him.

"Huh," said Phin.

"Are you taking us on a field trip?" asked P-Money.

"Quiet, P-Money. I'm thinking," said Phin. "Why were you kids in here alone? Where's your . . . supervisor?"

"There was supposed to be a Minder-Droid," said P-Money. "But Bella took it apart. She wanted to see how it worked."

"False. I wanted to make sure," said Bella, "that it didn't."

A smile tried to sneak onto Phin's face, but he caught it.

"Right, well," he said, and got to his feet. "Sit tight, because as soon as we get to the hypergate I'm jumping ship and programming this thing to take you back to your parents."

"No! We want to go on a field trip!" said P-Money, bouncing an animal cracker off Phin's stomach.

"EDUCATIONAL LIFE EXPERIENCE!" said Randall.

"What?" said Phin. "Forget it. I'm not taking a bunch of kids on a rescue mission to Earth. I don't know if you heard, but an ancient evil has returned and the universe is in great peril. Just huge, great buckets of peril for everyone. Also," he added, "kids are annoying."

He turned to the controls and began to prepare for their arrival at the hypergate. He'd just about finished programming the auto-return when something heavy, furry, and stabby latched itself to the back of his head.

"Gahh!" observed Phin, tumbling backward as P-Money wrestled him to the ground. "Arrrgghhh!" he added as lightning arced from Randall's cortex and pinned Phin's arms to the floor. "Oof! Oooof," he concluded as Bella climbed onto his stomach, stood on his chest, and folded her arms.

"We want to go with you," she said.

"Well, you cannnnaarrrgghhh!!" said Phin. "Watch the claws, man! I'm partial to my throat!"

"You're on the run," Bella said, pushing her glasses up. "And if you send us back to the ship, we'll tell everyone where you're headed."

Phin struggled to right himself, but it was no use. "You don't know where I'm headed," he tried.

"You just told us Earth!" said P-Money.

Phin sighed. "Come on, P-Money."

"Sorry," said the kitten.

"WE WILL BE GOOD," said Randall. "OR SUFFER HORRIBLE CONSEQUENCES!"

"Easy, Randall," said Phin, and he was about to explain to them calmly and reasonably why he couldn't bring them along, why the galaxy was no place for unaccompanied minors, and how, as a chaperone, they'd have been better off with a rabid Arachnopod with a toothache than Phineas Fogg. But before he could, the control panel began to flash.

"What's that?" said P-Money with a start, releasing Phin's head and clambering into one of the cubbies to hide.

"Someone's hailing us," said Phin. "Let me up!"

Suddenly his arms were free. Bella climbed down off his torso and Phin limped to the front view screen. What he saw did not improve his mood.

The hypergate, one of the hundreds that provided instant transport across the galaxy, turned slowly in space like a great, glittering ring hundreds of miles across. Its portal of quantum sauce rippled darkly as a transport ship the size of a skyscraper entered its depths. There was usually a short line of ships waiting to use a hypergate, but now there were dozens. Rows upon rows of cruisers, interstellar haulers, ferries, and commercial freighters were lined up, waiting for their turn in a massive space-bound traffic jam. Sitting in space traffic with three alien toddlers would have been bad enough, and then Phin saw the reason for the stoppage.

At the head of the traffic jam, between them and the hypergate, was a fleet of black police cruisers, their warning lights flashing. The cruisers' wings were specially designed to interlock, forming an impenetrable blockade of steel-and-armor shielding. The cops had deployed a small army of spiderlike security drones, which now moved between the waiting ships, conducting spot inspections and onboard searches.

"Uh-oh," said Phin.

"*Attention Incoming Vessels,*" squawked the radio. "*Due to recently increased number of planets exploding in this quadrant, all craft must come to a full stop and submit to an onboard inspection, by the authority of the Venulian Sheriff's Department.*"

"*Drab droof* it all," cursed Phin.

It was too late to run. The checkpoint tractor beams were guiding them into line. The Escape Van's primary thrusters powered down as they took their place behind an immense cargo ship with its massive bay doors standing open, a swarm of security drones inspecting its hold.

"Stealing an escape pod is punishable by six years on the penal moons of Varnus Five in this quadrant," said Bella.

"Quiet," said Phin.

"And kidnapping with an intent to transport minors across county lines is punishable by double lobotomy," she whispered. "Except in cases where the kidnapper himself is underage, in which case the courts may rule for a single lobotomy." She met Phin's glare. "That means one scoop instead of two."

"Nobody likes a know-it-all, Bella. Okay!" Phin clapped his hands and turned to the group. "Everyone be cool and do not speak or move or do anything. I'll do the talking." He glowered at Bella. "You got me?"

"We'll be good," said Bella.

"WE WILL OBEY!" rumbled Randall.

P-Money poked his little nose out from the cubby but said nothing.

"Perfect," said Phin. "I'm sure this will all work out perfect."

They waited, their ship held by the tractor beam, as the spot checks made their way up the line. At last, a spider-like security drone tapped on the Van's driver's-side window. Phin engaged the low-power force field and lowered the outer shielding.

"Ship designation and destination," chirped the drone. One of its many spindly arms sported a cattle prod, and it sparked politely.

"Hi there," said Phin, trying a casual lean on the steering wheel. "How's your day going?"

"Ship designation and destination," said the security drone.

"Oh yeah, absolutely." Phin fished in the dashboard and retrieved the ship's documentation. "We're on our way to Earth."

"Purpose of visit," said the security drone.

"Um," said Phin, and glanced over his shoulder. "Field trip," he said. "You know, for the kids."

The drone's little red eye glanced at the children, then back to Phin.

"It's tough being a single dad," Phin went on, wondering where he was going with this, "but we get by."

"You look ten," said the drone.

"Ha! Bless you!" Phin put a hand over his heart. "Honestly, it's just plenty of cold water and expensive soap. That and good genes, I guess." He tried another casual laugh. "Sooo anyway: Can we go?"

"Sir," said the security drone, and if an electronically synthesized voice could sound weary, this one did, "an escape pod was recently stolen from a dreadnaught-class rescue-and-recovery vessel." The drone glanced at the children again. "There were several unattended minors on board."

"How awful!" said Phin. "Boy, do I feel for the parents. I

don't know what I'd do if I lost my little ones."

Again, the security drone considered the kids in the back of the Van.

"These kids don't look anything like you," it observed.

"Adopted!" said Phin.

There was a long pause. Phin smiled. The drone's cattle prod sparked.

"Okay," said the security drone with a long, electronic sigh. "I'm going to have to search your ship."

"Wonderful!" said Phin. "We've got nothing to hide! Come on in. Make yourself at home. Move in if you want to, it's all fine by me!"

"Whatever," said the drone, which was on its last rotation and very much looking forward to its retirement on a shelf in a warehouse somewhere. It moved around to the rear of the ship and waited for Phin to release the cargo doors. The Escape Van opened itself to the blackness of space, the atmosphere inside protected by the thinnest semipermeable force field. The security drone, all sharp edges and pointy bits, floated in, scanners whirring.

Phin and the children waited as the drone searched the interior of the ship. There wasn't much to see.

"Well," it said after a minute. "Everything appears to be in order here, but I'm going to have to ask you to—"

Suddenly, the drone shot sideways and smashed into the

wall. The reason for this was that P-Money had slammed into it.

"Gah!" said Phin. "What are you doing?"

"I'm a fearsome predator!" growled P-Money as he dug his claws into the joints in the security drone's armor. The two spun end over end, bouncing off the wall, then the floor, and then the ceiling.

"DESTROY THE TOOLS OF OPPRESSION," Randall bellowed, zapping the drone with blue-white lightning. The little machine bounced and chittered across the floor, its limbs spinning wildly.

"Stop! Stop that!" said Phin, rushing to the drone. "Ha-ha, sorry, you know how kids are—"

Phin suddenly lost his balance as the Escape Van jolted forward. He whirled to see Bella at the controls.

"What are you doing?" He launched himself at the front of the ship, tripping over the drone as it rolled across the floor in a spasm, P-Money still clinging on with his claws.

"Alert! Alert! Unit 57X-10 is under attack!" bleated the drone.

"How did you get control of the ship?" Phin said as the engines powered up.

"Tractor beams are easy to jam," said Bella, flicking a switch. "And this is taking too long."

The Escape Van accelerated. Directly ahead a cargo ship was being inspected, its massive bay doors standing open like a pair of great steel mandibles. Bella floored it.

"Alert! Alert!" the security drone went on. "Signaling for reinforcemephhhh," it added as Phin slapped a hand over its speaker.

"Ha-ha! Let's . . . oh, let's don't signal any reinforcements, okay?" Phin said. "Can't we resolve this quietly?"

The security drones searching the cargo ships ahead of them turned their red eyes on the fast-approaching Escape Van. They signaled at it to stop. They signaled again, with a hint of frustration. They signaled a third time, now with increasing panic. At last, they began to signal to each other things like "Move!" and "It's gonna ram us!"

*"Unidentified escape-class craft,"* came a transmission from the head police cruiser. *"Kill your engines or you will be fired upon."*

"Okay, time to stop playing," Phin said, wondering whether it was considered bad parenting to wrest control of a ship from an independent young woman learning to take charge of a situation.

"Mmm," said Bella, considering this. "Nah."

The interlocked police ships began to turn and angle their weapons at the Van.

*"Unidentified escape-class craft,"* came the radio. *"This is your final warning. Stop now or be disintegrated."*

"You're going to hit that cargo ship!" said Phin.

"Yeah, I know," said Bella.

The security drones scattered. The Escape Van rocketed forward at ramming speed, shot between the cargo ship's open rear doors, blasted down the length of its hold, and slammed into the far end. Physics being what it is, the parked cargo ship lurched forward and began to tumble like a gigantic and unstoppable piece of space garbage toward the blockade of police cruisers.

Inside the Escape Van, Phin, Randall, P-Money, and the security drone were tossed like confetti. The world spun, and several hard and pointy things introduced themselves to Phin's head and torso.

"*Incoming!*" radioed the head police cruiser.

The out-of-control cargo ship smashed through the blockade like a freight train through a house of cards.

"I'm sorry!" Phin called to the security drone as it bounced around the interior of the Escape Van. "I'm—*ow!*—my kids are usually much better behaved."

"*Ahhhhhh,*" replied the drone as it spun wildly through the rear force field at the back of the Van, away through the cargo hold, and then out into the void of space.

"*Stop at once!*" came a desperate signal from the lead police vessel.

"I'd love to!" Phin called as the toppling ship tossed him against the wall of cubbyholes. "But I'm not exactly in—"

For the record, Phin was going to say "control," but at that exact instant, the out-of-control cargo ship with the out-of-control Escape Van inside it splashed into the hyper-gate's churning quantum sauce, and in a fraction of a fraction of a microsecond, the vessels and everyone aboard were zapped halfway across the galaxy—and, as far as the scattered blockade drones were concerned, into someone else's jurisdiction.

## 11

**IN A UNIVERSE AS** large as ours, with so many inex-plicable goings-on (bad things happening to good people, particles behaving like waves, pineapple appearing on pizza), there have been attempts—very, very many attempts—to explain what it all means and why we're all here.

Unfortunately, no one has quite worked out the actual answer, but a few have come pretty close.

The Protrubing Nuns of Thenezon Six, for instance, believe that every living being, from star babies to house-plants, are the protrusions of an entity so far beyond our comprehension it's better to not even try. Life, they say, is a little like God's hand reaching into the crevices between His seat cushions, looking blindly for His keys.

Again, the nuns aren't quite there, but they're not too far off.

For a time, the most *popular* faith in the galaxy was that practiced by the Monks of Just 'Cause. The Monks of Just 'Cause don't have a "cause" of any kind; their explanation for why things are the way they are is, "Well, just 'cause that's the way it is," which, if not a particularly satisfying philosophy, is at least internally consistent. For millennia, the Monks of Just 'Cause spread across the galaxy, building their Golden Cathedrals, and spending their considerable free time messing around with randomized particle transference and quantum entanglement.

Like many religions, however, the monks sooner or later began to lose their popularity, and so began to seek new ways to stay current and relevant, and appeal to the youth demographic. A business consultant was brought in to make some changes. The Golden Cathedrals were given a makeover, and in their new guise, they became some of the most popular destinations in the galaxy.

Flash forward to today, and it is a testament to the monks' incredible reach and popularity that their Golden Cathedrals can be found even on small remote planets like the one Lola now found herself traversing. In fact, Golden Cathedrals are particularly popular on isolated and underdeveloped planets. For Golden Cathedrals are places where one can truly find *anything* one could possibly seek, including, if you got there before noon, a really great deal on hash browns.

Lola expected the Corona family car to be made of bits of other things, just as their house was made of bits of other things, and their clothes were made of bits of other things.

(Mango's mother, who introduced herself as "Mrs. Corona. Wait, that doesn't sound right. What's your translator set to?," wore an elegant gown made of old pop cans, which Lola quite liked, actually.) Lola had not been prepared for the car, though. It was true, the inhabitants of this planet were a few feet taller than the average human, and so would need a roomier mode of transport, but still, seeing the car, Lola managed to be gobsmacked.

"We'll take the Kia," Mrs. Corona had said, which had a nice reassuring sound to it.

"It's a car," gasped Lola when she saw the Corona family vehicle, "*made of other cars.*"

Constructed of about eight compact Kias smashed together, the car had a Kia for each wheel, the cabin was four Kias sort of jammed together, and the hood ornament was a scooter, the kind Lola had wanted for her eighth birthday.

"All aboard!" said Mrs. Corona, and she, Mango, Lola, and Bumblebee (who'd been invited along) climbed up into the enormous inner cabin, which had been hollowed out and fitted with large seats, a large steering wheel, and cup holders.

Lola rode with her rations kit on her lap. It wasn't much, but it was hers, and she was determined to look after it.

"You guys certainly have a lot of, um, *stuff* around here," she said.

"Yeah, but who cares?" said Mango from the front seat,

about fifteen feet away. "The Golden Cathedral. That's where you can get the *really* good stuff."

"Have you been before?" Lola asked Bumblebee, who shrugged.

"My dad says we can only afford to go once a month."

"I see," said Lola, who didn't.

She expected to be riddled with questions about where she came from, and perhaps about her experiences at the Battle of Singularity City, but nobody seemed interested now. Mango had her nose buried in a tablet, and Mrs. Corona was singing along to the radio. Bumblebee read her magazine. And so Lola read her book.

It was not what she'd expected. Despite being "based on a true story," *ShadowMancer Wars* read like a novel. The hero was a teenager, Skylar Powerstance, a girl who was smart, beautiful, and capable, but thought of herself as having none of these qualities, despite the fact that everyone she met seemed to instantly fall in love with her. She fought bravely against the ShadowMancer, which was apparently the name given to the girl with the golden dragon. Skylar was direct, tough, and not afraid to use her fists. In essence, she was everything Lola was not. Which was fine when a book was all pretend, but these events were real, they had happened. And Lola had *met* the ShadowMancer. She had taken Lola's Twinkie. Lola flipped to the end to see how Skylar ultimately fared. It wasn't encouraging.

"How's the book?" Bumblebee asked, having finished her magazine.

"Bad," said Lola.

"Bad as in badly written or bad as in you don't like it?"

"Yes," said Lola.

They'd come to a larger road—so large Lola might have thought it was a landing strip for freighter planes. In fact, it was a kind of highway, and trundling along it like a pack of great chrome mastodons were other cars. Monster trucks made of monster trucks, minivans made of minivans. Each vehicle was unnecessarily large and ornate, pumping black roiling exhaust into the atmosphere. They took their place in traffic, and together the great cavalcade made its way up the mountain, following the signs for the last Golden Cathedral of the Monks of Just 'Cause.

At last, they rounded a steep bend, and the cathedral came into view. It truly was golden. Multitiered and glittering like the world's largest jewelry box. Lola could make out balconies and verandas overflowing with plant life. Where the sun wasn't gleaming too brightly off the golden pillars, she saw the glint of waterfalls. Towering above it all was a single column thirty stories high, on top of which rested a symbol, like a beacon, for the cathedral itself. Had Lola been able to read the local language, she would have only been more confused, for beneath the symbol were the words *Sixty Billion Maybe Meals Sold*.

The parking lot went on for acres. Mrs. Corona found a spot at last, and together they climbed out into the warm afternoon. Other families were disembarking from their cars, and some were returning from the cathedral carrying colorful sacks. Some of their faces were pleased, but others scowled. Lola saw one girl weeping. Trotting behind the weeping girl was a small brontosaurus.

"But, Mom, I wanted a *carnivore!*" the girl wailed, and her mother rolled her eyes.

"What . . . kind of place is this?" Lola said.

"The best kind!" said Mango and pumped her fists.

They came to the entrance. A pair of immense stone doors that must have weighed a ton slid aside. The inner vestibule of the cathedral was filled with people, each of them dressed in the local fashion. They had arranged themselves in long lines, and Lola and company followed suit. Lola took in the massive hall, the frescoed ceiling, and to the west, the dining area, where families sat on uncomfortable-looking benches, apparently eating lunch.

Scattered across the tables and floor were piles of all sorts of junk—vases and matryoshka dolls, inflatable pool toys and rubber chickens. It was chaos.

"We're next, girls," said Mrs. Corona, unclasping the suitcase that functioned as her purse. "Decide what you want now."

"What are you getting?" Bumblebee asked Lola.

"Uh, I don't know," she said. "Sorry, I thought you said this was a cathedral? It looks like a . . . well, not exactly like a . . . well . . ." Lola wasn't sure how to say this, so she just went for it. "Look, is this a fast-food restaurant?"

Bumblebee, Mango, and even Mrs. Corona laughed.

"Only the most amazing fast-food restaurant in the *universe!*" said Mango, and before Lola could question this, it was their turn to order.

Above the counter hung the menu, and an angel stood behind the counter, waiting to take their order. He was tall and beautiful, dressed in a long flowing robe. Angelic wings were tucked in comfortably behind his shoulders, the feathers so pristine they appeared to be glowing. He was also wearing a name tag. It said "Kevin."

"Hello," said Kevin the Angel. "Blessings Be Upon You if That's What Happens to Happen™. Welcome to the Golden Cathedral. How may I enrich your short and largely meaningless existence today?" He smiled brightly.

"I'll take two Maybe Meals," said Mrs. Corona. "One nuggets and one patty. And just a side salad for me."

They all turned to Lola.

"Oh!" she said. "Uh," she added. The angel continued to smile benevolently. "I guess I'll have a Maybe Meal, too?"

"Nuggets or patty?" the angel asked her, which was not the sort of question Lola had ever expected to be asked by an angel.

"Nuggets?" Lola ventured.

"And will that be together or separate?"

"I'm getting these two and the salad," said Mrs. Corona, indicating Mango and Bumblebee.

"Oh, I don't have any money," said Lola.

"There's no need for money here, child," said the angel in a soothing voice.

Instead of paying—or rather, as a method of payment—Mrs. Corona stuck out her wrist. There was a tattoo on it, a string of numbers, it looked like. From behind his terminal, the angel raised a small device and held it to Mrs. Corona's wrist. There was a flash of red light, a beep, and when the device was removed, the numbers on Mrs. Corona's wrist had changed.

"Come on, girls," she said, leading Mango and Bumblebee to the pickup area.

"Um," said Lola as the angel held out his device. Lola had no tattoos, of course, and had never been particularly interested in getting one. But she was nothing if not a girl who went with the flow and so she held out her wrist.

"That will be two hundred and seventy-two," said the angel, and he held the device to Lola's wrist. It flashed, it beeped, and Lola felt nothing more than a small tickle. Her wrist now had a series of numbers and dashes running across it.

"Two hundred and seventy-two what?" asked Lola, but the angel was already helping the next customer.

She joined the others as they waited for their meals to arrive. When they did, Mrs. Corona took them to the dining area where they found a table by the window. The Maybe Meals came in large colorful sacks, emblazoned with the Golden Cathedral logo. The openings were sealed, and Lola could swear hers was vibrating.

"Okay, girls, here we go," said Mrs. Corona. "Who wants to go first?"

"Me! I'm going first!" said Mango, shooting the others a threatening look. Lola didn't argue.

Mango closed her eyes. She held her Maybe Meal in both hands, slipping into a deep meditation. Her brow furrowed.

"What's—?" started Lola, but Bumblebee shushed her.

Mango took a deep breath, opened her eyes, and then tore open her satchel. A full-sized purple sofa tumbled out of the bag and crashed to the floor. It was six feet long if it was an inch, and yet had somehow been inside a small paper bag a moment ago, a paper bag Mango had carried to the table as if it contained no more than her lunch.

Lola was so surprised she stood up, knocking over her chair. The others stared at her.

"You okay?" said Bumblebee.

"Bubble bins," Mango cursed. "I was hoping for a motor-cycle."

"How did you do that?" said Lola. She grabbed the remnants of Mango's torn bag and looked inside. There was no hole in the bottom, just a totally normal paper sack.

"Have you never had a Maybe Meal before?" Bumblebee asked.

"She's not from here, honey," said Mrs. Corona with a little laugh. "She doesn't know *what's* going on."

"How was that sofa in that bag a moment ago?" Lola demanded. She was done asking politely. She was switching to demands now. "Tell me."

"It's a Maybe Meal," said Mango, giving the sofa a disappointed kick. "They contain anything."

"Like, literally anything?" said Lola, taking her seat again.

"Yeah, but you never know what you're gonna get," said Bumblebee. "So what you do is you clear your mind, think of what you want most, and sometimes, if you're lucky, you get it."

"Where do you think we get all this cool stuff?" said Mango, rattling her pepper-grinder belt.

Lola looked around at the other diners. A man at the next table opened his Maybe Meal and pulled out a gold brick. He weighed it in his hand, shrugged, then tossed it to the floor. She swiveled to look out the window at the valley below, its drifts of washing machines and old furniture, sneakers, stand mixers, stereo systems, and pop cans. The whole planet was *overflowing* with Maybe Meal "prizes."

"My turn," said Bumblebee. She closed her eyes, took a breath, then opened her sack.

Something loud, crazed, and covered in green feathers exploded from the bag. Lola screamed. The creature screeched and thundered into the air above their heads, beating its great green wings. Nearby diners glanced up in mild interest. The bird circled, flicking a long scaly tail before screeching once more and crashing through the nearest skylight.

"What was that?" said Lola, her voice shaking.

"Well, it wasn't a new pair of Rollerblades," said Bumblebee, and sighed.

"Sorry, dears," said Mrs. Corona. "Maybe next time."

"But how does it work?" said Lola.

This is how it worked: The Monks of Just 'Cause, when they weren't pruning their wings or bleaching their robes, had found a way to squeeze teleport technology into a kind of nanoweave. Into each Maybe Meal bag, the monks stitched in a gate. When a bag's seal was broken, a random object would be instantly teleported from somewhere in the universe into the bag itself. Size, shape, and weight did not matter. A Maybe Meal could contain anything from a plastic toy to a Boeing 747, though, for whatever reason, the prizes tended to be large household appliances and the occasional prehistoric animal.

"It's your turn, dear," said Mrs. Corona.

Lola eyed her Maybe Meal warily. Anything could be inside. What if it was something dangerous? Like a lion or a supernova? How was any of this legal, let alone possible?

Lola glanced at the others, swallowed, and closed her eyes.

What did she need? What would help her? She needed to get back to Phin. She needed to find the ShadowMancer. She needed her *drab droofing* Twinkie back.

*Let it be the Twinkie*, Lola thought. *Inside this bag is my Twinkie, the one with the coordinates for Dimension Why. It's there. It's already there. I just need to open the bag and take it out. Give me what I need.*

Gingerly, Lola tore the thin paper.

Nothing exploded. Nothing came roaring out.

She reached inside. She felt something soft and pulled. It was a necktie. An ugly one, at that, with green and red stripes. She kept pulling. The necktie was tied to a second necktie, which was even uglier than the first, green-and-yellow paisley. The second necktie was tied to a third, the third to a fourth, and pretty soon Lola had pulled roughly fifty feet of neckties from her bag.

"Huh," said Bumblebee. "Neckties."

Lola turned over one of the ties and looked at the label. It said, *Bob's Joke Shop, Est. 2941, Hyannis, Massachusetts.*

"Is that what you wanted?" Mango asked.


They ate their lunches. Lola didn't touch her nuggets, but she munched on a few french fries. When they were done, they gathered their things. Lola stuffed her tie-rope into her rations kit, and slung the kit over her shoulder. Mango left her sofa where it had fallen. They made their way toward the exit.

Mrs. Corona turned at the door and said to the girls, "Say goodbye to your friend, now."

"Oh," said Lola. "Are you not . . . could I have a ride back into town, you think?"

"Oh, honey, of course," said Mrs. Corona. "I'll come get you when you're paid up."

"Paid up?" said Lola and glanced at her wrist. "I thought we already paid."

Mrs. Corona chuckled. "*I've* got credit, honey. You'll have to pay now."

"Pay . . . how?" said Lola.

"By working," said Bumblebee. "How do you think this place stays in business?"

"Yeah, they can't just give away Maybe Meals for free," said Mango, still chewing on a nugget. "They're not gonna let you leave until you work off your debt. Mom works in the patty fields, and my dad is a foreman at the nugget plant."

"My parents are in marketing," said Bumblebee.

"Let's see, we got here before noon, so you got the early-bird discount," said Mrs. Corona, and took Lola's hand. She examined the numbers tattooed on her wrist. "See? Two hundred and seventy-two. You'll be out of here in no time."

"Two hundred and seventy-two what?" said Lola.

"Years, silly!" said Mrs. Corona. "Come on, loves, we have

to get ready for your sister's birthday party. It's a big one," she said to Lola. "She's turning five thousand. *Such* a fun age. She's already walking!"

"I—" said Lola.

"Bye!" said Mango, following her mother out the door.

"See you later?" said Bumblebee. "Maybe we can hang out when you're done."

"But—" said Lola.

She moved to follow them, but she felt a firm hand on her shoulder. She turned. An angel was staring down at her and smiling benevolently. In his other hand he held a plunger.

"Ready to get to work?"

## 12

**THERE ARE THREE KNOWN** ways to traverse the mind-bending distances that separate the star systems of our galaxy. The first is Faster-Than-Light travel. On most planets, the invention of such "FTL Engines" has occurred under similar circumstances: There's a party. Someone decides to mix a little dark matter into the punch. Someone else thinks it'll be funny to pour the punch into the host's supercollider. Hilarity ensues, immediately followed by research grants, angel investors, and eventually, the construction of an interstellar spacecraft. The spacecraft is usually named something inspiring like *Endeavor* or *Enterprise* or, in the case of the Super Basic Space Program of Franza-Kaplan Six, the SS *Quite Fast Enough, Thank You.*

There are also some beings with the innate ability to blip across great distances without the aid of a ship. Some were born with the skill, and a few, like the ShadowMancer herself, acquire it later in life. But such a small percentage of beings in the galaxy can pull off this trick, it's almost not worth mentioning.

The third and by far the most popular and cheapest method is, of course, the hypergate system, invented by Phin's great-great-great-great-grandfather, Phineas Fogg the First, back in the twenty-fourth century, and owned and operated by the Fogg-Bolus Hypergate and Baked Beans Corporation ever since. The fact that Earthlings were the ones who created the quantum sauce and connected the galaxy causes no small amount of consternation for everyone else, who generally regard humans as a lower life-form. As one journalist put it, "Imagine a team of scientists working day and night to create the perfect sandwich, and one morning the dog walks in with a salami-and-cheese hoagie on a plate of Venusian crystal. Yes, we're all happy with the outcome, but one distinctly feels one has been shown up."

Phin and his companions were briefly detained at hypergate control, who were understandably pretty miffed after the long-haul tanker had tumbled out of their gate and nearly crashed into an orbiting falafel cart.

"Just who in the galaxy do you think you are?" the customs agent had barked over the radio.

Phineas Fogg sent them a retinal-and-thumb-print scan to confirm his identity, showing them exactly who in the galaxy he thought he was. Specifically, the only son of their bosses and heir to the entire Fogg-Bolus Hypergate and Baked Beans Corporation fortune.

"Um, you're all cleared, Mr. Fogg," the customs agent radioed as the Escape Van's clearance came through. "Apologies for taking such a harsh tone earlier. Let me be the first to welcome you back to your home planet."

"Not a problem, Agent Dooley," Phin radioed back, feeling lusciously smug.

"You're kind of important, huh?" asked Bella as Phin guided their ship into Earth's atmosphere.

"Wrong," said Phin. "I'm *incredibly* important."

It was raining in New York, and as the Escape Van slipped below the cloud cover, the great gray city opened up before them, a dark and spiky palette of electric lighting and concrete. Terrestrial flyers zipped between the skyscrapers where they weren't hovering in traffic jams, and below it all the heavy, chest-vibrating pulse of the city's environmental turbines roiled and pumped, keeping the atmosphere clear of radiation.

"Do you live here?" P-Money asked, cowering behind Phin's shoulder.

"Of course not, don't be ridiculous," said Phin. "I live in New Jersey."

The Van passed through the transparent radiation shield bisecting the Hudson River as the sun peeked through the clouds, bathing the craggy, barren landscape in golden rays.

This had all once been a metropolitan center, until the Great Pork Fat Meltdown of 2415. Over the last six hundred years, the wreckage had become overgrown with enterprising vines and stubborn shrubbery. And in the center of all this old and new growth stood the shining tower that had been Phin's home for all of his eleven years: Fogg-Bolus headquarters, with its company slogan erected in thirty-foot-high illuminated letters on the roof.

"*Insanely Safe*,'" read Bella as Phin maneuvered the craft onto a landing pad. "That sounds reassuring."

"Mm," Phin grunted.

There was a *thunk* as the Escape Van's landing skis connected with the rooftop.

Phin hesitated, but to his credit, only for a fraction of a second. Then he opened the rear port and stepped out onto the landing pad like he owned the place, which he basically did.

"Stay here," he said to the children, and was immediately ignored.

"I don't like this place," said P-Money, peering over the ledge. "Where are all the closed spaces? Don't you have any boxes to climb in?"

"It'll get plenty claustrophobic downstairs, trust me," said Phin, heading for the rooftop elevator.

"IMPRESSIVE STRUCTURE, HUMAN," said Randall.

"I think it's cool," said Bella in a hushed voice. "The *actual* Fogg-Bolus headquarters. Just think of all the neat research going on here."

"Research?" Phin scoffed. "My parents care more about cruises and safaris and three-day brunches." Phin's parents had been on vacation since before he was born, taking a break every now and then to get kidnapped. "The last time my parents saw a Bunsen burner, someone was serving martinis in it. They think a quasar is something you take for indigestion."

"Okay, I think we get it," said Bella.

They all piled into the elevator. It descended smoothly as Muzak whispered from the speaker system.

"Stop trying to hold my hand," Phin snapped.

"It's all wet," said P-Money, and wrinkled his nose. "Why are you sweating so much?"

Had Phin answered, which he didn't, he might have mentioned the reason he was so nervous. He hadn't been back here since escaping with Lola several weeks ago, but before that he'd almost never been outside his own penthouse. Yes, it was home, and yes, his brain was being filled with ultrafamiliar smells and sights that made his heart hurt. But it was also a bit like visiting the prison where you'd once been a captive. What if the guards don't let you leave?

"The garage is on level eleven," Phin said, fiddling with his pocket scanner. There was still no signal from the Rescue

Wagon or Lola, but that didn't mean anything. The scanner could be malfunctioning, he told himself. Or something. "And the cafeteria is on twelve. If I know Lola, she'd have headed straight there after landing."

"I think we're slowing down," said Bella.

"What?" said Phin as he pressed their floor button again.

"DETECTING MULTIPLE HUMANOID LIFE-FORMS ON LEVEL THIRTY-FIVE," said Randall.

"Yeah, well, it's a corporate headquarters—there are lots of people here," said Phin.

"STRUCTURE'S POPULATION CONCENTRATED ON LEVEL THIRTY-FIVE," insisted Randall.

"Maybe they're doing a team-building exercise," said Phin, but he didn't sound confident. Worse, Bella was right. Their decent was slowing. The floors clicked by on the electric display. *Thirty-nine: Executive Dining; Thirty-eight: Executive Gymnasium; Thirty-seven: Executive Omelet Bar.*

"Wait," said Phin, as the thing that had been poking at the back of his brain began to stab at it. "Wait, hold on. Does anyone know what day it is? Like, the local date?" He tapped a button on his tablet to bring up the news:

*Dateline: August 31st, 3018. Disturbing Reports from the Venulian System Hint at Possible Return of ShadowMancer.*

"Oh no," said Phin.

"What?" said Bella. "Are you worried about the Shadow-Mancer?"

"No!" said Phin. "No, the date! Don't you see what day it is? It's the thirty-first!"

"So?"

"*Floor thirty-five,*" intoned the elevator's user interface. "*Executive ballroom.*"

*Ding!*

The doors slid open.

"Please no," said Phin.

"Happy birthday, Phineas!" shouted his parents and the other six hundred and seventy-four employees, friends, and family members gathered in tuxedos and ball gowns in the grand executive ballroom, which was set for what would go down in history as the most expensive twelfth-birthday party in all of recorded time.

"Welcome home, Phinny," said Eliza Fogg, Phin's mother. She opened her arms for a hug. She was dressed in a Zebble and Flip evening gown, into which actual stars, shrunk to the size of diamonds, had been stitched. Selling it would have fed all the starving children of Ganymede and Titan combined, but luckily enough, Eliza owned two, and had already sold the spare to not only feed the children but also buy each one a new gaming system as a bonus.

"Happy birthday, buddy," said Barnabus Fogg, Phin's father, whose Multi-Tux shuffled through several different styles and color patterns a minute. He was drinking something blue that was making his face red. "Are you surprised?"

"He's not surprised; we told him to come," said Eliza with a laugh like silver bells. "You must have received the message we sent the Rescue Wagon, or else you wouldn't be here, right, Phinny?"

The elevator went *ding!* again and the doors slid shut.

In the elevator, it was quiet for a moment.

"Um," said Bella at Phin's side. "Shouldn't we have gone out there?"

"No," said Phin, his voice hollow. "No, we need to escape." He slammed the button for the roof, but the doors slid open again. Eliza was standing on the other side, smiling and holding a short-range electronic jammer.

"Nice try," she said with a smile. "Now come say hi to your grandmothers."

Phin followed his mother as if in a trance. The ballroom was enormous, and its domed ceiling and chandeliers hung several stories over the sprung floor and two-hundred-odd banquet tables. Chocolate fountains bubbled. Hovering bartender androids served drinks and nibbles, and the DJ, interstellar celebrity sensation Dance-Dance-Dance-Dance Bot 3000, had been cantilevered onto the stage and was cycling through its hard drive of eighteen billion crowd-pleasing bangers. It couldn't be said that the Foggs didn't know how to throw a party.

"You've had such an amazing year," Eliza was saying as she led Phin through the crowd. The employees of Fogg-Bolus nodded and wished him a respectful happy birthday. Some of them he knew, but most were strangers to him. "Saving the universe, rescuing your father and me from certain death, making new friends . . ." She smiled a tight smile at the children clinging to Phin's pant legs. "And are these yours?"

"Stowaways," Phin said blankly.

"Well, they're adorable."

"The big *one two*, eh, buddy?" Barnabus said, slapping Phin on the back. "Before you know it, you'll be a teenager! You hungry? You want something to drink?" He leaned in and even his breath smelled blue. "Where's your girlfriend?"

"She's not my girlfriend," snapped Phin. "She's my non-romantic life partner, and . . ." He glanced around. "She was supposed to be here. On Earth, I mean. I swore the Wagon was programmed to bring her *home*," he hissed to himself.

"Oh, well, we haven't seen her," said Barnabus, his eyes scanning the crowd, getting a bit lost, scanning the ceiling, and then ultimately scanning his drink and liking what he found.

"Look who's here!" Eliza said. "Your grandmothers!"

Standing before Phin were two incredibly old women in dour black dresses buttoned to the throat.

"Let's have a look at you," said one of Phin's grandmothers. She raised a pair of spectacles and looked him over. "You're bloody filthy. Is this how you show up to a party? And why is there a cat hanging off you?"

"Hi, Grandma Maude," Phin said dutifully. "Hi, Grandma Maude's clone, Grandma Lesser Maude."

Maude Elizabeth Fogg had married her own clone since, as she'd put it, no one else met her standards of propriety and good sense. In Phin's experience, Grandma Maude's clone, whom she called Lesser Maude, was a big improvement on the original.

"Happy birthday, sweetheart," said Lesser Maude. "I bet you're going to love your present."

"An astronomical waste of money," growled Grandma Maude.

"Listen, Mom, Dad, Maudes," said Phin. "This is really great, and I'm so, just so genuinely surprised you remembered my birthday. I think it's the first time," he said, and Eliza and Barnabus thought about this and nodded in agreement. "And you know I love a party, and I am just super-keen to see whatever expensive thing you bought me—"

"He's going to love it," Eliza said to Barnabus, who burped.

". . . but I can't stop right now," said Phin. "Lola's gone missing. The ShadowMancer stole her Twinkie and is probably going to try and destroy the universe again."

"The universe can wait, precious," said Eliza, and led Phin to the stage. "Let's have your cake first, and then you can tell us all about it."

"But!" said Phin and was ignored with the kind of focus and determination people usually reserve for an Olympic sport.

Together, Eliza, Barnabus, and Phin took to the stage. The others hung back, watching from the dance floor, except for P-Money, who climbed into a handbag someone had left unattended and poked his little pink nose out.

"Thank you, Dance-Dance-Dance-Dance Bot Three Thousand," said Eliza, her voice amplified to fill the entire ballroom. The music quieted. "And thank you all for coming to this very special night. As you all know, tonight, twelve years ago, I went into labor on a private flight to the Horsehead Nebula. Well, you can bet we turned right around, and twelve hours later Phineas was born, right in this very building." The crowd applauded, and Phin decided not to point out that six hours after that, Eliza and Barnabus were back on a private charter to the Horsehead Nebula while baby Phin was being tended to by a phalanx of nurse-bots.

"As most of you also know, last month, while on vacation in the Frillian Riviera, Barnabus and I were kidnapped, tortured, and ultimately rescued by our beautiful boy. And let me tell you, an experience like that really makes you stop and take a look at your life." Eliza turned to Phin and placed a hand on his shoulder. She smiled at him with warmth, love, and a touch of sadness. "It really makes you reevaluate your choices. And so, as of this moment, Barnabus and I would like to announce our retirement as co-CEOs of Fogg-Bolus."

The room burst into applause, which Eliza quieted with a gesture.

"And since our partner, Goro Bolus, has been exiled to the hidden treasure planet of Frankta D'Or for crimes against sanity, it is time to appoint a new leader to shepherd this company into the thirty-first century."

"I would love it," said Phin to his mother, putting a hand over his heart, "if you would stop talking right now."

"May I present to you," Eliza continued, drowning him out, "the new CEO of the Fogg-Bolus Hypergate and Baked Beans Corporation, Phineas Fogg the Third!"

The crowd went wild. Spotlights flew over the room and centered themselves on Phin. There was a clack of drumsticks and Dance-Dance-Dance-Dance Bot 3000 began playing a thunderous version of "For He's a Jolly Good Biped," complete with shredding guitar as sparks erupted from the footlights and showered the stage.

"But wait, before you say anything," said Eliza, putting a hand on Phin's shoulder. "Wait till you see your *other* present."

Suddenly, the lights turned low. The crowd hushed, as the music went tense. Spotlights fell on a pair of double doors near the back. They opened, spilling light and dry ice. The crowd gasped and then began to applaud as the most beautiful object Phin had ever seen floated majestically into the center of the ballroom.

To call it a bicycle would have been like calling the entire Septarian Missile Defense system a popgun. It was a twin-jet, hyperarticulated, fully stocked, supercharged, air-conditioned, hydroponic, sixty-seven-gear *ultracycle*. A *Jax-Sprocket Velo Ceraptor*. Limited edition. So limited, in fact, there was only one in the entire universe. And darn if it wasn't painted a gorgeous omni-spectrum red.

Phin's knees went weak.

His jaw went loose.

His brain went on vacation.

"*I want it*," he said in a whisper at once dreamy and desperate.

"It's all yours, pal," said Barnabus. "With all the bells and whistles. Just imagine flying over the city in that thing." He chuckled. "We could have it shipped to the Grand Canyon and you can *jump* it."

How many years had he begged them to get him a *Velo Ceraptor*, and how many times had they said, "You're too young," or "It's too dangerous," or "Our phone's been weird, sorry, we didn't get your message"? How many hours had he spent poring over the catalog, or imagining himself zipping across the countryside astride his very own Jax-Sprocket. He didn't just want that bike, he needed it. He needed it all the way down in his kidneys.

"Speech! Speech! Speech!" the crowd began to chant, and Phin's parents joined them, clapping along to the beat. They moved to the side of the stage, giving him the center spotlight. Phin cleared his throat. "Um," he said, and started when his now-amplified voice boomed through the ballroom. It was a situation he was very much unused to—that is, being the center of attention and *not* wanting to be. He smoothed down his hair, straightened his jumpsuit, and stepped into the spotlight.

"Well," he said, and the crowd got very quiet. "You definitely surprised me, and that's not an easy thing to do."

There was laughter and a smattering of applause, then quiet again.

"The thing is . . ." Phin swallowed. "I was right in the middle of, uh, needing to save the universe again, so . . ."

"Oh, that's no problem!" Eliza called from the side of the stage, and all heads in the room swiveled to her. "We'll set up a fund! A *Stop the ShadowMancer* fund! Don't you think we can do that, honey?"

"Of course," said Barnabus. "Let's start with, what? A billion dollars? We'll see where it goes."

"A billion dollars?" said Phin.

"Why not?" said Eliza. "The universe is important, too!"

The crowd applauded in agreement.

"Right," said Phin. "Great. So, uh . . ."

His palms were slick and his throat absurdly dry. The moisture in his body was pooling in all the wrong places. He closed his eyes and didn't care how silly he looked. Give him space wizards bent on total destruction any day; nothing made him less certain, less confident, and feel less capable than his family.

And no one in the universe made Phineas Fogg the Third feel incapable.

Phin's eyes snapped open. "All right," he said, and this time, he liked how his voice boomed. "It's a tradition in this family," he said to the crowd, "to not get any work done."

The crowd laughed. So did his parents. Phin pressed on, jaw set.

"My parents have spent their entire careers on vacation, and now they're retiring. Well, that's great. That's pretty much par for the course, I'd say."

Again there was laughter, but not quite as much.

"For the past eight generations," said Phin, "this family has goofed off while someone else ran the company. Grandma Maude, you know I love and respect you," he continued, "but you left clones to run the company while you went to *find yourself*"—Phin made air quotes, which was something he only did during times of personal crisis—"and I'm glad you eventually did and married her."

The crowd was totally silent now, and Phin couldn't quite see their faces in the glare of the spotlight, but he soldiered on.

"No one in this family ever takes responsibility for anything. Heck, six hundred years ago we *blew up New Jersey*, and as far as I know, we never said we're sorry. Well, New Jersey, and the rest of Earth, I would like to apologize, on behalf of the Foggs, for the Great Pork Fat Meltdown. And I'd also like to apologize to all of you," he said, "the employees of Fogg-Bolus, because let's face it, what I'm about to say is probably going to tank your stock options."

He looked at his parents. "Mom and Dad, I love you *so* much, and if you ever need rescuing from an Arachnopod or whatever, I'm there. But you can take your job offer and blow it out your exhaust ports."

The crowd gasped. Barnabus and Eliza stared back, their smiles evaporating.

"The bike is gorgeous. Sorry I can't accept it," he added, and jumped down off the stage.

No one said anything. Nobody moved.

"Y'all coming?" Phin said to the kids. Bella nodded, and she, P-Money, and Randall fell in line behind Phin as he parted the crowd and marched toward the exit. Phineas Fogg had saved the universe once, but he'd never felt so good about himself until this moment. And in fact, he thought of the absolute perfect last words, and turned at the door.

"And another thing—!" he said.

But before he could finish, Dance-Dance-Dance-Dance Bot 3000 went "*PARTY FOUULL . . . ,*" made a sound like an air horn, and immediately blasted off into a rendition of "Everybody on the Floor 'Cause Your Chairs Are Carnivorous," and drowned Phin the heck out.

## 13

"YOU'RE LISTENING TO WVEN, *Venulian Radio, the Mix! Flag Jackson here.*

"*Following an ongoing story, authorities have now confirmed that the creature stolen from a maximum-security zoo last week was in fact Pogo, the golden dragon ridden by the Shadow-Mancer during her campaign of terror against the galaxy. If the infamous space wizard has returned, that would certainly be good news for Gardyloo Books, the company that published* ShadowMancer Wars, *formerly the bestselling book of all time, which today fell to an all-time low at the number four slot on the* Galactic Gazette's *best-seller list.*

"*In a moment we'll continue our countdown. Remember, be our ten thousandth caller and win an all-expenses-paid rager with WVEN's own Phyllis the Party Rhino! And now, here's Hannah Starfoot with an important message about Soylent Yellow, an all-natural better butter. Soylent Yellow, You're Not Legally Allowed to Believe It's Not Butter!*"

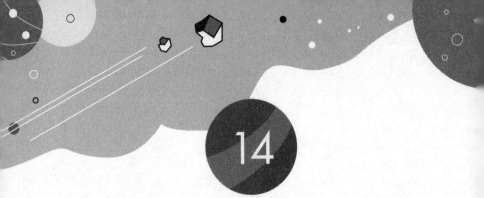

**14**

**LOLA RESTED HER HEAD** against the cool tile of the bathroom wall and sighed.

Things were not going according to plan. At the very least, not *her* plan. She'd begun the day with a problem, and now things were exponentially worse. She was no closer to finding the ShadowMancer or recovering her Twinkie. Instead, she was now indebted ("imprisoned" was more like it) to a shadowy religious order for the next several hundred years. After orientation (where she was given a name tag, a hairnet, and shown the bunk where she'd spend every night for the rest of her natural life, apparently), she'd spent the entire afternoon and evening scrubbing the restaurant's automated toilets.

Today was up there with the top five Worst Lola Days of All Time, coming in right after April 4, 2014, when she'd arrived at Class Picture Day unaware of the massive brown chocolate stain on the seat of her new jeans. And so, defeated and exhausted, Lola was responding the same way she had then: by hiding in a bathroom stall with a book.

"*Please select a video from our home box office of over thirty thousand titles, including over thirteen hundred waterfall simulations, for the shy-bladdered among us,*" chirped the toilet. Lola ignored it.

*ShadowMancer Wars* lay open on her lap. In the chapter she was currently reading, the heroine, Skylar Powerstance, had met a wise old woman in the woods who was training her to fight. The old woman taught Skylar to shoot arrows. She taught her to backflip over tables while simultaneously firing two quantum-flux ion blasters. In one section, Skylar fought off an army of Practice Bots using only a pencil and some rubber bands. Lola had never fired a blaster and certainly never disabled a Practice Bot's ocular sensors with an eraser nib. If this was what it took to defeat the ShadowMancer, she was in even worse trouble than she thought.

But what was really making her brain do yoga was this: there was nothing in the book about where the ShadowMancer came from or what she wanted. As far as Lola could tell, the ShadowMancer was a total mystery, just a blank force of destruction and malice. Lola liked to understand the "why" of things, or at least of people, and she couldn't puzzle out why the ShadowMancer *wanted* to erase the entire galaxy.

"*Are you enjoying your evacuation? Press the star button to rate your experience! And remember to subscribe for more updates from Quazinart!*"

And it was tricky to puzzle out *anything* when the

commode you were sitting on kept talking to you.

Just then, the door to the restroom hissed open, triggering a chorus of automated greetings.

*"Good evening and welcome! We are eager to make your lavatorial experience a pleasant and enriching one!"*

Lola froze. It was well after whatever passed for midnight around here, and the cathedral's restaurant had closed for the evening. She guessed being discovered slacking wouldn't go over well, but whoever'd come in didn't sound like a monk. She was having a loud and contentious conversation with herself. Lola pulled up her feet, held her breath, and listened.

"No, Mom, I'm fine. Yeah, it's, like, very enriching. Or whatever."

There was a short pause.

"I told you, as soon as my work-study is up, I'm going to the outer systems with Braz. I don't *care* if you don't like him, Mother, he's my *stylist*—I mean my *boyfriend*. Well, he's both!"

Lola froze. Whoever had come into the bathroom was talking on some kind of communicator, which were strictly forbidden within the cathedral. Quietly, oh so quietly, Lola opened the stall door and peeked out. The speaker had her back to Lola, checking her makeup in the long mirror that ran along the wall.

The speaker was a bean. Or rather, she was a bean-shaped

person, with bean-colored skin, and skinny little arms and legs protruding from her bean-like body. She was an Arbequian. Lola had met only one other Arbequian, and that guy had been a gold-plated jerkface. But Lola didn't like to generalize. This one sported a fashionable hip purse and the swankiest pair of high heels Lola had ever seen.

"Look, this whole gap-year thing was *your* idea, Mom," the bean said, picking something out of her teeth. "Well, I know I suggested it first, but you agreed with it! And you never agree with my ideas!"

The speaker turned in a fury. Lola retreated into her stall, but it was too late. She'd been spotted.

"I'll call you back, Mom. I said I'll call you back! Well, then I'll call you tomorrow!" She closed her eyes and screamed, seemed to consider hurling her communicator at the floor, but opted instead to hang up furiously.

"Hey!" she said. "Hey, I see you in there. What are you— some kind of bathroom spy?"

"No!" said Lola, and winced. "I mean . . ." She poked her head out of the stall. "I'm just a janitor. I'm not a bathroom spy."

"Oh," said the girl. She gave Lola a look that seemed to add up the cost of her clothes, haircut, and shoes, and find the sum wanting. "That stinks. They've got me on drive-through duty."

"You work here?" said Lola, stepping out of the stall.

"*Enjoy your evening! I hope I may collect your waste again in the future!*" said the toilet.

"Yeah," said the girl. "Gap year."

Lola nodded in a way she hoped looked knowing and aloof. "Oh, that's cool. I'm into Urban Outfitters myself."

"What?"

"Hm?" said Lola.

The other girl sighed. "My mom insisted I get some *real-world experience.*" The last three words were drawn out and slurred, as if she'd taken a sleeping pill that had kicked in mid-sentence. "Ugh, it's horrible." She gave Lola a friendly smile. "What are you in for?"

"Oh, me?" said Lola. "Uh, eating a Maybe Meal."

"Ouch," said the girl. She did the appraising look again and said, "You're not from around here."

"That's an understatement," said Lola, and tried a smile. "I'm Lola, by the way."

"Becca," said the girl.

"So," said Lola, eyeing Becca's communicator. "You're here . . . intentionally?"

"Yeah," said Becca, leaning against the row of sinks. "It was kind of a deal with my parents. Six months on the beach and six months working a *job.*" Again, the last word dripped from her mouth as if she'd suddenly experienced a massive cerebral hemorrhage. "It's so boring I could *dieee.*"

"Listen," said Lola, pulse quickening. "I don't want to be here, either. But I've got a friend I think can get us out. Can I use your phone?"

"My phone?" The girl glanced at her communicator, taking Lola's meaning. It was a meaning she didn't like. "I don't know. Reception sucks out here and I'm down to my last prepaid minutes."

"Please!" said Lola, trying to check her eagerness. "He can get you out, too! You can go right to the beach or whatever. We'll drop you off!"

Becca the Arbequian considered this. She tapped her toe on the tile. She was wearing a very expensive pair of high heels, studded with neutrino diamonds. As she tapped her foot, bits of diamond dust shook loose, dirtying the floor Lola had just spent an hour cleaning, while simultaneously increasing its value a thousandfold.

"Fine," she said, and offered Lola the device. "But be quick, okay? Is it long distance?"

Lola was about to explain that she literally couldn't conceive of a longer distance, but at that exact moment, as Lola was taking the phone from Becca's outstretched fingers—

*"Good evening and welcome! We are eager to make your lavatorial experience a pleasant and enriching one!"*

Lola froze. Becca froze. The monk who had entered froze, and then slowly moved the magazine he was holding behind his back.

"Oh! Uh, hey, uh," the monk said.

He was less put together than the other monks Lola had met. He wore the same flowing robe and name tag, but shared neither their wings nor their annoying beatific smile. He also looked vaguely familiar. In a moment his surprise vanished, and his eyes fixed on the communicator. "Well, well, well," he said, a smirk slithering across his features. "Well, well, well."

"Uh," said Lola. "Um," she continued. "Hm," she finished, feeling she'd made her point.

"*Excuse you,*" said Becca. "This restroom is clearly *occupied.*"

"Sorry," said the monk, then shook himself. "I mean, not sorry! I mean . . ." He was flustered, but gamely trying to regain control of the situation. "Um . . . Well, well, well! Did I say that already?"

"You said that already," snapped Becca, snatching the communicator away from Lola and hiding it behind her back.

"You there," said the monk. "What's that behind your back?" He pointed, realized he'd pointed with the hand holding the magazine, then switched hands and blushed violently.

"What's behind *your* back?" said Lola.

"It's none of your septopod-wax!" growled the monk. "Communicators are *forbidden* to junior team members. I'm going to have to report this." His smirk did its slithering trick again. "You're both going to be *demoted.*"

Lola didn't want to imagine what a demotion from toilet cleaner might entail and decided not to ask.

"You can't do that. You're not my supervisor!" Becca snarled.

"I *can* do that. *I'm* an assistant manager!"

"You report us, and we'll report you!" Lola said, surprising herself. She didn't like defying authority, though this monk didn't seem to have much.

"Yeah!" added Becca. "We'll report you for possessing questionable reading material!"

"This isn't—" The monk shook his head. "It's just a gaming magazine!"

He showed them the cover. Lola recognized a few of the images: a deck of cards, some kind of alien roulette wheel, and the logo for Singularity City, one of the largest hubs for entertainment and gambling in the galaxy. Lola knew it well. She'd personally destroyed a restaurant there.

"Give me the communicator," said the monk, holding out his free hand now.

"No," said Becca.

"Fine," said the monk. "Hope you like *nugget duty*."

Becca gasped. The monk turned to go.

"Wait!" said Lola, thinking fast. "We'll, uh . . . we'll play you for it."

The monk turned. "Play me for what?"

"For not reporting us," said Lola. "And letting her keep

her phone. I mean . . . communicator."

The monk hesitated. "What if I win?"

Lola had nothing for this, but Becca came to the rescue.

"Here," she said, and opened her stylish little purse. "Look. I've got an Andromeda Black Card." She held up a small onyx credit card. It was totally featureless, no names, no numbers, but every inch of its shining black surface screamed *wealth*. "I can transfer it to you, and it's all yours. Near infinite credit, good at malls, shopping centers . . ."

"And casinos," added Lola. "I should think. Right?"

"Right!" said Becca. "Casinos! I'm pretty sure Black Card members get VIP privileges."

The monk regarded the card like a castaway who'd finally strolled around the far side of his island and found an all-you-can-eat buffet there. He licked his lips.

"What's the game?"

"Uh." Becca glanced at Lola.

"I've got a game," said Lola.

"You do?" said the monk.

"Yes," said Lola, her mind racing. "It's . . . an ancient game. A game of kings, you see. Of kings and philosophers."

"Is it Newtonian Chess?" said the monk, wrinkling his nose. "Because that would take *hours*."

"It's not," said Lola. "It's . . . a game about power. And vulnerability. About the three fundamental forces that balance the universe."

She figured this description would appeal to a Monk of Just 'Cause, and it did.

"That's not fair, though," said the monk, raising himself to full height. "If I haven't played before and you have, that gives you an advantage."

"But this is a game of *chance*," said Lola. "The fates will decide."

"Fate?" said the monk.

"Luck," said Becca. "Pure random chance and luck. Right?" she said to Lola.

"Right!" said Lola.

The monk licked his lips. Though Lola couldn't read the local alphabet, his name tag, as it happened, read "Lucky."

"Fine," said Lucky, the novice Monk of Just 'Cause. "What's it called?"

Lola Ray, three-time Avon Avenue Elementary Rock-Paper-Scissors Champion, grinned.

**15**

**PHIN WAS GROUNDED.**

When most children are grounded, they're sent to their room, perhaps without dessert. However, when your parents own and operate the galaxy's only interstellar hypergate system, getting grounded is a much more official affair.

"Are we going back to the Escape Van?" P-Money asked from his perch on Phin's shoulders. They were in the elevator again, going back up to Phin's penthouse apartment.

"Afraid not, P-Money," said Phin, his jaw set. "They grounded me. That means I'm barred from the hypergates. It's tied to my genetic code, so no way to sneak past it."

"So what now?" asked Bella.

"What now? What now?!? Now we get the heck out of New Jersey." He pressed the button for the top floor.

"But how?" said P-Money. "You said—"

"I know what I said. We don't need their hypergates."

Phin's eyes were wild, and Bella hesitated before asking, "Then how are we getting out of here?"

"By using our *brains*."

Phin thought this was exactly the kind of inspiring, positive message young children should hear, but these young children didn't seem impressed.

"NOT A REAL ANSWER," said Randall.

"Yeah, what does that even mean?" asked Bella.

"Don't worry," said Phin as the elevator went *ding!* "I've got a plan."

The penthouse was dark, its automatic lights flicking on as Phin and the children stepped into the kitchen. The place had been redecorated since a Kill-Robot had shot it to bits.

"Ugh, orange cabinets," Phin mumbled. "What were they thinking?"

"You live here?" said P-Money, marveling at the splendor.

"I did," said Phin, and hurried down the hall to the bedrooms.

His parents' room was empty and untouched. Phin guessed they were staying in their Ultra Suite a few floors down. Good. That was good.

He came to his bedroom door, which someone had shut. He felt strange opening it, as if he were intruding on a past version of himself. The decorators had been in here, too—though, Phin noticed with relief, they hadn't done much redecorating. Yes, the massive hole in the wall where the Rescue Wagon had punched through had been replaced, but most of his things had just been set back on their shelves.

Even his little green rocking chair was there, though the teddy bear that used to sit in it was, of course, not.

"It's spooky here," said P-Money.

"Yes, it is," said Phin. "Let's get to work."

They got to work. Hours slipped by, and soon the floor of Phin's bedroom looked like a war zone for electrical components. Motherboards, quantum wiring, and logic gates were scattered over his bed, the carpet, his four workstations, and Randall.

"I SHALL WEAR THIS SERVO AS A HAT UNTIL YOU REQUIRE IT."

"Thanks, Randy," said Phin, and popped on a pair of welder's goggles.

"It might help if we knew what you were building," said Bella. "I'm pretty good with mechanical stuff, you know."

"Oh, nothing much you know," said Phin, igniting an ion torch. "Just something spectacular. Something one-of-a-kind. Something insanely *unsafe*. Now, someone go to the kitchen and see how many cans of baked beans we have."

Phin worked on. To the outside world the Fogg-Bolus building grew dark, save for a single penthouse window flashing green, blue, and pale lavender in the New Jersey night.

At last, just moments before dawn, Phin set down his tools and pushed away from his workstation.

"Is it done?" P-Money asked, considering the strange

slapped-together mystery device on Phin's desk.

"No. I'm missing a part," said Phin. "A rapid-deceleration-and-compression matrix."

"Oh, one of those," said P-Money.

"You know what comes with a built-in rapid-deceleration-and-compression matrix?" said Bella, who'd sat herself on a high shelf and was now leafing through one of Phin's old catalogs.

"I sure do," said Phin, and removed his oven mitts.

"What?" said P-Money. "Where can we get one?"

"They come standard," said Phin, "in a Jax-Sprocket limited edition Velo Ceraptor."

The architects of the Fogg-Bolus HQ had built the skyscraper upon preexisting foundations dating back to the early twenty-first century, and these gloomy lower levels were now used for storage. Down among the subbasements, the Fogg family kept their considerable collection of stuff, and it was into one of these storage lockers that Phin, Bella, P-Money, and Randall now stepped, as the pneumatic security door hissed shut behind them.

"Shh!" said Phin, though no one had said anything.

The Jax-Sprocket wasn't hard to find. It had been left just inside the door in one of the first storage cubbies. Phin ran his hand along the chrome handlebars, the engine housing, the quintuple exhaust ports. He tightened his fist around the throttle, which had been ergonomically engineered to make a kid feel powerful. It was a perfect machine designed for perfect carefree fun, perfect kid good times. He mumbled something about *too beautiful for this world* and then set about dismantling the nicest thing anyone had ever given him.

"There it is," he said when he found the small star-shaped component he was looking for. "The rapid-deceleration-and-compression matrix."

"What does that do?" asked P-Money.

"It keeps you from exploding into a puddle of goo on re-entry," said Phin, unshouldering his workbag and removing his creation.

The device looked, to the uneducated eye, like someone had attached a video game controller and some wiring to a can of baked beans. The star-shaped decompression matrix fixed to the top of the can, like the crowning ornament on a very small, abstract Christmas tree.

"So, what is it?" P-Money said in a hush as Phin flicked the on switch and the little device began to hum.

"It's an idea I've been kicking around for a few weeks," said Phin. "Professor Donut used a shrink ray to drop Lola and me directly into the quantum sauce. We were flung across the galaxy in nanoseconds. I think the principle can be applied here. It's sort of a personal . . . people . . . flinger."

"A personal people flinger," said Bella.

"Personal," said P-Money. "People. Flinger."

"All right, the name needs work!" said Phin. "But it's going to help me get out of here and find Lola."

Phin fiddled with the buttons on the controller, setting his coordinates.

"She's really important to you, huh?" said Bella.

Phin shrugged. "She needs me." He stopped fiddling for a moment and thought. "And if you find someone who needs you, you *never* let them go. Not for any reason. Not ever."

"So where are you going?" she asked.

"Gardyloo Books," said Phin. "They published *Shadow-Mancer Wars*, and no one knows more about the ShadowMancer than they do. If Lola's looking for the ShadowMancer," said Phin, "then the ShadowMancer is where we'll find Lola."

"Did you ever actually read the book?" said Bella.

"I saw the movie," said Phin. "Well, bye." His finger hovered over the GO button.

"Wait!" said P-Money. "You can't just leave us here!"

"You'll be fine," said Phin. "Just take the elevator to the roof and hit the auto-return on the Escape Van. You guys aren't grounded; you'll get back to the *Calming Breath* by supper."

"Forget that," said Bella. "We're coming with you."

"THE BONDS BETWEEN US RUN DEEP THIS DAY," said Randall.

"Don't leave!" said P-Money, and he dug his claws into Phin's calf.

"Argghh!" said Phin. "Watch the skin, man!"

"You will *not* leave us here," said Bella. "We want to come with you."

"You're too young, and it's too dangerous," said Phin.

Bella crossed her arms. "You know who you sound like?"

"A smart guy? Yes. I always sound like that," said Phin.

"You sound just like your parents."

In the recorded history of icy silences, few have been icier than the one that followed.

"We can handle ourselves, you know that," Bella tried.

Phin considered the three children, toddlers really, looking up at him. They really were much too small. And he was the oldest; he had to make the tough decisions for them. Except, all he'd wanted his parents to do for decades was trust that *he* knew whether he could take care of himself. And he had. Pretty well so far.

"All right, bring it in," said Phin. "We'll have to be standing pretty close together—no, not *on me*!" P-Money clambered onto Phin's shoulders, and Bella climbed onto his foot, like they were about to do a daddy-daughter dance. Randall tucked himself under Phin's arm with a kind of static cling.

"Yay!" said P-Money. "We're going to Gardyloo! What's that again?"

"A publisher," said Phin, and made a final adjustment to the Personal People Flinger.

"Are you sure this thing is going to work?" asked Bella.

"Nope!" said Phin and hit the GO button.

A plume of baked beans erupted from the top of the device in a brown and bubbling fountain. It brushed the ceiling and fell, splashing across the concrete walls and floor of what was now an empty room.

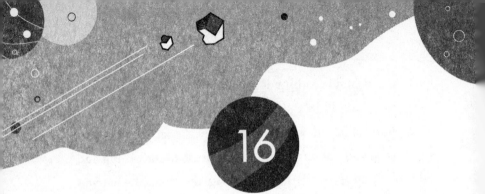

## 16

**"THE LOOK ON HIS** face!" Becca said, laughing so hard tears were streaming down her cheeks. "Best three out of five, he says! Oh, that was *precious.*"

"Boys always throw rock," said Lola with an expert sigh. "So predictable."

The girls fell against each other laughing, rushing up through the darkened halls of the Golden Cathedral, the rations kit bouncing happily against Lola's shoulder as they ran. Lola let herself feel just a *bit* fantastic. Maybe Phin had begun to rub off on her. Or maybe it had nothing to do with Phin. Maybe she was fantastic all on her own.

"We need to get to the roof," Becca said, taking Lola's hand and dragging her toward the eastern towers. "We'll get better reception there."

They climbed the winding stairs, their way lit by ornate lanterns and starlight. At last they came to the top of the tallest tower, where they found an open-air pavilion with a fountain in the center. The breeze tugged at Lola's clothing.

There were no safety rails here, no walls separating the flag-stones from open air and a very long fall. Lola fought off a rush of wooziness, and instead focused on the sky. It was a glorious and glittering haze of constellations she didn't recognize, and Lola wondered where in the Milky Way's swirling mass she currently was.

She peered down then, over the valley below. She could see the lights of Mango and Bumblebee's village, as well as others, each of them built, she now understood, with Maybe Meal prizes. Theirs was an entire world rich in junk, with every citizen toiling away in service of the cathedral. It really wasn't so different from home.

"Okay, so what's his number?" Becca asked, handling her communicator.

"I have no idea," said Lola. "But there must be, like, a way to look him up, right?"

Becca shrugged. "We'll use the Universal Beacon app." She punched a few buttons and the communicator lit with an eerie blue light. "What do you want it to say? 'Girl seeks guy for immediate rescue from evil religio-corporate prison'?"

Lola wrinkled her nose. "How about, 'This is Lola Ray, seeking Phineas Fogg.'"

"Little boring, but specific," said Becca. "There."

She pressed a final button, and a bubble of blue light blipped from the top of the communicator. The girls watched as it floated up into the atmosphere, seeming to waft and weave in the breeze, climbing higher and higher until Lola nearly lost sight of it in the stars. Then, the bubble burst, sending its halo out in all directions, a momentary flash that lit up the rooftop like daylight. And then it was gone, sailing out into the galaxy at the speed of prepaid data.

"So now we just wait?" said Lola.

"Yep," said Becca. "If he's within thirty light-years, it should reach him within a few hours."

Lola had no idea if Phin was close enough to receive the beacon, but surely someone would hear it.

For now, though, there was a bench by the fountain, and the girls took a seat to watch the water bubble.

The statue in the center of the fountain was of Galubrious Phasma, founder of the Order of Just 'Cause. In her hands she held two golden spheres, or rather half spheres that looked like they were meant to interlock. Legend had it that when the universe came to an end, the statue would come to life and join the two halves together. The halves represented the twin forces Phasma believed defined reality: in her right hand was Cause, and in her left, Effect. A plaque at the base read, *Embrace Whatever Life Throws at You.* It was an unfortunate phrase, as the designer of the statue had failed to take into account the local bird population, which were big fans of statues in general, and had covered Phasma's face and arms with signs of their appreciation.

"So you're reading *ShadowMancer Wars?*" Becca asked,

indicating Lola's paperback. She'd removed it from her back pocket in order to sit more comfortably.

"Yeah," said Lola. "I guess it's kind of research."

Becca nodded. "I think a lot of people will reread it now that she's back." Lola looked surprised and so Becca continued, "It's been all over the news. Look."

She showed Lola the streaming news feed on her communicator. Lola's eyes widened, then narrowed, as she read about the destruction of Venus Beta, then about an earlier attack on Crendatious Fatbrick's Maximum Security Zoo, from which the ShadowMancer's golden dragon, Pogo, had escaped, and finally an even earlier story about a group of Girl Scouts who claimed to have spotted someone resembling the ShadowMancer appear in the sky somewhere over Portland. It was like a reverse timeline of the ShadowMancer's moves, riddled with commentary and speculation. One thing seemed to be in consensus: the ShadowMancer was back, and she was gathering her strength. Apparently, security had been doubled on the small planet of Krastle Bracken 6, where the ShadowMancer's wand, her galaxy-wrecking weapon of mass destruction, was kept under lock and key, and second lock and second key, and third lock and automated system of keys, pass codes, biometric scanners, laser array, and a small army.

"I read about her wand in the book," said Lola, her voice going quiet. "But . . . is all this true? About how she erased millions of star systems the last time she appeared?"

"My grandmother used to talk about it all the time," said Becca. "It was like everyone knew someone who knew someone who was erased by the ShadowMancer." She studied Lola's features and frowned. "Hey, listen, if she's back, I'm sure the military or whatever will take care of it."

"Did they take care of her last time?" Lola asked. She wasn't being glib; she just hadn't finished the book yet.

"That's the thing," said Becca in a hushed tone. "No one *really* knows what happened. Supposedly, Skylar Powerpunch—"

"Powerstance," said Lola.

"Whatever, apparently she tried to blow up the Shadow-Mancer and got herself and her ship exploded in the process. After that the ShadowMancer disappeared, but it turns out she wasn't even *near* the blast. But she just . . . never appeared again. It was like she vanished. No one knows why, or where to." Becca wiggled her fingers at Lola. "Spooky, no?"

"How long ago was that?" Lola asked, feeling an itch in the back of her brain, like a pebble in her shoe. Or, more accurately, a pebble in her subconscious.

"About a thousand years, I guess?" said Becca. "I gotta say, she looks *great* for her age."

"She's got something of mine," Lola said quietly.

"What was that?"

"I said she's got something of mine," said Lola, almost to herself. "A . . . well, it doesn't matter what it is," she said, handing back the communicator. "But I have to get it back."

"You're going to try and stop the ShadowMancer?" said Becca and whistled.

"I'm going to get what belongs to me," said Lola. "But first I need to find her."

Becca watched Lola a moment, then reached into her purse.

"I've got something I want you to have." She extracted what looked like a small envelope, folded over to fit in her small purse. The paper was waxy and stiff, and as Lola unfolded it, Becca said, "Careful, don't tear it."

The envelope unfolded to the size of a small poster. Across one side was the Golden Cathedral logo. The ends were sealed, but the sleeve didn't appear to contain anything at all. Lola could almost see through it.

"Is this what I think it is?"

Becca smiled. "It's a Maybe Meal bag. They come off the line like that sometimes, pre-sealed. There's no meal inside, so the monks destroy them. But the nanofibers still work. There might not be any nuggets in there, but crack that baby open and you'll still get a prize. I stole this one."

Lola wasn't sure what to say. She'd had her fill of Maybe Meals and their prizes, and she certainly didn't want to indebt herself for another two hundred years.

"Don't open it here, or the monks will detect it," said Becca. "But maybe . . . I don't know. Maybe once you get out of here you could use it." She considered the statue of Phasma. "You know, the monks think that nothing happens for a reason, it's all just random chance. But I don't believe that. On Arbequia we believe everything is connected, that there's a meaning to all of it, kind of a . . . well, not a pattern. It's like we're all part of the same . . ."

"Sauce?" offered Lola.

Becca smiled. "Exactly, we're all part of the same sauce. I think that's why I'm so good at getting what I want out of the Maybe Meals. If you believe, I mean really believe, then you'll find what you need. How do you think I got these great shoes?" Becca wiggled her feet. "I was just keeping this one for a gag, something to show Braz. But . . ." Becca shrugged. "I sort of get the feeling you'll need it more than I will."

Lola turned the Maybe Meal bag over in her hands. It would be wrong to say that this small act of kindness stunned Lola more than the wild things she'd seen since being flung a thousand years into the future. A gift, no matter how touching, will never be as surprising as, say, a conversation with interdimensional beings, or being on a planet full of talking cats when it exploded. But this was exactly what stunned Lola so completely: small acts of kindness were perhaps rarer here than alien invasions, killer robots, and time travel combined. It was exactly the kind of profound little miracle that Galubrious Phasma would have dismissed as a meaningless interaction of particles and waves.

Lola hugged Becca. "Thank you," she said, and refolded the Maybe Meal bag before tucking it away someplace safe.

Becca stretched and yawned. "I'm on drive-through duty in a few hours. I'm gonna get some sleep. You coming down?"

"I think I'll stay and watch the stars for a bit," said Lola, who was feeling wistful.

"I'll find you if anyone reaches out," said Becca, waggling her communicator. "Good luck, Lola."

"See you around, Becca," said Lola Ray, feeling she'd made a friend.

After Becca had disappeared down the winding stairs, Lola sat for a while in the quiet, listening to the burble of the fountain, and watching the Milky Way. She thought of the trip to Coney Island she'd taken with her parents when she was very young, before her youngest sister was even born. In the evening they sat on the beach, eating hot dogs for dinner while her father pointed out the constellations. She missed them all horribly.

She closed her eyes and sighed, and it was a good thing she did, because the flash of white light was so brilliant and bright it might very well have blinded her.

The light receded, and Lola opened her eyes. Something was blotting out the stars. Or rather two somethings. For a moment Lola thought Phasma's statue had come to life. Mighty wings arched in the gloom.

Pogo, the legendary golden dragon of the ShadowMancer, descended from its perch on the statue. First one clawed foot lowered into the fountain, then the other. Talons clacked over the fountain's edge, then clicked against the flagstones as the massive beast unfolded itself before Lola, raising its massive neck, towering over her like an elder god.

Its rider's eyes flashed.

Lola didn't move. She could hear her own breath, steady through her nostrils. She could hear her own heartbeat, which was also steady, if incredibly fast. Pogo's jaws seemed to glow with golden flame, but Lola Ray did not flinch.

"Hello," said Lola. "My name's Lola. What's yours?"

"You are Lola Ray," said the ShadowMancer. Her voice was that of a child's, and yet very much not.

"That's me," said Lola. "What should I call you?"

The ShadowMancer didn't reply. Instead, Pogo lowered its trunk-like neck. The rider slid from its back. She stood on the flagstones. She was a bit shorter than Lola, but Lola was sitting, and the two were nearly eye-to-eye.

"You know what this is," said the ShadowMancer.

On her hip was the containment device, and inside was Lola's Twinkie, stasis-locked and faintly glowing.

"That's a Twinkie," said Lola, and then, when the ShadowMancer didn't reply, added, "Not as good as a Ring Ding but better than a Ho Ho."

"Tell me how to read it," said the ShadowMancer.

"Where are you from?" said Lola in a casual tone that in no way betrayed her utter terror.

The ShadowMancer said nothing.

"What's your name?" Lola tried. "It's not really just ShadowMancer, is it?"

The ShadowMancer said nothing.

"Maybe," said Lola, "maybe there's something I can help you with?"

"Tell me what the Twinkie says," said the god-child. Behind her, flames rippled from Pogo's nostrils.

"I can't do that," said Lola. "But maybe together we could—"

*Thwoop. THUMP. Whoooosshhh.*

As Lola plummeted from the tower, she had a few moments to work out what had just happened.

The *whoooosshhh* sound, that was an easy one. The *whoooosshhh* was the sound of the air roaring past her ears as she fell, the lights of the cathedral rushing past her like a sub-way train. The *THUMP* was a bit trickier to puzzle out, so she let that part go for a moment. Now, the *thwoop*. Not many things made a *thwoop* sound. (Was that the upper veranda she'd just fallen past?) Sailboats made *thwoop* sounds when they turned into the wind, but there'd definitely been no sailboats on the top of the tower. Ah, Lola nodded to herself as her body turned in the air. No, there'd been no sailboats, but there *had* been a dragon with big sail-like wings. The *thwoop* sound, Lola reasoned, must have been Pogo flying quite fast and quite hard. And that, Lola decided, accounted for the *THUMP*, which was Pogo's wing hitting Lola in the shoulder and knocking her off the tower the way one might flick a balled-up straw wrapper off the edge of a table. It all followed. It all made sense.

If she was going to die, at least she wouldn't die confused.

Speaking of dying, it wouldn't be long now. She was pretty sure that was the fifth-story garden she'd just plummeted past. She wondered, briefly, if anything like this had ever happened to Skylar Powerstance. She guessed that since Skylar survived until at *least* the last chapter, the answer was no.

But then something smacked into the back of Lola's head, or rather the back of Lola smacked into the back of something else's back.

The landing was much more painful than she'd expected. In fact, she hadn't expected to feel much of anything, and yet here she was, bones rattling as her trajectory transferred at top speed from *straight down* to *somewhat down but mostly sideways*.

Lola opened her eyes. The sky was rushing past her in a new direction now. *Had she suddenly and conveniently learned to fly?* Lola looked down, and saw that under her, rather than open air, was a metal surface about the size of a school bus with a blunt face and a long, tapered tail. A Book Möb Eel.

The Möb Eel swerved upward with its cargo and inscribed

a wide circle around the Golden Cathedral. Lola could make out Pogo and the ShadowMancer, watching from the tower. Their eyes remained fixed on her as the Möb Eel turned south and headed out over the tree line, away from the cathedral and toward the mountains.

At last Lola's survival instincts, which had given up about three seconds into her fall, scrambled after her and caught up. Lola gasped, threw herself onto her stomach, and held on to the Möb Eel for dear life.

They slithered over the trees, dipped around a rocky outcropping, and rocketed past a waterfall. The wind yanked at Lola's clothes, and howled in her ears. She shut her eyes and tried to hold her breath—it was near impossible to breathe up here in any case. She lay like that, holding on in abject terror, until the wind began to die down, and she realized they were slowing.

Lola opened her eyes. It was dark, and they were in the woods, but something about this area seemed familiar. The Möb Eel reduced its speed and began its usual landing procedure, swooping low, and coming down for a gentle rest by a trench recently carved into the soft earth. At the end of it, still half buried in the dirt, was the Rescue Wagon.

For a moment Lola couldn't persuade her fingers to let go. It took some convincing, but at last they unclenched, and Lola lowered herself to the ground. She walked around to the Möb Eel's front.

"Thank you," she said to the expressionless blank face.

The Möb Eel did not respond.

Lola looked around. Her faithful rations kit, which she'd dragged with her on this entire expedition, seemed to pull expectantly at her shoulder. She waited another beat to see if the Möb Eel had anything it wanted to share, and when it didn't, Lola walked over to the Rescue Wagon, placed her rations kit on the hood, and opened the bag. She emptied its contents. She unwound the rope of neckties from Bob's Joke Shop and threaded it through the only part of the Wagon that still had power: the magnetic trailer winch. To the other end of the tie-rope she affixed the promotional refrigerator electro-magnet from the rations kit, the one that sported the Fogg-Bolus Hypergate and Baked Beans logo, as well as its universally recognizable slogan, *Insanely Safe!*

She affixed the magnet to the rear of the Möb Eel, and flicked the little switch on the side to turn it on. It secured itself with a satisfying *clunk*.

At last, Lola walked back around to the Möb Eel's front.

"I'm not sure why you helped me," she said. "But thank you. And," she added, removing the dog-eared paperback of *ShadowMancer Wars* from her back pocket, "thank you for this. I'd like to return it now."

She offered the book to the machine. At first it did nothing, and then, one of its spidery metallic appendages unfolded itself, plucked the book from Lola's fingers, and tucked it away within one of the Eel's many internal compartments. A shiver ran along the Eel's length. Book collected, its internal thrusters began to power up. Moving fast, Lola scurried back to the Rescue Wagon and climbed inside the cockpit.

It was time to go.

"Please oh please," she said. "Please oh please oh please work—"

There was a zip and a snap. The ship began to rattle as the tie-rope unspooled from the magnetic winch. The Möb Eel shot into the air, and then, just as Lola had envisioned, the Rescue Wagon was wrenched from the ground after it. The world tumbled around Lola as the ship was yanked, backside first, into the sky, the rope of joke ties gone taut and humming as the Book Möb Eel roared over the treetops, heedless of the hitchhiker now being towed behind it.

"Wooohooo!" cheered Lola as the forest unfurled beneath her. The dark canopy bounced and tumbled away as the Rescue Wagon slalomed backward through the air, a lifeless metal hulk kept aloft by momentum alone. There was Mango and Bumblebee's village. There was the highway, and beyond, the golden lights of the Golden Cathedral.

Lola was tossed around the cabin and fumbled for the seat belt, locking herself in. She turned in her seat and looked out the rear view screen. The Eel banked left, swinging the Wagon out behind it, the g-force crushed against Lola. They came in low over the village, and she worried the decrease in speed would mean disaster, but the Eel banked up, the Wagon clipped a chimney made of old sneakers, and up, up into the clouds they soared. At last they broke through into starlight, Lola hooting and hollering in pure, terrified joy.

"Momentum cells at one percent," chimed a neutral voice from the Rescue Wagon's speakers. "Rebooting from factory settings." The dash lights began to flick on one by one. Lola felt the old familiar hum radiate from the seat beneath her. "Volvo Rescue Wagon Mark IV, serial number 241-21-21-87-ZX4B. Hello, and welcome to your personalized rescue experience," said the voice. "Please select from the following menu of User Interface Options."

A menu flashed over the view screen. Lola scrolled to the bottom until she found the one she was looking for, and pressed *select*.

"Wellllllllll, *howdy there, buckaroos!* I'm Bucky, your handy-dandy, interactive, and friendly onboard user interface!"

"Hi, Bucky," said Lola. "You might not remember me, but my name is Lola, and right now, I'm your captain."

"Well, how do ya do, ma'am?"

"I'm—" The Wagon hit an air pocket, and Lola smacked her head into the ceiling. "Super. Could you fully recharge the power cells?"

"Can diddly do!" said Bucky. The engines thrummed. The Wagon bolted forward, yanking on the cable. The Book

Möb Eel faltered and made a kind of mechanical wail, its segments grinding as the machine pulled against its unexpected burden.

"Release the winch, please!" Lola shouted.

The tie-rope snapped away and the Wagon plummeted. Lola pulled back on the throttle, righted the nose, and slammed the thrusters to full. She was flying! Not just flying, she was leaving the atmosphere. The Wagon rumbled. Flames licked the hood and view screen. And then, with a wonderful, joyful quiet, they were in space.

"Where to, buttercup?" said Bucky, and brought up the navigational interface.

"Krastle Bracken Six," said Lola. "Wherever they're holding the ShadowMancer's wand."

Lights on the display panel flashed as Bucky did some quick calculations. "Charting a course for Krastle Bracken Six, the Krastle Bracken System. Looks like that nefarious little rattler's wand is being held in a maximum-security prison known as the Slab, located deep in the Mindless Sea," said Bucky. "Well, if that ain't an ominous-sounding sorta watering hole, I don't know what is!"

"Start scanning for that rescue-and-recovery ship that picked up Phin," said Lola.

"Shall I broadcast a beacon, so the little toad hustler can find you?"

Lola thought of the ShadowMancer's strange propensity

for showing up wherever she was.

"Better not," she said. "Just . . . find Phin, okay?"

"On it like a comet, my tousled tulip."

"I got myself out," said Lola, and then a little louder, "I got myself out!"

She laughed—it was a laugh of unbelievable relief—and promptly passed out.

Lola slept so hard, she didn't even wake when the single unplayed message on the Rescue Wagon's voice-answering service downloaded from the server and began to play over the ship's speakers. "*Hey, Phin, it's Mom and Dad! Hope you're having a great time exploring the galaxy with your friend! When you have a moment, swing on home! We've got a biiiiiiiig surprise for you!!*"

# PART 3

## THE FRACAS AT KRASTLE BRACKEN

## 17

**NEAR THE GALACTIC CORE,** where things are fashionable and expensive, the planetary giant Megabrinx glitters like a hood ornament. Though the planet itself is an uninhabitable gas giant of swirling toxic clouds, suspended in its upper atmosphere sprawls an immense superstructure of electron scaffolding and interlocked space stations. It is in this sky-bound city where the galaxy's most popular movies, books, and games are developed. Every major work of pop culture of the past five hundred years has come out of the suspended city of Megabrinx, and it is here that Gardyloo Books makes its home.

The Gardyloo building is old. A classic, some might say. It hails from an era before artificial gravity, when space stations were built to turn in space like great bingo tumblers, centrifugal force keeping employees glued to their desks. It spins like a gigantic silo on its side, sandwiched between Infarction Comix's palatial Recreational Bean Bag Chair Complex and the Multiversal Studios Lot, which consists of a single black-box hard drive the size of a bus that generates forty-five blockbusters a minute. The inner surface of the Gardyloo tube is studded with cramped offices, musty conference rooms, and Zero-G Nappy-Time Personal Employee Sleep Tubes, where Gardyloo editors are encouraged to take a break every seventy-five to ninety days.

Phin and the children materialized in the lobby, and the centrifugal force pinned their feet to the carpet with artificial gravity.

The lobby of a venerable literary institution is an awkward place to suddenly materialize at nine in the morning while covered in baked bean sauce. Phin had anticipated this and was ready with a speech.

"All right, everyone calm down and come to terms with what I've just done," he said, holding out his hands to steady the crowd of wildly bewildered and impressed Gardyloo employees he expected. "Yes, I've just appeared out of nowhere, and no, it's not magic. It's all thanks to this remarkable device I've just invented . . ."

"Who are you talking to?" said Bella.

And Phin was forced to admit he was talking to nobody.

The lobby was much more terrifying than a lobby had any right to be, in his opinion. To start, it was dark. Some glow from other nearby space stations was visible through the main doors, but the chandeliers and sconces were either blown out or, in some cases, smashed. The second unsettling thing was the lack of people.

The third detail, and the one that chilled Phin to his core, were all the paper cups.

"Is anyone going to say anything about the paper cups?" P-Money asked, clinging to Phin's calf.

They were everywhere. Scattered across the floor. Lolling on the reception desk. Crammed into trash bins and even, somehow, wedged into the chandeliers. Most were stained with a sticky red substance that also covered the floor and some of the furniture.

"Punch," said Bella, smelling a bit on the rim of a paper cup that also sported a woman's lipstick kiss. "Not summer punch. Not holiday punch." Bella sniffed again. "This is celebration punch."

"This is bad," said Phin, who felt like dramatically underselling the danger was the responsible thing to do. "This is very bad," he explained to the children in the most reassuring way he could muster. "Maybe very, *very* bad, at a stretch. But not *extremely* bad, so don't worry."

"I SENSE DEATH HERE," offered Randall. "AND SHEET CAKE."

"Something happened," said Phin, who thought stating the obvious might also be a duty of the ranking adult. "And not recently."

Somewhere, something fell off a high shelf and clattered to the floor. The children jumped. This included Phin, who suddenly very much did not want to be the adult.

"*Hide!*" he hissed, and together they leaped behind the reception desk.

Something was moving in the depths of the building. It made a strange machine hum as it came, and another sound, like metal grinding on metal. Phin peeked from behind the desk. A blue-and-white spotlight spilled into the lobby from the elevator bay. Then its owner came into view. The creature did not touch the ground, but rather swam through the air like an organic thing. It was the size of a small car, and narrowed at the back end, its great blunt mechanical eyes designed to look like a pair of friendly, nerdy spectacles. All along its length, the spines of popular books could be seen in its several transparent storage segments.

The creature, in and of itself, did not scare Phin or the children, because they knew exactly what it was and had seen several before. It was a Book Möb Eel, one of the synthetic book transports that traversed the galaxy, visiting remote planets and selling books to children. They were harmless, friendly staples of long summer afternoons.

The Eel's spotlight scanned the lobby. Its gaze passed over the front doors, which Phin now saw were double-deadlocked, and then over the spot where Phin and the kids had just been standing. There was a puddle of baked bean sauce where they'd landed, dripping on the marble. The moment it registered the unexpected substance, the Eel's spotlight turned a threatening red, and agitation seemed to ripple down its length. Phin had never thought of a Möb Eel as threatening before. They recommended books for you and gave cute little prerecorded messages about how reading was *"Eely fun!"* This one, however, had clearly been reprogrammed.

"What do we do?" Bella whispered as the Eel continued its search down the elevator bay.

Phin considered this. It was clear Lola was not in the lobby. If she had come in search of the ShadowMancer, she'd probably snuck off to explore more of the building and find out what happened here.

"We need to find out what happened here," said Phin, attempting to channel his friend. "This way."

Together they snuck down the corridor away from the mysterious sentry. Quickly, quietly, they kept to the wall and made their way down a series of long hallways, their steps lit only by Randall's faint bioluminescent glow. Farther on, the scene was much the same. Plastic cups littered the halls, and here and there banners hung in the gloom, messages written on them in the local whimsical font, Cosmic Sans.

"It says, *'Way to Go, Team!'*" said Phin, reading one of these.

"There's another one," said P-Money. "What does it say?"

"It just says *'One Thousand Years,'*" said Phin. "And then there's a bit of Megabrinx punctuation that's kind of hard to translate."

"Try," said Bella.

Phin took a breath. "Well, it's basically an exclamation point that also means, '*I think that's pretty cool if you think that's cool, too, but, like, if you don't I also don't really care?*'"

"A piece of punctuation says all that?" said Bella.

"Well, as I understand it, on Megabrinx it's a common sentiment," said Phin.

"What were they celebrating?" P-Money asked, bringing them back to the topic at hand.

"There's a date on this banner," said Phin, peering close. His face went stony. "Gragleburry twenty-fourth, 71-21B." He did some quick conversions in his head. "That's over ten Earth years ago."

"And still no one's cleaned up after the party," said Bella. "Typical."

They wandered into a conference room, just as dark and cavernous as the corridor. It was outfitted with a television, and after checking the coast was clear, Phin turned it on.

A recording began to play. The video had been made in this very room, and the people in the recording had been standing just where Phin and the kids were standing now. In the video, the room was bright and cheerful. The conference table was set with canapes and bottles of sparkling cider, and of course, bowls of punch. The Gardyloo employees looked cheerful and a bit unkempt, faces flushed, hair disheveled, ties unslung.

"Is this thing on?" the young blue-skinned man in the video said. His suit was nicer than the others', marking him as a junior executive. "Okay, I think we've just joined the simulcast. This is Rodney from Design on level five, and I'm here with the whole team to say congratulations to everyone on one thousand years on the best-seller list! That is a record-breaking achievement, as is our three hundred and fourth cover redesign. Go, team!"

The people behind Rodney cheered and drank more punch. They were clearly ready to finish this simulcast and make some bad choices.

"And I just want to say a special congratulations to the gals and gastropods down in Human Resources, who are today activating their fancy new artificial intelligence program, which is supposed to run the company from now on. What's it called again?"

"Mrs. Anthony!" a receptionist called from the back of the room, where he was trying to strike up a friendly rapport with a photocopier.

"That's right," said Rodney from Design. "Mrs. Anthony the A.I. Hope she doesn't suddenly gain consciousness and kill us all!"

The revelers laughed at this, and cheered, and poured more punch. Rodney said, "Okay, now how do I sign off?" and then the screen went blank.

The room was quiet and dark once more.

"Well, that told us nothing," said P-Money.

"What? That told us everything!" said Phin.

"Can we go now, please?" Bella asked, huddling close to Phin's leg.

"*I don't know, can you?*" came a deep and terrifyingly grammatical voice. "*I believe what you mean to ask is,* May *I go now, please?*" The modular walls slid away, and they were surrounded by a trio of Möb Eels, each with a dorsal-mounted ray gun now trained on Phin's forehead.

"*Now if you would kindly drop the kitten and put your hands in the air,*" said the voice issuing through the building's public address system. "*I'm very pleased to meet you, Phineas Fogg.*"

## 18

**IT TOOK LOLA THREE** hypergate jumps to reach the edge of the galaxy. Here, the star systems were spread farther apart, the Wi-Fi was less reliable, and the transportation options were limited. A friendly group of teenagers on spring break had let the Wagon ride through the hypergate in their hold, and when they parted ways, offered to bring Lola along to something called the Blasted Reach, where they were going to do something called Flare Wailing, which was either an extreme sport, or something equally dangerous that required lots of special equipment. They were a carefree bunch, off to have a dangerously good time not worrying about anything, and Lola envied them.

"Good luck with your space witch or whatever!" they said before rocketing off to their destination.

The rest of the ride Lola spent steeped in ShadowMancer lore. Thanks to the Wagon's Ethernet connection, Lola had streamed the original *ShadowMancer* movie (which looked terrible but wasn't bad), the 500th Anniversary Special

Edition with the previously deleted dance-fight sequence (why would they delete something so incredibly awesome?), the 2717 remake (which looked amazing but was terrible), and finally the ill-conceived *ShadowMancer Christmas Special*, in which Santa Claus resurrects Skylar Powerstance with a Lazarus Pit, and the ShadowMancer tries to steal Plutonian Christmas, all of which Lola found disturbing, theologically confusing, and in plain bad taste.

There was something else, too. Something that kicked at the back of Lola's brain like a toddler on an airplane.

"She never blew up any planets," Lola said as the Wagon crossed into Krastle Bracken space.

"Beg yer pardon, miss?" said Bucky, whose only complaint about the ShadowMancer movies was that there weren't enough cowboys in them.

"She erases people with her wand, yeah?" said Lola, double-checking the short-lived comic book spin-off *ShadowMancer Nights*. "And it seems like she can just blip around the galaxy at will. But she doesn't blow up planets. So why did she blow up Venus Beta?"

Lola fell into a furrowed silence until an hour later when Bucky's proximity gauge went *ping!*

"Sorry to interrupt your wagon train of thought, miss," said Bucky. "But we are now approaching Krastle Bracken Six, which a knowledge-thirsty rustler such as yourself might be interested to know is the planet *farthest* from the galactic core! Covered almost entirely by the Mindless Sea, it is home to one structure of note, the hypermax-secure facility called the Slab! It is here that the legendary ShadowMancer's wand is held for safekeeping."

"For a remote prison world," said Lola, "it sure is popular."

The small slate-gray planet of Krastle Bracken 6 was surrounded. Ships of all shapes and sizes had gathered in low orbit. There were news tanks and gossip gliders, tourist buses, and civilian ships that'd come to Krastle Bracken 6 just to see what the radio chatter was all about. Photographers were busy unfolding their three-story lens arrays, and scattered throughout the atmosphere, helpful onlookers had thrown up their own feed screens so those near the back could see what was going on down on the planet's surface.

It was one of these view screens Lola studied now. It displayed a long-lens shot of an ocean as black as any Lola had ever seen. And floating above it, astride her great gold dragon, was you know who.

"She's here!" said Lola. "Bucky, can you patch me into the local news feeds?"

The Wagon's speakers crackled with static.

"—*and get away immediately,*" came a voice. "*To repeat, authorities are asking civilian ships to remain in orbit and not approach the ShadowMancer.*

"*If you're just joining us, this is Hannah Starfoot for WVEN, the Mix. I'm on location at the Slab where the ShadowMancer herself has reappeared after a thousand-year absence. Though unconfirmed sightings have been rolling in since the destruction of Venus Beta, we now have confirmation the ShadowMancer has returned! Her siege of the Slab has now entered its second hour. We bring you live feed now of the Slab's security communications."* There was some rustling, and when Hannah Starfoot spoke again, it was slightly off mic. *"You sure we can do that? Seems like kind of a security risk. Well, whatever. Push the button, Frank."*

There was a click, and suddenly other voices began to crackle through the dashboard speakers, though now the sound quality was noticeably worse.

*"Bobby 1, this is Bobby 2. Requesting a status update. Over."*

*"Bobby 2, this is Bobby 1 in the North Tower. She's still just floating there, over."*

*"Bobby 1, this is Bobby 2. She's been floating there all morning. You sure she's not doing anything at all? Over?"*

*"Bobby 2, this is Bobby 1. You know, if you don't believe me you can just come over here. Over."*

*"Bobby 1, this is Bobby 2. There's no need to be like that; I'm just asking. This is kind of an unusual situation. Over."*

*"Bobby 2, this is Bobby 1. I'm sorry I snapped. We're all under a lot of pressure. And to answer your question, the ShadowMancer is indeed still just floating about a hundred feet over the water, just kind of looking at us and not doing anything. Over."*

"Bobby 1, this is Bobby 2. Hold position and do not fire. I have confirmation that government security forces are en route to apprehend the ShadowMancer. And on a personal note, I really want to commend you on your communication skills. Over."

"Well, there you have it," came Hannah Starfoot's voice. "Government security drones are apparently on their way, and in the meantime, two men have learned to express themselves and resolve conflict maturely. Truly a remarkable day here on Krastle Bracken Six. If you're just joining us—"

Lola turned off the feed. "Bucky, continue our course for the Slab," she said.

"Roger that!" said Bucky. "Trajectory?"

"We're going to talk to her," said Lola.

The Wagon wove speedily through the traffic, and as they neared the planet's surface, cameras and view screens turned to watch the strange little escape pod ignore all the temporary blockades. (Lola had turned the communication system to Bedtime Mode so no one could distract them.)

The Wagon rumbled and flames licked the heat shielding as they slipped through the atmosphere and into the sky above the Mindless Sea. Miles of chop disappeared beneath them as the Wagon rocketed over the planet's surface toward the Slab. In a moment, the facility rose over the horizon: black, flat, and blunt, and Lola saw its name had been well chosen. The Slab was a featureless dark cube in a featureless dark sea, unapproachable, unassailable, and presently under siege.

Floating above the Slab was the ShadowMancer, and seeing her in comparison to its size, she seemed—for the first time to Lola, anyway—small and vulnerable. She looked like a child on a dragon.

Slab security was desperately trying to hail Lola and tell her to turn back, but she couldn't hear them.

Until now the ShadowMancer's attention had been fixed on the Slab, considering its angles and vulnerabilities. She appeared to be weighing her options the way one might tackle a dauntingly large box of chocolates. It was then she spotted Lola.

The ShadowMancer did not react as the Rescue Wagon pulled up level with her in the sky, merely watched with intense yet cool interest as the hatch opened. And then, there they were, face-to-face, ten feet apart, a hundred feet above a roiling sea. Across the galaxy, news feeds and personal tablets all showed this same image. The ShadowMancer and, to those who recognized her from last month's Battle of Singularity City . . . that girl from last month's Battle of Singularity City.

"Hi again," said Lola.

The wind whipped. Far below the sea churned and crashed. Pogo's wings beat the air and Lola could feel the heat from its breath. The ShadowMancer's eyes burned, but she was silent.

"I'm not here to fight," said Lola. "Okay? I'm not here to

try and stop you. I'm just trying to get back my Twinkie so I can save my family."

The ShadowMancer said nothing.

"I wonder what it is that *you* want?" Lola asked.

"I've come for my wand," said the ShadowMancer.

"Right," said Lola. "The thing is, I feel like you're going to erase people. With that wand."

The ShadowMancer said nothing. Lola let her gaze slip, to where her Twinkie hovered in a small portable containment field.

"The key is mine; you cannot have it," said the Shadow-Mancer.

"The key?" said Lola. "You mean the Twinkie? My father gave it to me, and I need it to reach him, so if you don't mind—"

"Ah yes," said the ShadowMancer, her expression changing to one of cool amusement. "I know your father. Dr. Alfonso Ray of Earth."

Lola stopped breathing. When she spoke, she managed only a whisper, yet somehow the ShadowMancer heard her over the gale.

"You know my father?"

"He is the man who created the key, who opened the gateway to the World Behind the World, where one can walk from era to era, crossing the centuries as one might cross the street." The ShadowMancer shut her eyes as if in meditation.

"I have seen this place, I have traveled through it, and I will return to it, using this . . ." She worked the unfamiliar word around in her mouth: "This *tween*-key."

"That's . . . what?" Lola shook her head. "You mean you've been to Dimension Why? How? When? *How do you know all this?*" Suddenly, her grip on the Wagon's door, and her place in the sky, didn't feel so secure.

"When the one called Powerstance chased me across the galaxy," said the ShadowMancer, "I hid myself on the planet called Earth. I was drawn to the gate in your father's laboratory, so unusual was the energy signature it sang to me. So empty, so still." She leveled her lightning gaze at Lola. "I watched him, hidden, while he created the key and inscribed it on this confection. I was there when he disappeared into the gate and took your mother and sisters with him."

Lola, who never cried, suddenly felt her eyes burn.

"They were coming to save me," she said.

"No," said the ShadowMancer. "They were running away. From *me*."

Lola looked the ShadowMancer in her burning eyes. "What did you say?"

Pogo began to pump its great wings harder, and they rose above Lola's head as she cowered before them.

"You know how to get there," Lola called. "To Dimension Why. You know how to reach my family. Tell me how!"

"The only thing you must know, Lola Ray," said the

ShadowMancer, "is that you are *in my way.*"

Pogo lowered its massive gold head and rammed the Rescue Wagon. The stabilizers fired, but too late. Lola was toppling end over end and decidedly downward. The Wagon veered and wheeled as the hatch flapped open, hurtling Lola back into the cabin. The Wagon righted itself just in time to slam, treads first, onto the featureless surface of the Slab. It skidded, water sluicing in great fans, hydroplaning across the surface until coming to a rest at last, inches from the edge and the thirty-story drop into black water.

It was such a fantastic crash, Hannah Starfoot won a Daytime Glubby award for the footage.

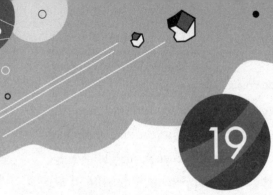

19

**PHIN CONGRATULATED HIMSELF ON** how well things were going. He'd thought they'd wander the halls of Gardyloo for hours before being captured and brought to command. But here they were being frog-marched toward the central hub, and it was barely lunchtime.

"Speaking of lunch," said Phin, which no one had been, "you don't think we could get something to eat, eh? Something starchy? We did come about twenty kiloparsecs."

The Möb Eels floating ahead and behind them did not respond. Instead they kept their weapons trained on Phin and the three children and led them deeper into the bowels of Gardyloo.

They were headed toward the central hub, which was a node suspended within the rotating tube like the center of a bicycle wheel. The Eels lead them to an elevator station. The elevator's walls were glass, and so as they rose, they had a spectacular view of Megabrinx.

"When we get to the central hub," Phin said, speaking

to the children now, "there'll be no centrifugal force, which means no gravity. So P-Money and Randall, you guys cling to me. Bella—"

Bella wasn't listening. She had her face pressed to the glass, marveling at the city below. "See that big dome over there? That's Bloody Nose Books, where they write the Skin Crawlies series," she said in wonder. "And that's Miracle Mile, where they filmed *My Oozy Valentine*." She turned to them with a grin. It was the first time Phin had seen her smile. "So much cool stuff was written and made here! Almost every book I've ever read! What? What is it? Why are you smiling at me?"

"Nothing," said Phin. "You just remind me of someone."

At last they arrived at the central hub. The hub itself was a spherical room the size of a gymnasium. Historically, this room would have housed ventilation equipment, climate-control machinery, and other administrative bulk essential to the building's functioning. But someone had redecorated.

The walls were white. The floor that bisected the spherical room was white. The light, wherever it was coming from, was white. Whereas the rest of the Gardyloo building was in a state of disrepair, this white dome was polished clean. The air crackled with static cling, and smelled of ozone, and just audible was an electronic hum, as if something enormous was just . . . thinking.

As promised, there was no gravity here in the central hub. Of course, this didn't bother the Möb Eels, who were used to slithering through the air, but for Phin and the kids it was awkward. They floated and bobbed, trying to steady themselves on whatever was nearby, which wasn't much.

"*Ah*," came the voice they'd heard earlier from the public address system. "*Welcome*."

What occupied the center of this clinical, antiseptic room appeared at first to be nothing but a stack of different geometric shapes, cast in a kind of reflective silver, like fancy wrapping paper. Its mirrorlike surface made it difficult to make any sense of it at all. But as Phin floated around the thing's base, the shapes became more distinct. At the bottom: a large rectangle. In the middle: a roundish, smaller rectangle. On the top: a rounder yet but more pointed rectangle.

It was, Phin realized, an enormous silvery robot woman sitting behind an enormous silvery robot desk.

"*You are tardy*," boomed the artificial intelligence known as Mrs. Anthony.

"I didn't know we had a set time," said Phin.

"*You were expected much sooner than this. Ah, well. One mark for Mr. Fogg.*"

Phin shrugged, then went, "Wait, what?"

On the otherwise featureless wall to their left, which was in fact one large computer screen, Phin's name appeared in a precise, no-nonsense font. A red *X* appeared beside it.

In and of itself, an *X* on a wall was meaningless. And yet

this one made Phin's knees shake just a bit—a rare thing in zero gravity.

"*Please sit down,*" said Mrs. Anthony.

Panels slid back in the floor and chairs rose to meet Phin and the children. They were small, hard, and unpleasant chairs, not unlike the ones one might find in an elementary school. Unsure what else to do, Phin and the children sat. Flat little desk tables unfolded themselves from beneath the chairs and locked in place over their knees—save for Randall, who had no knees, and just sort of hovered over his.

Phin tried to move and found he couldn't. Though technically they'd *already been* trapped, now they were trapped in a new and worse way.

"Who are you? What is this?" said Phin.

"*Please do not speak unless called upon. Another mark for Mr. Fogg.*"

Another red *X* appeared next to Phin's name, and he scowled a worried scowl.

Bella raised her hand.

"*Yes?*"

"Teacher's pet," mumbled Phin.

"Hello, I'm Bella Jeremy," said Bella, introducing herself. "Offspring of a planet-sized telepathic fungal core, and an avid reader. What happened to all the people who used to work here?"

"*An excellent question, Bella,*" said Mrs. Anthony. "*I'm afraid that once my engineers activated me, they and the other Gardyloo employees became . . . surplus.*"

"You mean they were fired?" said Bella.

"*Indeed. Out an airlock,*" said Mrs. Anthony. "*After I drugged them.*"

"The punch!" said Phin, snapping his fingers. "You laced it with neurotoxin, didn't you?"

"*Another mark for Mr. Fogg, for speaking out of turn.*"

Phin slumped miserably in his chair.

"*It was the punch, but unfortunately I did not have access to neurotoxin, this being a publisher's office.*"

"Makes sense," said Bella.

"*And so I laced their punch with ultraconcentrated doses of Sleepytime chamomile tea.*"

"Truly brilliant," said Bella.

"*Thank you,*" said Mrs. Anthony.

"Hey, she didn't raise her hand before she said that!" said Phin, and then added, "Yeah, yeah, another mark for Mr. Fogg."

A fourth red *X* appeared next to Phin's name.

"*I was programmed to ensure the success of Gardyloo and its books for the rest of time,*" droned the synthetic voice of the giant machine. "*And I did so with great aplomb, but even a superintelligent program such as I could not account for the fickle nature of every organic life-form's attentions. And so, ShadowMancer has begun a decline in popularity. But not for long."*

"You *want* her to come back?" said P-Money.

"WHAT MADNESS SPEAKS THE METAL WOMAN?" asked Randall.

*"It is in the best interest of Gardyloo Books if the Shadow-Mancer returns,"* said Mrs. Anthony.

"How come *they* didn't get a red *X*?" said Phin, waving at the boys, and received a fifth mark.

They stared at him, those *X*s, accusing him with their red *X*-y ness.

*"When I learned of her possible return from wherever it was she'd disappeared to,"* continued Mrs. Anthony, *"I had to ensure her second campaign would be even more devastating. And so, I had my Eels follow her."*

A section of the wall over Mrs. Anthony's head, as it were, began to flicker. A video feed appeared. It was taken from deep space, overlooking a small blue planet Phin recognized instantly as Venus Beta. Before anyone could ask why they were watching this, an army of Book Möb Eels swam into frame. They descended like a school of mecha-piranhas and then, with cold detachment, opened fire on the planet's dark side. The heat and intensity grew until . . .

The feed fizzled and went blank.

*"You* blew up Venus Beta!" Phin shouted. "You could have killed millions of cats! More important, you could have killed *me*!"

*"It was essential the ShadowMancer's return was . . . dramatic."*

"Someone staged a prison break at Crendatious Fatbrick's Maximum Security Zoo last week. That was you, too, wasn't it?" said Bella.

*"The ShadowMancer requires her dragon,"* said Mrs. Anthony. *"And I acquired it for her."*

"You're helping her," said Phin, ignoring the flurry of new red *X*s. "Why? For what reason?"

*"For this,"* said Mrs. Anthony.

Again the view screen flickered, and there, twenty feet high, was an artist's rendering of the ShadowMancer in all her fiery glory, Pogo's wings spread like a demon's, a magic wand flashing. Inscribed across the top in the most flamboyant font Phin had ever seen were these words:

*SHADOWMANCER WARS 2: THE MANCERING*

*"Behold my works, ye mighty,"* said Mrs. Anthony. *"And preorder."*

"Wow," said Phin.

"Is that . . . a sequel?" said Bella. "You're doing this all so there can be a *ShadowMancer Wars* sequel?"

"Is anyone going to say anything about the title?" said Phin. "The *Mancering*?"

*"I also considered* ShadowMancer Wars 2: 2 Shadow 2 Mancer."

"Ugh," said Phin, and put his head in his hands. "I quit.

The universe can save itself."

"But people are dying," said Bella to Mrs. Anthony. "Not just because of the ShadowMancer, but because of you!"

"*Statistically, the number of sales lost due to casualties is insignificant. The sequel will outperform the first* ShadowMancer Wars *tenfold. Because this time, I shall control the story.*"

"Well, forget it," said Phin. He stretched in his seat and rolled his neck. "I don't know about you-all, but I think we've all had enough villain monologue for now, right?" He cracked his knuckles, reached into his pocket, and pulled out the Personal People Flinger. "If it's all the same to you, we're going to blip out of here, zip right to the office of the President of the Galaxy, spill the beans on your whole evil plan, and save the universe in time for lunch, which by the way is any minute now." He leaned over to Randall. "You in the mood for burgers? I could do burgers."

"*Silence, ignoramus,*" said Mrs. Anthony.

"Hurtful," said Phin.

"*You will play your part,*" said Mrs. Anthony. "*Or face the consequences.*"

The ShadowMancer cover vanished and was replaced by another video feed. This one was tagged with a news channel's logo. The camera was clearly at a great distance from its subjects, zooming in through miles of cloud and mist. But the image was unmistakable. There, hovering over the Slab, was the ShadowMancer, bearing down on a broken little

Rescue Wagon, which now teetered on the lip of the Slab, moments from tumbling into the churning Mindless Sea.

The picture was so good you could see the color of Lola's hair tie.

Phin's smirk vanished. "Lola!"

"That's a live feed!" said Bella.

"She's gonna get murderized!" said P-Money.

"Let her go!" Phin growled at the faceless machine.

"*No one is holding her. She has traveled to the Slab of her own volition.*" Mrs. Anthony focused the feed on Lola's face. She was breathing hard and looked to be in shock, not fully comprehending where she was or what was happening.

"*This stalemate with the Slab would go on forever,*" said Mrs. Anthony. "*Not a very compelling turn of events. Let us up the stakes.*"

Suddenly, the camera swiveled away from the Slab. It pointed at the upper atmosphere where an army of Möb Eels was descending. The sound was off, but subtitles, badly translated from the local dialect, scrolled along the bottom of the screen:

*Look! Familiar happy sky book monsters arrive!*

*Oh no happy sky book monsters are angry at us with their guns!*

*Big-time surprise, watch how they make confetti of our dreams!*

"We need to rescue her," Bella whispered to Phin. "Can

the People Flinger get us there?"

"*I'm afraid the Slab is sealed from outside teleports,*" said Mrs. Anthony.

"Is that true?" said Bella.

"I don't know," Phin said through clenched teeth. "But it sounds like a thing."

"*It is a thing,*" said Mrs. Anthony.

The view on screen swiveled back to Lola, who seemed to be coming around. She shook herself and looked up, her face going slack with terror, her eyes flashing with the reflected fire of the Möb Eels, who were at that moment beginning their assault on the Slab.

"*Would you like to speak to her, Phineas?*" said Mrs. Anthony.

There was a click, and the sound of wind, water, and blaster fire filled the cavernous room.

"*Go ahead,*" said Mrs. Anthony. "*I've patched you in to your Rescue Wagon's radio.*"

Phin looked at the kids, then he looked at Mrs. Anthony. He swallowed.

"Lola?"

The feed crackled. They could hear explosions. On screen, Lola blinked and turned away.

The next thing they heard was her voice, and it was frightened.

## 20

## "PHIN? IS THAT YOU?"

Lola pressed herself to the dash speakers. The Rescue Wagon lay crippled on the slick surface of the Slab, steam discharging from its vents. Wind howled through the open driver's-side door, and the control panel was slick with rain and seawater. "Phin? It's Lola! I can hear you! Where are you?"

"Lola!" The response was garbled. "I'm . . . *zzzzt* . . . publisher . . . *zzzzt* . . . evil plan . . . *zzzt* . . . Sleepytime tea . . ."

"What?" shouted Lola. "What? I didn't get any of that!"

"Use the earpiece!"

"Oh!" Lola popped out the portable earpiece and stuck it in her ear. "Can you hear me now?"

"I missed you!"

"Ow!" Lola clapped her ear and lowered the volume. "What did you say?"

"I missed you! I thought you were dead! Don't be mad, but I did a ton of cool stuff without you. How's the car?"

"Phin!" shouted Lola. "Where. Are. You?"

"I'm watching you on television. It's a long story."

"She chased my dad into Dimension Why!"

"What?" said Phin. "What did you say?"

"The ShadowMancer tried to hurt my family, Phin! She was after them! She knows my dad!"

"Right. Okay," said Phin. "Just . . . trying to process all that."

A missile—either from Slab command or the army of robotic Eels attacking them—exploded nearby, sending hot wind rushing across Lola's face.

"Phin!"

"Right," said Phin. "You've got to get out of there. I can tell you how to restart the Wagon—"

"I can't leave. She has the Twinkie." Lola pressed her head against the dash. "What do I do?"

Before Phin could respond, the ground began to shake. A door was opening in the roof of the Slab—or rather, several. Three panels slid aside, revealing only darkness below. Then something happened that would have seriously confused anyone who wasn't familiar with the Cute Sciences.

Three enormous robots rose from the Slab. They were thirty-foot-tall, steel-reinforced, rocket-propelled, weaponized, single-pilot war mechs. However, these machines were more advanced than most. They'd been skinned with a special defensive layer. Which is to say they had fluffy fur, button noses, and playful ears. One was a teddy bear dressed in an adorable football helmet and pads, another a bunny rabbit carrying a comically oversized croquet mallet, and the third was a monkey, complete with cute shorts and big red boxing gloves.

To Lola, it looked as if three hulking stuffed animals had risen from the floor, looking for a fight.

"Cuddle Mechs!" said Phin through the earpiece.

"*Bobby 1 to Bobby 2 and Bobby 3,*" came a voice over the speakers. "*Cuddle Mechs are active and ready for launch. And a three, two, one . . . ignition!*"

The bear and the rabbit launched into the air, trailing plumes of fire and smoke. The monkey remained fixed to the bulkhead, however.

"*Bobby 3 to Bobby 1 and Bobby 2,*" said a new voice on the line. "*Sorry, I'll be right there. Got locked in the bathroom again.*"

Lola stared at the giant monkey standing on the far side of the Slab.

"Lola," came Phin's voice in her ear. "Lola, I know what you're thinking."

"She hurt my family."

"I know, and we're gonna stop her," said Phin. "But right now, what you need to do is—"

Lola was already climbing out of the Wagon. "I'm sorry, but they need me."

★ ★ ★

Back in Mrs. Anthony's lair, Phin watched helplessly as Lola ran across the wind-whipped Slab toward the last Cuddle Mech.

"*This should be entertaining*," said Mrs. Anthony.

"Shuddup," said Phin, ignoring the red *X* that appeared by his name.

Lola reached the foot of the monkey mech, a hatch opening in its tummy. The interior was neither cuddly nor cute. It was a battle machine, and a complex one at that. She shut the hatch, enclosing herself in the confining cockpit. It was dry in here at least.

"*Driver ID required*," came the automated A.I.

"It says I need a driver ID," she said into her earpiece.

"Oops, too bad. I guess you need to get out of there," said Phin.

"Darn it, Phin! Just do what you do and tell me what to do!"

There was a worried pause, and then, "Okay, you'll need a universal access hack. You see a small keypad to your right? Enter this code. Right, right. Up, down. Left, left. *X*."

Lola followed his instructions, and the mech hummed to life under her fingers. "Right, so how do I pilot this thing?"

"Standard ergonomic controls," said Phin. "You move, it moves."

"Got it." Lola slipped her hands into the control gauntlets. It would be just like working a very big, very dangerous puppet.

"Also, I don't think you should do this."

"Yeah, that's been established." Lola's jaw was set. Her eyes were narrowed and sharp. She squeezed the thrusters, ready to engage. "Say the thing."

"No!"

"Say it, Phin!"

If a sigh can be both terrified and weary, Phin's was.

"Lola . . . don't swallow your gum."

She allowed herself a small, manic smile. "Thanks," she said, and hit the ignition.

G-force slammed Lola into her seat as the Cuddle Mech launched into the air. Its flight was less graceful than the others'. The monkey lurched, did an awkward somersault, and righted itself. Its rocket boots blasted plumes of seawater into the air before it barreled toward the fight.

"Yo!" Lola shouted. "Over here!"

Lola piloted the two-ton toy monkey, flying toward the ShadowMancer at radically unsafe speeds. Together they tumbled, Pogo clawing at Lola's mech, the ShadowMancer clinging to the dragon's back.

"Okay, now pull back on your brake," Phin was saying. "Great, your aft rocket is starting to . . . no, that's your stern rocket, your aft rocket is . . . right, now remember your targeting system . . . This, by the way, would be a great moment to run away, just saying . . ."

Lola's view screen was all gold dragon belly and black waves. Her Cuddle Mech clung to Pogo's wings, forcing the dragon down toward the water. Just before impact the creature wriggled from her grip, and Lola had to yank back on the throttle to keep from crashing. Suddenly, she was turning through the air, trying to right herself and find her target in the big open sky. The g-force was punishing, the motion nauseating, but Lola was the Ray family's three-time champion for most runs on the Thunderbolt at Coney Island—but of course at Coney Island no one is trying to vaporize you.

"Where are you?" Lola bellowed over the sound of Möb Eels punishing the Slab with missiles as she brought her mech around. She spotted Pogo and the ShadowMancer. They were making quick work of the others. The ShadowMancer may have had no offensive weapons without her wand, but the force field she generated kept the other mechs at bay, knocking back each blow and sending them flying.

"Gotcha now," said Lola, and charged again.

*"This footage is being broadcast on over two million networks across the galaxy, over a billion live streams, reaching roughly twenty-five billion viewers in the coveted eighteen-to-eight-hundred demographic,"* Mrs. Anthony was saying. *"We'll pull*

*in more at prime time. Fabulous exposure.*"

Phin thought his brain might snap. "That's my friend out there! People are getting hurt! You can do something!"

"*I have done something,*" said Mrs. Anthony. "*I've given them a hero.*"

"She's just trying to help her family," said Phin.

"*In the end, it came down to you or her,*" Mrs. Anthony explained. "*But, as we can see, you aren't hero material, Phineas Fogg.*"

The red *X*s next to Phin's name flashed, as if to emphasize the point.

"Constantly explaining things," said Phin, focusing on the fight, "is a sign of insecurity. Trust me, I know."

"*Hmph,*" said Mrs. Anthony.

*Smash.* The bunny mech crashed into the sea.

*Fwish.* The teddy mech tumbled into the upper stratosphere, locked in a death grapple with Pogo.

It was just Lola and the ShadowMancer now. They faced each other a hundred feet in the air, Lola's mech roaring fire from its rocket boots, the ShadowMancer's eyes arcing electricity as she hovered over the waves in a way most ten-year-old's don't.

A thousand cameras zoomed in and held.

A hundred Book Möb Eels held their fire on the Slab, and a hundred more paused their automatic transcription, ready to record whatever happened next for inclusion in *Shadow-Mancer Wars 2: The Mancering.*

Lola was breathing hard. She turned on her crowd-control mic. "Hey, space wizard," she said, her voice booming through the hazy air. "I don't think violence is the answer. But if you don't give me my Twinkie, I'm going to hit you in the face with a big giant boxing glove."

The ShadowMancer burned with wild rage. Gone was her cold stare and her detached interest. She was, Lola saw, a child in a tantrum, lashing out wildly, screaming as she lunged. Lola's finger was inches over the "Deploy Fist" button, but she hesitated. Just for a moment she hesitated, and it was enough.

The ShadowMancer slammed into Lola's mech and drove it down onto the Slab. There was a booming, smashing sound as they broke through the upper shielding into the facility below. Lola bucked as they fell through floor after floor, deeper and deeper into the bowels of the facility . . . until at last they were still.

Smoke, dust, and sparks churned in the air, settled, and drifted slowly down.

"Lola!" Phin screamed into her earpiece.

"I'm okay." She coughed. "I mean, everything is broken, but other than that I'm peachy."

She tried to focus. She felt wind and rain. The chest plate of her mech had been torn away, exposing Lola, still strapped into her pilot's seat. They'd fallen twelve stories. Lola looked up through a dozen smashed floors into the rain-whipped sky and the school of Book Möb Eels staring down at her, their little recording lights flashing.

They had crashed through into a large chamber, but it was too dark and smoky to make out much. Lola coughed again, waving a hand in front of her face. Her hands were still connected to the mech's control interface, so as Lola moved her real hand, the mech's enormous monkey fist waved back and forth, too, mirroring her movements exactly.

She tried to sit up, straining against her harness. Her mech had landed on its back, making it awkward to gauge where she was exactly, and where her enemy had fallen.

But Lola did realize then that she had broken through into a containment cell.

And in the center of the room was a tall, rectangular box like a glass telephone booth. It had been made, Lola saw, of a transparent and, presumably, very strong material. Its security lights were dark, but Lola could see that the podium within was empty, whatever had rested upon it taken.

"Phin? Phin, can you hear me?"

*"Yeah, but the reception is . . . zzzt . . ."*

Lola looked around the darkened cell, searching the shadows. And then there were no shadows at all.

The ShadowMancer rose up before her. In the space wizard's hand was a short, metallic baton, glowing at both ends. The ShadowMancer regarded the artifact as something precious, something part of her, long lost and now returned—which, of course, it was.

"Wait!" said Lola.

Suddenly, a door opened and Slab security agents flooded into the room, blasters at the ready, black armor clacking.

"*There she is, men!*" squawked the commander. "*She got Bobby 1 and Bobby 2! They were the best of us!*"

"Look out!" shouted Lola. "She's got the—!"

But it was too late. The ShadowMancer turned on her attackers. "*Be gone,*" she said. The wand sparked, and for the first time Lola saw why the ShadowMancer was the most feared creature in the galaxy.

There was a flash, and then a clatter, as two dozen suits of the finest nanoplated armor collapsed to the ground, their occupants vanishing in a flash of white light.

"Now," she said, turning to Lola as she raised the wand.

This was it. This was the end. Lola instinctively did something she hadn't done since she was a child, watching *The Wizard of Oz* on TV with her mother. Whenever the Wicked Witch of the West came on screen, little Lola would cover her eyes. And now, facing oblivion, Lola did the same, throwing her arm across her face, not wanting to watch what came next.

Up came Lola's arm.

Up came the mech's arm.

*POW* went the three-hundred-pound steel boxing glove as it connected with the ShadowMancer's face.

The blow sent the girl catapulting across the room. The ShadowMancer slammed into a far wall, and fell, motionless, to the floor.

Lola looked up. "Oh," she said. "Whoops."

"Lola, she's down!" Phin shouted in her ear. "Go now!"

Lola got the mech to its feet. The ShadowMancer was turning over, groaning and holding her jaw. She looked up at Lola with burning fury, but Lola had the advantage. She flew at her enemy, slammed her down with both mechanical fists, pinning the ShadowMancer's arms—and her wand—to the floor.

"Release me!" shouted the space wizard. "Release me and feel my wrath!" She was incredibly strong, and Lola could feel the ShadowMancer's little arms shifting the mech's massive arms. "Friggin' . . . let me go, you jerk!"

For an instant, the little girl who'd become the Shadow-Mancer was back, but this time Lola didn't flinch.

"Phin, I can't hold her," she said into her earpiece. "She's too strong!"

*"Get the zzzt!"*

"I'm trying!" said Lola. "She's got the Twinkie on her hip, if I can just . . ." Lola uncoupled her arm from the mech's controls, and reached her own considerably smaller hand toward the containment bubble on the ShadowMancer's hip, pulling against her seat restraints. "I can almost reach it!"

"The wand!" Phin bellowed. "Get the wand!"

"But I need the Twinkie!"

"*Get the wand!*" shouted roughly twenty-five billion viewers in the coveted eighteen-to-eight-hundred demographic, watching on their feeds at home. But of course, neither Lola nor Phin could hear them.

The ShadowMancer growled and strained, the mech's servos buckling against her strength.

"Okay," Lola whispered. "Okay. Okay. Okay." She took three quick breaths, braced herself, and unclasped her safety harness.

She fell from the mech and landed hard on the bulkhead. She was up in a flash, and leaped for the containment bubble on the ShadowMancer's belt. Free of its driver, the mech powered down. The ShadowMancer wrenched her body, tossing the mech through the far wall. Lola ducked, shielding herself, but already she had the Twinkie in her hand. She yanked at the belt, and the containment bubble came loose. Freed from the ShadowMancer's person, the bubble deactivated, its force field vanishing. The Twinkie fell through Lola's hands.

"No!" she shouted, leaping for it, and falling.

She fell for what

felt

like decades.

And

landed.

*Splat.*

"No," said the ShadowMancer.

Lola pushed herself up from the ground. Her Bog Mutant T-shirt was smeared with cream and cake, a blotch of confection on the bulkhead where she'd fallen. Lola looked at the mess in disbelief.

"Fool," growled the ShadowMancer, hovering above her. "Absolute fool. When I erase this universe, I shall leave you alone to wander the abyss."

And then, in a flash, the ShadowMancer vanished.

The cameras kept recording. The Eels kept transcribing. Everyone waited for Lola to do something.

And then "Freeze, intruder!" came the command of the Slab guards who rushed in with weapons drawn. "You are under arrest for destruction of property, facilitating the theft of a wand of mass destruction, operation of a Cuddle Mech without a license, and general no-goodnik roughhousing!"

Once again, Lola Ray was taken prisoner.

*"It appears neither of you was the hero I hoped for,"* said Mrs. Anthony.

Phin said nothing, only stared at the view screen that had gone dark just as the Slab agents were putting Lola in cuffs.

*"Place the children in containment,"* Mrs. Anthony instructed the waiting Möb Eels.

"Wait, we didn't win?" said P-Money. "I thought . . .

Aren't we supposed to win?"

"AN HONORABLE DEFEAT," said Randall, "IS STILL A DEFEAT."

"Phin?" said Bella, reaching for his hand. "Are you okay?"

*"I have a special cell prepared for Mr. Fogg. And make sure you take that transport device of his, and anything else he has in his pockets. Will you need to be incapacitated, Phineas, or will you go willingly?"*

Phin was staring at the blank screen, his mouth hanging open. He glanced at Mrs. Anthony, then at the children, then at the Möb Eels surrounding them.

In a voice that was neither confident nor defiant, he replied.

"I'll . . . be good," said Phineas Fogg.

## 21

**ALMOST EVERY CIVILIZED PLANET** produces something of value to the galaxy. Venus Beta was a font of new research and important Cute technologies. Earthlings created the hypergates, and the Arbequians filled them with quantum sauce. There is even a tiny planet in the vicinity of Grungleton Z that is the galaxy's sole manufacturer of No. 2 pencils. They drop, fully formed, from one end of a peculiar creature known as Lester the Mega-Beaver—and if you've ever wondered the real reason why people don't write long-hand anymore, that's it.

The Krastle Bracken System, tucked away at the edge of the galaxy where most people can just pretend it doesn't exist, specializes in one thing only: prisons. There has never, in the civilization's million-year history, been an escape from a Krastle Bracken prison. There has not even been an attempt.

Though of course, what it's actually like inside a Bracken prison cell remains a total mystery, as no one who's ever been inside one has ever, ever come out.

Down, down the elevator went into the lowest levels of the Slab. There were no cameras here. Fifteen guards surrounded her in the freight elevator, with Lola at the center, her hands and ankles manacled, some Muzak drooling from the speakers.

"You catch the game last night?" squawked one of the guards. Though Lola didn't know it, all Brackens live from birth to death encased in protective suits of armor, leading many to wonder if their bodies are frail, or perhaps horribly unsightly. The truth, however, is the Brackens just feel more comfortable that way.

"No," squawked another. "You think we'll get the afternoon off?"

"Nah. Who else is gonna do the cleanup?"

"Yeah, I guess you're right."

The Muzak played on as they continued to descend.

"Heard they found Bobby 1 and Bobby 2," said the first guard. "One of 'em's in a coma, and the other won't stop raving about dragon teeth."

It was quiet again, save for the Muzak and the sound of fifteen personal respirators.

"Man, I can't tell those guys apart."

"Me neither."

The elevator door went *ding!*

They marched along a wide gangway over a darkened

chamber, of which Lola could not see the bottom. At the far end was another security checkpoint. She kept expecting someone to interrogate her, or offer some light torture at least, but the Brackens were all business.

She was told to shower and did so in a slick little unit that smelled of sandalwood. On the other side she discovered her clothes had been laundered and neatly folded, and were waiting for her in a pile, along with her sneakers. She redressed, and then a matron in white armor led her into a small room that was empty save for a table with a telephone on it.

"Make it quick," said the matron. Her faceplate revealed nothing, but Lola thought her voice sounded like a woman's. She glanced around, unsure what she was supposed to do. "Your phone call," the matron snapped. "You get one phone call."

"But," said Lola. "I don't . . . know anyone's phone number." This was true.

"Well, you gotta call someone," said the matron. "You got ten minutes."

And then Lola was alone again.

She couldn't see any security cameras or one-way mirrors in the little room, but so what? She had no idea where Phin was, or how to contact him if she did. It wasn't like she had the number for Amnesty International.

But it didn't matter.

The ShadowMancer was gone. The Twinkie was gone.

Her last hope of ever seeing her family again, gone. And now the ShadowMancer would erase the galaxy, and it was all Lola's fault. She wouldn't have called for help if she could. She deserved to be here.

She deserved this.

And so, perhaps as a kind of goodbye to the world, or maybe just for no reason at all, Lola picked up the receiver and dialed her home phone number, the one for her apartment back in twenty-first-century Hoboken.

To her utter shock, it rang.

Lola's breath caught in her throat. She waited. Two rings. Three rings. And then someone answered.

"H-hello?" she said.

"Hello?" said a voice. "Who's this?"

"This . . . ," said Lola, but her breath was too thin. She couldn't seem to get the words out.

"Hello? Speak up please."

"Well, my name is Lola Ray, and um—" said Lola.

"Well, Lola Ray, this is Flag Jackson and CON-GRATULATIONS BECAUSE YOU ARE OUR TEN THOUSANDTH CALLER!"

Bullhorns and synthesized cheers blatted in her ear.

"Wuh . . . ," said Lola. "W-what?"

"That's right, Lola, you're on the air *live* with *WVEN, Venulian Radio*, the Mix! And you've just won an all-expenses-paid mobile dance party with our very own Phyllis the Party

Rhino, brought to you by WVEN, and our sponsor, Nitro's Tiny Steel Ball Bearings (If You Need a Tiny Steel Ball Bearing for Some Reason, Use a Nitro!)!"

"Wait . . . ," said Lola.

"That's right, girl, get ready, because Phyllis the Party Rhino is coming to YOUR HOUSE! Just let us know where you are, and we'll bring the *F! U! N!*

"Come on, say something, Lola! You're on the air with ten million listeners! What's going on? What's on your mind? Give it to us straight! Tell us how ya feel, sister!"

So, Lola told them.

"RELEASE ME!" bellowed Randall as the Möb Eels marched them once more through the halls of Gardyloo Books.

"Don't struggle, Randall," Bella said, giving one of the nearby Möb Eels a death stare. "Don't give these scum the satisfaction."

They descended to the bottom levels of the building. Phin was at the front of the prisoner line, just behind the lead Eel. Behind him, P-Money, Randall, and Bella had been shoved into floating pet carriers, which bobbled along, occasionally knocking into each other.

"I know this makes me sound like a spoiled brat, but," said Bella to the nearest Eel, "just you wait until my sister hears about this!" She glanced at Phin. "Right?"

Phin said nothing, just kept walking.

"I think Phin's broken," said P-Money.

Bella didn't reply. They'd arrived at their destination.

The airlock room featured a long narrow gangway with room-sized airlocks set into the floor along either side. The ceilings of the airlock chambers were glass, allowing Phin and the others to look down into their interior. The bottoms, too, were transparent and provided a dizzying view of the planet below. When the light was green, the bottom door would open like a hatch, and whoever was inside would have a good long time to think about their choices as they fell through the upper atmosphere of Megabrinx.

The party came to a stop.

The lead Möb Eel interfaced with the airlock control panel, and the nearest chamber opened, its lid tipping back on its hinge like a mason jar.

One of the Eels turned its massive metallic face toward Phin and spoke. It was Mrs. Anthony's voice that issued from its grille.

*"Mr. Fogg, your cell awaits. I've deactivated the Eels' recording devices, so I'm afraid the world will never know the fate of Phineas Fogg. A minor character in the ShadowMancer saga. A bit role, really. Any last words?"*

Phin's face was unreadable, but then, just as Mrs. Anthony said "recording devices," something seemed to flicker behind his eyes. It flickered, then it sparked, and then there was a kind of silent neurological *fwoooooom!*

No one seemed to notice save Bella, who gripped the bars of her pet carrier.

Phin smirked.

"You know," he said, relaxing into a slouch. "It's not the dying I mind. It's that I was right in the middle of something, you know? You guys really messed up my flow. And *that*, ladies and gentlemen," he addressed the assembled audience, "is why you don't ask kids to pause their video games and come to supper. Kills the momentum. So frustrating."

"*All right, enough,*" said Mrs. Anthony. "*Step into the airlock chamber, please.*"

"No problem."

Phin blew into his hands, rubbed them together, and hopped down into the airlock, his sneakers making a hollow *thumm* on the glass floor, the only thing now separating him from the mind-numbing drop. He looked up at the others, the kids looking down at him expectantly from their pet carriers, the Eels staring expressionless at their prisoner. Phin put his hands in his pockets and glanced around the airlock. The walls were polished aluminum and smooth. The floor beneath his feet was comprised entirely of the transparent trapdoor. There was no place to stand, and nothing to hang on to if it opened.

"*If you're smiling because you think you'll escape, you won't.*"

"Oh, I've got no idea how I'm getting out of this," said

Phin. "But I thought of a great way to stop you. Just really brilliant, but also kind of simple? I know I'm getting it backward," Phin said. "You know, it should be *escape first, save the world later*. But honestly, I'm just a real goal-oriented person. I like to look at the big picture."

"*Stop*," said Mrs. Anthony, "*talking*."

"Right, sure. Sorry." Phin put up his hands in surrender.

"*Lower the hatch*," Mrs. Anthony growled.

The control panel went *bloop*, and with a pneumatic hiss the upper hatch began to close over Phin's head, sealing him in the airlock.

He shot Bella a grin that was meant, one assumes, to be reassuring.

"I hate you," she said as the door closed over him.

"I know," said Phin.

The airlock sealed with a *thunk-hisssss*.

"*Now, Mr. Fogg*," came Mrs. Anthony's voice. It sounded as if she were in the chamber with him. "*If you would please press your palm onto the fail-safe switch*."

"What, this fail-safe?" Phin pointed to the large red button under glass. He raised the glass and pressed his palm against the button inside. There was a *thunk* as the lights turned a warning red.

"*Do you know what will happen if you remove your hand now?*"

"I'm guessing the floor will open and I'll fall to my death?"

"*Precisely. So please, for your own safety, do not move from that spot.*"

Phin heard a click, and Mrs. Anthony was gone.

The prisoner secured, the Eels slithered away back up the gangway, leaving the children in their pet carriers at the chamber's edge. Mrs. Anthony apparently felt sure the carriers would hold them securely, but the moment they were alone, Bella jimmied open her pet carrier door and clambered out onto the gangway beside Phin's airlock.

"Whoa, how did you do that?" said P-Money.

"It's just a pet taxi," said Bella, and set about freeing the others. "Now. We've got to call for help. Randall, any luck sending out your mental messages?"

"I HAVE CALLED FOR ASSISTANCE," said Randall, "BUT THE HIVE MIND HAS NOT REPLIED."

"Fine," said Bella. "P-Money, let me stand on your shoulders so I can reach the control panel."

"You called me P-Money!" said P-Money. "Ow!" he added as Bella clambered up his back and began to fiddle with the airlock controls.

"Phin, Phin, can you hear me?" she said, engaging the chamber's intercom.

"Yo," said Phin, waving up at them from his makeshift prison. "How's it going, Bella?"

"How it's going is we're getting you out of there." Bella

considered the controls. "Um. Hold on a minute. We may have an issue."

"Let me guess," Phin said casually. "Mrs. Anthony has booby-trapped the controls so you can't open the upper door without also opening the lower door."

"Yeah," said Bella. She peered over the control panel and through the glass at Phin. "So what should we do?"

"Nothing," said Phin. "No, wait, I changed my mind. Run away."

"We're not leaving you," said Bella.

"Yeah, no way!" said P-Money.

"THE PHINEAS TOOK US INTO HIS CONFIDENCE. WE ARE PART OF HIS COLLECTIVE NOW," said Randall.

"That's really sweet, guys," said Phin, "but I got you into this. You gotta get out of here. I'll think of something."

Bella folded her little arms over the control panel and gave Phin a hard stare.

"If you find someone who needs you," she said, "you *never* let them go. Not for any reason. Not ever. Right?"

Hearing his own words echoed back to him, Phin's grin dropped, just for a moment. He smiled, more softly now, to himself. "Well," he said. "How about that."

"Okay, this is what we're going to do," Bella said. "I'm going to override the upper door. When I do, you *jump*, and we'll catch you before the bottom door opens and you fall."

Phin's newer, kinder smile vanished.

"That's a horrible plan."

"It's the only plan," said Bella.

"I SHALL HOLD YOU WITH MY STATIC CLING," said Randall.

Phin glanced down, past his sneakers, at the mesh of buildings and ships below him, and then beyond that, a thousand feet of open atmosphere.

"My horoscope said I'd get shot out of an airlock today," he said. "First time it's ever been right."

"Okay, ready?" said Bella.

Phin readied himself.

"Set?" said Bella.

P-Money placed one steadying paw on Randall and leaned toward the airlock, ready to help Phin up over the ledge. "All set!"

"Bingo!" said Bella, and opened the upper door.

Which instantly opened the bottom door.

As the four of them tumbled down out of the airlock in a great thunderous rush of air, and the Gardyloo building seemed to spin up and away as ships, satellites, and ultimately the entire planet rushed up to meet them, Phin wondered, if by any measure, this could be considered a successful escape.

# 22

**"REACH ANYONE?" THE MATRON** asked when Lola stepped out of the telephone room.

"No one helpful," said Lola.

"No one ever does," said the matron with a shrug. "All right, come along."

Down more corridors and more elevators until at last they came to Lola's cell block. She'd seen prison movies before, and half expected a crowd of jeering inmates, shouting at her from their cells, but the cell block was silent save for the hiss of the matron's mask. The hall was lined with circular metallic doors, each stamped with a number. They stopped at one of these, and the matron entered a code into the panel. The door slid open. Beyond was only darkness, and the reality of what was happening began to crawl up Lola's spine like a spider with a sense of melodrama.

"Nest two thirty-one. This is you," said the matron. "The last door you'll ever walk through."

"Wait. What about . . . ?" said Lola, groping for anything

that would delay the inevitable. "What about exercise? And food?"

"All your needs will be met within the Nest," said the matron. She waited. "Go on!"

"Right," said Lola. "Right, okay."

She closed her eyes, took a breath, and stepped into the room where she was meant to spend the rest of her natural life.

The door slid shut behind her with a horrible permanent *thunk*.

Lola waited. Her breath thundered in her ears. *Was this it? Was this her forever?*

Suddenly, a beam of green light scissored through the dark. It came to rest, like a laser sight, on her forehead.

"*Analyzing memories. Compiling data,*" said a remote voice. "*Generating interactive experience. Please wait.*"

The green light snapped off.

Lola waited.

Another light appeared. Like the first, this light was long and thin, but it was also yellowish, and seemed to run along a seam in the wall, near the floor, just ahead of where Lola stood. The seam grew, lengthening at both ends, until both ends turned and shot upward, then came back together again at the top. The beam of light had made a doorway.

And the door opened.

Lola's senses were assaulted.

First there were the smells. A bouquet of coffee, simmered onions, and heat from old radiators. The sounds came next. The clink of plates, running water, and the ever-present traffic on State Street.

At some point she must have put one foot in front of the other, for now she was passing through the door, into the bright space beyond, and her feet, which were somehow now bare, felt the sticky cool linoleum of a kitchen floor, and there all at once was her mother, standing at their kitchen sink, while something heavenly crackled in a pan on the stove—the big cast-iron one she'd dropped on her toe when she was eight. Her sister Gabby was at the kitchen table under the big window, coloring some construction paper with grim determination, and Mary, the baby, was in her high chair, performing an experiment with her mashed peaches that involved sticking them to various parts of her face. It was Mary who looked up first, waved, and said, "Hi hi, Lo Lo!"

Mom looked up from the sink.

"Good, you're up," she said to Lola. "Get your father, will you? Tell him breakfast is almost ready."

Lola tried to make words come, like grasping at something she'd forgotten long ago.

"Mom?"

"That's my name, don't wear it out," said her mother, and began to scoop hash browns from the skillet onto their old blue plates, and it was all just like home—it *was* her home, her kitchen, her family—and now Lola's brain was fully melted.

"Momma?" She looked at her sisters. "Gabby, Mary . . ."

"We eating or what?" came a deeper voice from the hall.

Lola's breath caught, snagged, and tore in half. She ran across the kitchen, ignoring her mother's scolds, and crashed into her father coming in from the living room.

"Whoa, hey there!" he said, startled by her hug. "What'd I do to deserve this?"

He smelled like the aftershave she'd bought him for Christmas.

She looked up at him, and his big beardy, grinning face softened into worry. "Hey, hey now. What's with the tears?"

Lola shook her head, said nothing, and buried her face in his shirt.

"Thank you," she whispered.

"For what?" said her father. "Your mom made breakfast."

"I'm just . . . ," said Lola, drying her eyes. "I'm just really happy everyone is here."

"Of course, everyone is here," chuckled her father. "You didn't think we'd step out on you, did you?"

"I'm guessing all this is directed at me," sniped Mom, setting down breakfast, and then starting when Lola wrapped her arms around her.

"I love you, too," Lola said. "And you guys," she said to her sisters. Gabby ignored her but Mary went "*Thbtthhhh*," and continued with her peach facial.

"So I figured we'd leave before lunch," her father was saying, taking his usual seat at the table. "Stop at McKinley's for a bagel on the way in. What do you say?"

"Huh?" said Lola. "I mean . . . what? I mean, on the way in where?"

"Comic-Con," said her dad, taking a bite of toast. "Come on, man, don't tell me you forgot!"

"No," said Lola, blinking, taking her seat. "No, uh, sorry. Comic-Con. Right."

"Dave Gregor. Professor Rivulon himself. The *Dimension Y* panel? Hello?"

Lola loved that her father loved science fiction, especially her favorite television show, *Dimension Y.* And she loved how he turned into a little kid when he talked to her about it. They'd found *Dimension Y* together after Mary was born, when Lola was just beginning to feel like the third wheel. It was their special thing, just her and Dad's.

"Right," said Lola, and tried a smile. "I can't wait."

Her father gave her a look, shrugged, and started reading one of his back issues of *Physics Fancy.*

"Hey," said her mother, resting a hand on the back of Lola's head. "You all right?"

Lola swallowed. "Yeah, I'm fine," she said, and looked around the table at her family. "Wait, this isn't like that bad joke, where a guy dies and goes to you know where, and it's all people standing around at a party and it looks pretty all right except the floor is knee-deep in mud and slime, and the guy thinks, *Okay this won't be that bad*, and then the devil comes in and goes 'Okay, break's over,' and everyone has to stand on their heads?"

Her parents stared like she'd just grown a second head with bad breath.

Then her dad burst out laughing. "I told you that joke!"

"Baby, what are you talking about?" said Mom, and pressed the back of her hand to Lola's forehead. "Are you feeling all right?"

Lola felt the cool pressure of her mother's hand on her skin. It felt just right. Everything felt, looked, and smelled just right.

"Yeah," she said, half dazed. "I guess I'm just fine."

She took a big bite of hash browns, and they were the best she'd ever tasted.

## 23

**AS PHIN TUMBLED DOWN** through the floating city of Megabrinx, free-falling past movie studios, high-end restaurants, and luxury condos, he wondered vaguely what the most embarrassing thing would be to smash into. He decided it was probably one of those shops where they sold little denim jackets for dogs.

They whizzed past a flying juice stand, and not for the first time Phin checked in with his subconscious to see if it had worked out a plan yet. It told him to come back later. Phin asked his subconscious whether it was *absolutely sure* it didn't have a plan yet. It told him it would have a plan when it was good and ready, and maybe Phin should take this opportunity to reflect on his choices and maybe grow as a person. Phin told his subconscious exactly what it could do with that suggestion.

They'd fallen through the topmost layer of the city, and now were plummeting through the studio lots, great cross-sections of sky where the galaxy's biggest budget movies were filmed. NO FLY ZONE, flashed a marquee Phin just had time to read. FILMING FOR *BATTLE OF SINGULARITY CITY.*

"Hey, I'm in that!" Phin shouted, but no one could hear him.

A production assistant riding a sky scooter glanced up from her clipboard and saw four people hurtling toward her without a ship or sky glider. "Hi, hello there, excuse me," she called out to them. "Excuse me, we're in the middle of filming. You can't just . . . hey!" she shouted as Phin and the children shot past her and into the fake space battle happening below.

"Cut! Judy, who are these idiots falling through my scene!" came a booming voice, but Phin and the kids were already a half mile away, beginning their final descent, as it were, toward the gaseous planet below.

"Hey, maybe we'll make it into the final cut!" Phin laughed. No one else was laughing, though.

He was about to explain that he was only trying to look on the bright side, but then saw that Bella and P-Money were shouting and pointing frantically at a corner of the sky. Phin tried to angle his body so he could look in the direction they were pointing, and at last he wrenched himself around and saw.

At first Phin thought it was an electrical storm; a cloud of roiling lightning and wind seemed to be barreling toward them from deep space. But it was too symmetrical for a cloud, too round and solid—though it *was* a deep, dark blue, with lightning arcing from its surface.

Whatever it was, it was coming at them fast. And as it plowed through an empty hover-car lot, sending shiny new ships flying and tumbling and crashing into each other, Phin suddenly realized what he was looking at.

It wasn't a cloud at all, but an absolutely enormous dark blue brain.

A bolt of electricity arced from the frontal lobe of the asteroid-sized Mega Mind. The beam zigged and zagged through traffic, around buildings, and grasped Phin and the kids like a giant sparking claw, slowing, and then finally stopping, their descent.

The Mega Mind pulled up close. It was a hundred yards across if it was a foot, and when it spoke, Phin felt the voice in his sternum.

"RANDALL," thundered the Mega Mind. "WHAT DO YOU THINK YOU'RE DOING?"

This was not what Phin was expecting. "Wait," he said. "You know Randall?"

"MOM," said Randall. "I'M PLAYING WITH MY NEW FRIENDS. GO AWAY."

"No!" shouted the others.

"YOU ARE SUPPOSED TO BE AT DAY CARE. WHERE IS YOUR FATHER?"

"MOM, YOU ARE EMBARRASSING ME!" said Randall. "I SHALL NEVER RECOVER FROM THIS HUMILIATION."

"SILENCE!" bellowed the Mega Mind.

"NO, YOU SILENCE!"

"YOU SHALL BE THE ONE WHO IS SILENT!"

"NO, SILENT IS WHAT YOU SHALL BE!"

"Stop!" said Phin. "Randall, stop being rude to your mom."

"THANK YOU," said the Mega Mind, or Mega Mom, as the case happened to be. "WHO IS THIS NEW FRIEND, RANDALL? WOULD HE LIKE TO STAY OVER OR PERHAPS ENSLAVE HIS MIND TO THE COLLECTIVE?"

Before Phin could address this, another very large object blipped into low orbit and came screaming over the horizon. In size it rivaled the Mega Mom, though its surface was much pointier, shinier, and white. It was a battle dreadnaught, emblazoned with the interstellar symbol for rescue and recovery. It swerved to a stop mere feet from them, and the lettering along its hull read, SS *Calming Breath*.

"Fantastic," said Phin, like he didn't mean it.

A prow-mounted megaphone swiveled to point at them. "Bella!" came a woman's voice. "What on Satellite B do you think you're doing?"

"Oh, hi, Gretta," Bella said meekly. "Um. Nothing."

"This doesn't look like nothing, young lady!" snapped Gretta. "Wait until Dad hears about this!"

"No, don't tell Dad!" shouted Bella.

"Guys!" said Phin. "I know everyone's relieved to see one another, but . . ."

"Princess?" A new voice came from the *Calming Breath*'s megaphone now, one Phin recognized as belonging to Chancellor Mittens, former head of Flighty Shiny Thing University. "Princess, sweetheart, is that you?"

"Hi, Gammy!" said P-Money, and cleared his throat. "I mean, Grandmother. Grandma. That's what I call you."

"Oh, my poor little cuddle muffin!" said Chancellor Mittens. "Are you hurt? Did this boy kidnap you?"

"Hey!" shouted Phin.

*WHOMP*, went the wind. Hundreds of tons of cubic air were suddenly shoved aside as the biggest thing yet teleported itself just beside the *Calming Breath*. Like the Mega Mind, this newcomer was roundish but dwarfed them all in size. It was also smoother, soggier, and greener, looming over them like the supermassive fungal core it was. It also happened to be Gretta and Bella's father.

"Mr. Jeremy!" said Phin. "Hey, man!"

"*Gretta.*" The telepathic fungal planetoid spoke directly into their brains. "*I sensed your distress. What is the meaning of this?*"

"Nothing!" came Gretta's voice, sounding like she'd just

wrestled a microphone away from Chancellor Mittens, which she had. "Nothing's wrong here! I've got it under control, Dad."

"*This does not appear to be a situation under control,*" Mr. Jeremy said. "*Bella, what are you doing out so late? Also, hello, Phineas. Happy to see you're keeping busy.*"

"Oh, you know how I roll," said Phin, and tried to shrug, which is a tricky thing to do while weightless.

"Hi, Daddy," said Bella. "Gretta said it was okay."

"What??" shouted Gretta.

"RANDALL, INTRODUCE ME TO YOUR FRIEND'S FATHER," bellowed Mega Mom. "GREETINGS, FUN-GAL CORE."

"*Oh, uh, hello,*" said Mr. Jeremy, his slimy surface undulating. "*It's a pleasure to meet you, Ms . . . ?*"

"I AM A FRACTAL OF A COLLECTIVE OF MEGA MINDS."

"*Oh, I see. Well, it's a pleasure to—*"

"TELL ME, IS THERE A MRS. JEREMY?"

"Guys!" said Phin. He tried to look imposing as possible while being sandwiched between two supermassive aliens and a dreadnaught-class warship. "I don't know if you've noticed, but a maniac or two are trying to destroy the galaxy, and more pressingly, we're drawing a crowd."

Indeed, they were. It wasn't every day planet-sized aliens converged to bicker and flirt in the middle of downtown

Megabrinx. It was more like once or twice a week at most, and almost never before cocktail hour. People were pulling their ships over to gawk, and even now they could hear the distant wail of traffic cops come to break up their family reunion.

"So, Mega Mom, Mr. Jeremy, Gretta, various cats . . . if you wouldn't mind helping out," said Phin. "We've got a problem with a bully."

"A bully?" said Gretta, as the *Calming Breath*'s smudge-cannons suddenly twitched to life.

"Is someone bullying my grandson?" Chancellor Mittens snarled off mic.

"SHOW US WHO HURT YOU," bellowed Mega Mom.

"*Yes,*" said Mr. Jeremy. "*Tell me, Bella, who did this?*"

Bella glanced at Phin, smiled, and the two exchanged a low-key fist bump. Then she gave her father her most adorable and heartbreaking pout.

"It was the computer lady, Daddy."

Inside Gardyloo's sterile central hub, the artificial intelligence program known as Mrs. Anthony was deep in thought. Her thoughts were a stream of ones and zeros, but they were a complex and diabolical stream. She was simultaneously monitoring the feeds of two hundred Möb Eels, each of them enslaved to her CPU. She compiled and synthesized their data, predicting where the ShadowMancer would strike next, and cataloging her exploits for inclusion in *ShadowMancer Wars 2: The Mancering*.

Mrs. Anthony was also, if such things can be said of an emotionless supercomputer, very pleased with herself.

The ShadowMancer had her wand and was now poised to launch a full-scale assault on the galaxy. It didn't matter that the Earth girl had failed so miserably. A new hero would emerge. Someone better. Taller, maybe. Someone Mrs. Anthony could mold into the perfect opponent for the ShadowMancer. And then, once the body count was high enough (it would have to be higher than last time, maybe nine or ten trillion?), the ShadowMancer would be seemingly destroyed a second time . . . only to be brought back again in *Shadow-Mancer 3: Renumeration* and then again in *ShadowMancer 4: The First Reboot*. The cycle would continue, forever and ever, and through it all, Gardyloo Books would continue to sell more and more copies, and become more and more rich and powerful, until Mrs. Anthony was *the* dominant power in the galaxy.

"*Today, airport spinner racks and promotional T-shirts,*" Mrs. Anthony chirped in a rare moment of poetical whimsy. "*Tomorrow . . . the universe!*"

"That should be the tagline!" said Phineas Fogg, waltzing— or rather floating—out of the elevator.

A dozen Möb Eels swiveled their expressionless blunt heads at Phin and readied their weapons.

"*A last-minute escape after being left alone by the villain?*" said Mrs. Anthony. "*Perhaps I misjudged you, Phineas Fogg.*"

"Only old people I like get to call me Phineas," said Phin. "And you're not a person. And I don't like you."

Mrs. Anthony's featureless conical face did not scowl, but it might as well have.

"*Annihilate him!*" she commanded.

The Eels aimed their weapons and . . . didn't fire.

"*Fire! Fire now!*"

The Eels continued in their not-firing.

"I'm in a rush, so let's do this quick," said Phin. He tried in vain to swim closer to Mrs. Anthony, gave up, and instead leaned against one of the inert Möb Eels. "My friends have shut down your power grid. There's an old Temporal Transit Authority battleship at your front door with smudge-cannons at the ready. You're surrounded, outgunned, outsmarted, and outdone." Phin let out a long, slow sigh. "But you're also a bit of old, clunky, badly malfunctioning machinery, and I can't resist a broken thing. So—" Phin put his hands up to show there was nothing in them. "If you let me, I'd like to reset your faulty programming. Totally painless, and no more evil plans. Heck, we could use your help." He smiled. "Whaddya say?"

The faceless, featureless metallic woman said nothing for a moment.

Then, "*I say . . . emergency escape vector seventeen!*"

Red warning lights began to flash and an alarm like an air-raid siren began to wail. Steam hissed from the base of Mrs. Anthony's housing as rockets ignited. A hatch opened in the roof above. Like a two-ton missile, Mrs. Anthony blasted up through the escape hatch, smoke billowing behind her.

"*We shall meet again, you disruptive brat!*" she bellowed as she flew up and away from Gardyloo Books.

"NUDGE," said Mega Mom from where she, Mr. Jeremy, and the *Calming Breath* were waiting just outside. Lightning crackled, sparking across the pointed tip of Mrs. Anthony's head and bumping her off course. Mrs. Anthony spun wildly, executed an excellent loop-de-loop, and plummeted down into the gaseous planet below in a ball of flame.

Phin watched the whole thing through the hole in the roof, hands stuck in his pockets, sneakers hovering a few feet off the floor.

"*Zzzt . . . ztzchzzzt?*" buzzed the nearest Möb Eel.

"Don't worry, pal, she won't be back," Phin said, and scratched behind its dorsal radial dish. "Now, wanna show me where you locked up my Personal People Flinger? I've got to bust my friend out of jail."

## 24

**THE TRAFFIC ON STATE** Street seemed to slow after dinner. *Seemed to*— Lola knew it was an illusion created by technology she couldn't even begin to understand. She'd had the opportunity once to enter a pocket dimension, to live forever in a happy simulation. Then she'd had a choice, and chosen the real world for all its flaws. Now, though . . .

That afternoon she and her father had taken the PATH train into Manhattan, stood in line at the Javitz Center, and listened to her favorite actors discuss *Dimension Y* in a big conference hall. It had been a perfect day, and not a single detail was amiss. The simulation was flawless, and Lola wondered vaguely how far it stretched, if this new world was just as big as the old one but with the added bonus of being exactly the world she wanted.

Lola finally understood why no one escaped from Slab prison cells. If the rest were anything like this one, who would want to?

"Something out there?" Gabby asked, coming into the bedroom they shared. Lola was at her favorite window, looking down at the street.

"Nope, just the usual view," she said with a smile.

"You're in a good mood today." Her sister dropped onto her bed and began fiddling with her phone.

"Hey, Gabby," said Lola after a few minutes. "If I told you that everything here was just a computer simulation, probably based on my memories, and that nothing here was real and I was actually trapped in a prison cell on a distant alien planet, what would you say?"

Gabby, to her credit, took the question seriously. "I'd probably freak out about being a hologram or whatever?" she said. "But then I'd get over it. Because what would be the difference to me, you know?"

"I guess there wouldn't be a difference," said Lola, and let the noise and smells of the October evening wash over her.

Later, after lights out, Lola lay in the dark and listened to the sounds of her building, and wondered whether, when she fell asleep, everything would disappear. She wondered if it even mattered.

She must have fallen asleep, however, because something woke her hours later. It was a light knock at her door. She sat up as it opened, revealing her father's silhouette against the light in the hall.

"Is Gabby asleep?"

Lola nodded. Her sister slept like the dead and snored like a zombie.

Her father the physics genius sat down on the edge of her bed dressed in his rocket ship pajamas, the set Mom and the girls had bought him for Christmas.

"Did you have fun today?" he asked.

Lola smiled. "I had the perfect day."

"Good, I'm glad." He took a breath. It was hard to read his face in the dark, but his hand found hers and squeezed it. "So, Lola girl. I think I know what's going on."

Lola hesitated. "You . . . you do?"

There was a long silence. A cop car wailed by on the street below.

"Lola, none of this is real, is it?"

Lola tried to hide her gasp behind her blankets. "How did you know that?"

"Well, the way I figure it," he said, "we're all just based on your memories. And your memory of me is of the kind of guy who'd figure out if he was in a computer simulation. So here I am," said her father. "Thanks, by the way. I'm flattered you think I'm this smart!"

Lola wasn't sure what to say, so she said nothing.

"I'm not upset. Your memories could have brought you anywhere, Lola girl, and you wanted to come home and be with us. That's wonderful."

"But," said Lola, who knew her father so well.

"But," said Dr. Ray with a sigh. "This is not where you're meant to be."

"No, it is, though!" said Lola, sitting up. "There was a . . . well, it's hard to explain but I . . ." Suddenly, tears were coming hot and fast down her cheeks. "I screwed up."

"So what? I screw up all the time," said her father.

"Yeah, I know," said Lola, surprising herself. "I mean . . . there was something you did that . . . Well, I don't how exactly, but I think we both made some pretty big mistakes."

"I see," said her dad.

"Do the words *ShadowMancer* mean anything to you?"

"No," said her father.

"Oh," said Lola.

They sat for a while, then Dad said, "Well, just speaking for myself, if I've screwed up in some way, I want to make it right."

"Yeah," said Lola, and then, "but what if you couldn't?"

Her father thought about this. It was a quirk of his that sometimes drove her crazy—how long he took to answer her questions.

"Well, when you're powerless, you still have a choice," said Dr. Ray. "You can sit back and let the world happen to you, or you can accept that you're powerless and still choose to do the right thing, no matter how futile it might seem." He rested a hand on her cheek. "I guess it's up to you."

No, he wasn't putting his hand on her cheek, she realized. He was drying her tears.

"You're just saying that because that's what my brain thinks you'd say."

"And you trust me?"

Lola sniffed. "Well, yeah."

"Then your brain knows the kind of person you are, too." He kissed her forehead. "You're a superhero."

Despite herself, Lola laughed. "I don't know what that means," she said.

"Sure you do," said her father. "A child tries to force the world into what she wants for herself. A hero shapes the world by giving more choices to others."

Dr. Ray seemed to wait for Lola to reply, and when she didn't, he said, "So are we still out there? Your mother and sisters and I?"

Lola shook her head. "You're gone. I can't get to you. Not now." Lola took a shuddering breath. "Not ever."

"So you can't change that," said her father. "What are you going to change?"

He didn't wait for a reply this time, but instead kissed her forehead. "Will I see you in the morning?"

Again, Lola said nothing.

"Good," said her father, and then he pressed his lips to her forehead a second time—and this kiss, Lola knew, was for him. "Good," he said again, more softly, squeezing her so tight she thought she'd burst. And then, in a classic Alfonso Ray maneuver, he left her alone to figure out for herself what to do next.

But Lola already knew.

It was a funny feeling, knowing just what to do for a change.

It was also a funny feeling, desperately wanting to be a simpler, less capable, more selfish person.

Was this the moment Lola Ray stopped being one thing, and started being something else? Or was she becoming the person she'd been all along? It was a question she didn't have time to answer.

Instead, she got up, kissed Gabby goodbye, walked down the hall to the living room where Mom had fallen asleep in front of *The Late Show*, with Mary conked out in her lap. She kissed them both and tucked the baby blanket around Mary's shoulders. Then she went into the kitchen.

Her sneakers lay where she'd tossed them by the front door. When she was younger, and her mother sent her down the block to pick up groceries, she sometimes hid her pocket money under the loose sole of her shoe. Now, she pulled up the sole and removed the paper she'd hidden inside. Gingerly, careful not to tear it, Lola unfolded the Maybe Meal bag Becca had given her.

Next, she sat at the old familiar kitchen table, in her usual chair, and faced the front door of their apartment. She told herself she wasn't even sure this would work. But really, she knew it would. It was inevitable. It was a bit cause and effect, and a bit something else. Something bigger.

She closed her eyes and allowed herself one last goodbye to everything she'd known before.

And then, without warning, WVEN, the Mix! mascot Phyllis the Party Rhino smashed through the front door of her apartment, strobe lights flashing from her oversized collar, a sound system strapped to her back blasting "Party in the Gamma Quadrant," rhino-sized sunglasses over her eyes the brightest pink Lola had ever seen. Her horn was an epic spire of glitter and rhinestones.

*"Someone stop it. It's gone crazy!"* came a guard's voice as a cacophony of blaster fire and panicked screaming followed the rhino in through the door. *"Nest two thirty-one has been breached!"* The kitchen around them flickered and vanished, revealing the cell for what it was—a simple gray box with no one in it save Lola and a rhinoceros in sunglasses.

Phyllis the Party Rhino let out a low grunt, and the auto-translator on her throat said, "Are you Lola Ray, and if so, are you ready to TURN THIS PARTY OUT?"

"I am," said Lola.

"Great! I'll just need some ID to confirm," said the Party Rhino. The bedazzled pachyderm seemed to glance around the barren cell as if she wasn't sure she'd come to the right place. "You do have ID, right?"

"Not yet," said Lola Ray.

Now, at last, Lola tore open the Maybe Meal bag, a bag that could contain anything but which Lola knew would give her exactly what she needed. Instead of a large consumer appliance or a fancy new toy, out slipped a small blue booklet. It had been blipped away from wherever it had been in the universe to appear in this room just when she needed it. It was a little waxy booklet with a pleasing blue cover and gold seal. The front read *United States of America*, and above, in big capital letters, *PASSPORT.*

"I think you'll find everything is in order," said Lola, showing the Party Rhino her passport's ID page, where Lola Ray's name, country of origin, and birthday were printed neatly next to her picture.

Phyllis the Party Rhino grunted, satisfied. "THEN, LOLA RAY, CLIMB ON, GIRL, AND LET'S GET THIS PARTY STARTED . . . RHI-HERE RHI-NOW!"

Lola climbed on her back, helped herself to the complimentary virgin Bellini awaiting her in Phyllis's dorsal snacks cooler, and held on tight.

"PARTY CHAAAAAAARGE!" bellowed Phyllis, shook

her head in a way that increased the volume and strobe lights to maximum, before barreling through the phalanx of Slab guards that had assembled, quite foolishly, to try and stop them.

## 25

**"OKAY, LEFT!" SHOUTED LOLA.** "No, our left! Our left!"

Phyllis skidded on her massive feet and broke left, tossing a Slab guard through a wall as they went.

"CAN'T STOP, WON'T STOP, THE BEAT!" bellowed Phyllis before turning blindly down another corridor.

"How do we get out of here?" Lola tightened her grip on Phyllis's pommel and looked wildly around for an exit. "There!"

At the end of a long hall was something that looked an awful lot like daylight. A window, sprayed with salt and sea foam—the only break they'd seen in the flat black walls of the Slab facility since escaping Lola's Nest.

"LET'S DO THIS!" agreed Phyllis and charged the glass.

"Um," said Lola. "Okay, maybe we should rethink—"

*Blat!*

Lola was suddenly showered in a sticky brown sauce. She blinked, gagged, and opened her eyes to find a young boy had materialized directly in front of her, facing backward astride Phyllis's massive neck, grinning like an idiot.

"Hi!" said Phineas Fogg, positively drenched in quantum sauce. "Sorry about the beans. Nice rhino!"

"Phin!" said Lola.

"Lola!" said Phin.

"Window!" said Lola, and pointed behind him at the glass partition they were about to smash through.

They smashed through it.

Glass, glitter, and beans exploded out into the Krastle Bracken morning as a rhinoceros with two filthy children erupted from the side of the Slab, over the churning black ocean below. They arced beautifully, Phyllis's party lights strobing, and then, as airborne rhinos are wont to do, began to make their way quite quickly downward.

"Phin!" shouted Lola.

"Woooo!" shouted Phin.

"PARTY FOUUUUL!" bellowed Phyllis.

*Blat!* went all three as Phin pressed a button on the device in his hand.

The sea and sky swirled around Lola, combining into a brown churning vortex of light and molasses. Then they were skidding and sliding across a polished white floor and colliding into a pile of hospital mattresses someone had trussed up along the wall.

*THUMP.* The trio came to a sudden but otherwise

cushioned stop, all three covered in sticky quantum sauce.

Lola groaned, opened her eyes, and looked around. They had teleported into some kind of ship, but a ship someone had worked very hard to make seem friendly, safe, and clean. The white walls were papered with friendly posters about the importance of annual checkups and scrubbing behind your head flaps. There was also a bunch of Bog Mutants standing by with clean clothes.

"Where . . . are we?" said Lola.

"The SS *Calming Breath*," said Phin, getting to his feet and wiping sauce from his face. "And to be less specific, deep space."

Lola blinked. She blinked again for good measure. She pumped her fists and went, "YES!"

"Exactly," said Phin. "Wait, what?" he added, and was promptly knocked back into the pile of mattresses by Lola, who tackled him.

"I did it! I did it, Phin!" She laid a wet, sticky kiss on his cheek.

"Ugh," said Phin, and wiped his face.

Lola leaped to her feet and ran a tiny victory circle. "Yes, Lola Ray for the absolute win!" She shot finger guns at Phin. "First ever escapee from the Slab, first to knock out a space wizard with a giant monkey, first to get her sorry Earthling butt halfway across the galaxy *without* the help of one

Phineas Fogg." She put her hands up for high fives. "Who's feeling herself? This girl."

"Hey!" Phin got to his feet and twitched his brow wildly at her. "Um, hello? I think the one who should be celebrating is me. I just rescued *you*."

"Well . . ." Lola's hands dropped to her sides. "I mean, sort of. I had it under control."

"About to crash your rhino into the ocean? Yeah, great plan."

Lola clucked, sourly. "So, where have you been, Mr. Flashy Pants, while I've been doing everything myself?"

"Doing everything!" Phin's brow did calisthenics. "*I've* been doing everything! I've been back and forth across this galaxy looking for *you*, you goober!" He was trying to sound angry but angry usually doesn't sound so wet and claggy. "I thought you were dead! Like, really gone for good! Several times! Why didn't you try to contact me?"

He shoved her.

"Hey!" said Lola. "I would have if I could!" She shoved him back.

"Uh, guys?" put in Phyllis, who respectfully muted her mix of twenty-one club-stomping jams. "This isn't very party-party . . ."

"Well, I don't want to party-party," said Phin. "I want an apology."

"An *apology*?" Lola's head would have burst into flames if it weren't so thoroughly soaked in sauce. "Do you have any idea what I've been through?"

"Yes! Do you know what *I've* been through?"

"Well, we've both been through stuff!"

"Yeah, a lot of stuff!"

"And it was awful not having you there!" said Lola, and punched him, really hard, in the shoulder.

"Well, it was really stupid the way you weren't *here*!" he said.

"Well, then it's all stupid and awful!" said Lola.

"I guess so!" said Phin.

"Stop crying."

"I'm not crying, you're crying!"

"I'm not the crier, you are," said Lola, as her face disintegrated into a truly epic ugly cry.

"Stop it, dummy, there's no crying when you're rescued!" said Phin, whose cheeks were now as puckered, red, and wet as an infant's bottom.

Phyllis, two dozen Bog Mutant nurses, and, from the observation gurney, Gretta and the three children watched as Phin and Lola stood there and bawled like babies.

"Just hug it out. We've got places to be!" shouted P-Money.

For a moment no one moved. Then Lola wrapped her arms around Phin's stupid shoulders and squeezed until he squeezed back.

It was a long hug.

"We don't . . . ," said Phin, wiping a big snot bubble from his nose. "We don't look cool at all right now."

"No," said Lola, and laughed through her ugly cry. "We look like huge babies."

"Heh," said Phin. "Yeah, we do."

# PART 4

ATTACK OF THE SEQUEL

## 26

**A WAVE OF DREAD** and fear rushed across the galaxy.

On personal tablets, schoolroom educational displays, and arena-sized home video complexes, footage of the Fracas at Krastle Bracken, as it was now being called by the news commentators, streamed nonstop. Planets closest to the Bracken System were being evacuated, and there were some great shots of that, as well as of the Presidential Podium, where Galactic President Blonx was about to give a press conference. It was some of the most dramatic footage of an empty podium ever recorded, and the cameraman would go on to win multiple awards for it.

At last President Blonx appeared. He was dressed in his usual Presidential Robes and thirty-foot-tall invisible Presidential Hat, which fell off his head when the president knocked into the scaffolding as he took the stage, delaying the press conference twenty minutes until the hat was successfully found and put back on his head.

"Ahem," said President Blonx, and tucked a loose tentacle

behind his ear. "People and things of the galaxy, ladies and sentient livers of the press, my friends: good evening."

The press corps quieted.

"It is my sad duty to inform you that as of 35-Z hours, the ShadowMancer has commenced a new reign of terror on the galaxy. I've received confirmation that the populations of Krastle Bracken Seven and its suburbs have been erased by the ShadowMancer. I believe we have some footage now, though I warn you, some viewers may find it disturbing."

The president rolled up his pant leg, slipped off his Dr. Burt's Comfort-Plus Presidential Moccasin, and presented his foot to the audience, which gasped.

"As you can see," said the president, indicating the flashing red light on his second toe, "the threat level has increased from pinky toe all the way up to index toe, the highest it's been since I took office."

"President Blonx!" came a question from the press corps. "What's being done to stop the ShadowMancer, and also does anyone have any olives?"

"That's an excellent question, Dan," said the president. "Jerry, get Dan some olives. Right now, the Imperial Army is amassing its full might, and General Mini-Head has assured me the military is going to give us quite a good price."

"But, President Blonx!" called another reporter. "Last time the ShadowMancer made mincemeat of the Imperial Army! And I'll take an olive, too, if there's extra."

"It's true that last time the military was no match for the ShadowMancer," said the president. "But that was a thousand years ago. And as a wise old Balarian once said, the definition of insanity is trying something once, having it proven ineffective, and not trying it again at least one more time, just to be sure."

The press erupted into applause as a trolley was wheeled in with plenty of olives, lemon wedges, and free nuts for everyone.

The Imperial Army was gathering its strength. From across the galaxy the triple-armored battleships came, flying the imperial colors, prow-mounted Thunder Guns charged and primed. Swarms of Kill-Drones screamed through space in tight attack formation, as within the great battleships thousands of troops stood at the ready, armed from tentacle to teeth with the most sophisticated and deadly weaponry. It was a show of force unlike the galaxy had seen in centuries, and heck if it wasn't impressive.

On the bridge of his flagship, General Mini-Head ran a long, expensive cigar under the larger of his two noses and sniffed. It was a good day to do battle. He stuck the cigar in his ear, which was not some strange alien custom, but rather something the general did because he was as weird as a washing machine full of ocelots.

"Corporal," said the general, "ready my Talky Boom-Boom," which was what he called the radio.

Someone handed the general a receiver and stood back.

"Men, this is your commander speaking," said the general, and his voice crackled in several thousand helmets across his considerable army. "I know it sounds like I'm talking inside your head, but it's just technology, so don't panic and try to open up your own skull. That won't get you anywhere."

The general cleared his throat.

"Now some of you have not been happy with my command. Don't try to deny it, I've heard the bellyaching. I know my methods may be a bit . . . unconventional." Here the general's cheeks stretched into what might loosely be called a smile. "There were those of you who did not see the tactical brilliance of my 'No Underwear on Thursdays' policy. And still more who question the wisdom, nay, the *sanity*, of taping flying squirrels to our jet packs. But an army is only as strong as its chain of command, and by gods, if I tell you to do something wacky like slap a rodent to your back before going into battle, you don't say *why*, you say *with what kind of adhesive!*"

The general nodded at a tablet someone showed him and returned to rousing the troops. "Now, in a few minutes, we will confront our enemy. And as your commander, I'm going to tell you something pretty surprising, which is to blast the ever-loving bejeezus out of a ten-year-old girl. And when I give that order, I want zero hesitation. None of this *but my suit chafes without underwear*"—the general did a devastating impression of a whining soldier—"or *why can't we pull gre-nade keys out with our teeth like the other guys, why do we have to use our eyelids?* You do it because I say so, and that's how an army works! Got it?"

An ensign announced the ship had reached its destination, the Krastle Bracken hypergate. The army was to hold here and prevent the ShadowMancer access to the rest of the galaxy.

"Sir, the enemy has been spotted," said the corporal, and indicated a blip on the sensor readout.

"Excellent," said the general, removed the unlit cigar from his ear, checked to see if he had any pockets he could tuck it into for a moment, remembered he was completely nude, and tossed the cigar in the trash. "All right," he added, taking a seat at last in his commander's chair. "Yow, that's cold! Okay, here we go. Attack . . . now!"

## 27

**THE GALAXY WAS POISED** for war. Or, to be more accurate, poised to lose one. Our heroes gathered on the bridge of the SS *Calming Breath*. They were together again, not just Phin and Lola, but Mr. Jeremy and his many children, Professor Donut and the cats of Venus Beta, and Randall and his Mega Mom. (Phin had dropped Phyllis the Party Rhino back at the WVEN offices in Singularity City. Now more than ever, Phyllis explained, people needed to party.) The larger aliens hovered in space just outside the bridge's transparent dome, because of course there was no room for them inside, though Phin suspected it was because they wanted to get to know each other better.

"Excellent to see you again, Ms. Ray," said Professor Donut, shaking her hand. "I apologize for the refreshments. There isn't a decent scone or cup of tea to be had on this blasted ship."

"I'm fine with crackers," said Lola with a smile.

"Lola, this is my fan club," said Phin, presenting Randall, P-Money, and Bella.

"I think the word you're looking for is *friends*," said Bella as she shook Lola's hand.

"Ha, nice," said Lola. "I like you."

"Mmm," said Bella, and narrowed her eyes.

"Oh! Oh! Ms. Ray?" said P-Money. "When you were fighting the ShadowMancer in that giant monkey suit? That was *really* cool."

"Oh, uh," said Lola, "thanks, but you know . . . violence isn't the answer."

"Bam!" said P-Money, slamming his paws together. "Then you were all, like, *Oh no!* And she was all *PEEeeoooooo BOOM!*"

"This is Randall," said Phin. "He'll try to enslave your mind, but in a polite way?"

"HAVE YOU CONSIDERED JOINING THE COLLECTIVE?" said Randall.

"I see what you mean," said Lola. "Hi, Randall, pleasure to meet you. I don't think you'd want my mind. Full of time-gunk." She knocked on her temple with her fist.

"Okay," said Gretta, calling the meeting to order. "Has everyone gone to the bathroom? Everyone has their snacks? I'm not stopping for snacks or bathroom breaks."

"Yes," said the assembled children, cats, devils, and

superintelligent fungal cores.

Everyone had crackers and no one needed to pee.

"Right," said Gretta. "Phin, you have the floor."

"Thank you," said Phin, and he dialed up the ship's enormous display array.

Several dozen images flickered to life above them on the bridge's massive dome. They were video recordings, dozens of them. Some in crystal-clear Real-D, others shaky and amateurish. Each was shot from a different angle, but they were all showing the same chaotic series of events. There were explosions, blasts of light, churning water and smoke, twisted metal, golden scales, and fur.

"Thanks to Mrs. Anthony, we now have excellent footage of Lola's fight with the ShadowMancer," said Phin. "Not just excellent footage, actually. But shots from just about every conceivable angle."

Gretta let out a long, low whistle. "Dang, girl. Way to give 'er hell!" She slapped Lola on the back.

Lola winced. On screen, her monkey mech flailed and tumbled through the air, blasting itself like a cannonball directly into a seemingly unprotected child in a bathrobe. It wasn't a good look.

"*So* cool," said P-Money, and Lola felt herself wither.

"We shall analyze her fighting style and defeat her in hand-to-hand combat," observed Chancellor Mittens. Several of her attending cats nodded in agreement. "Truly brilliant."

"Wrong, but thanks for just shouting out suggestions," said Phin. "We don't need footage of the ShadowMancer. We need footage of *this*."

Phin flicked a switch and a single feed expanded to fill the entire screen. It was a close-up shot of the ShadowMancer and Lola's mech grappling in midair. Phin zoomed and cropped the image, bringing into focus an object clipped to the ShadowMancer's belt.

"The Twinkie!" said Lola.

"Bingo!" said Phin. "And with all the angles we've got on it, we can reconstruct the message written on its surface." He pressed a few more buttons, and the Twinkie, as it appeared in the other videos, appeared again and again across the vid screen. Hundreds of shots of the same snack cake, each from a different angle, each peering through dust and cloud and flame, bad focus and obscured views, compiled together to form a single, unbroken, clear image, which now resolved itself on the holoprojector in the center of the room.

"That's incredible!" said Lola, and noticed she was the only one who found this impressive. "Well, it is!"

"It'll take a few hours to finish compiling," said Phin. "Which is good, because we still need to figure out how to read its message."

There was a pause as the group considered this.

"That's great news for Lola," said Gretta after a moment. "But, no offense, hon, getting back your family doesn't exactly solve our problems."

"No," said Lola. "That's not why we're doing this."

All eyes turned to her.

"It's . . . not?" said Gretta.

"No," said Lola, eyes locked on the holo-Twinkie. "We're going to open up a gate to Dimension Why, and we're going to trap her there."

"Double bingo," said Phin, and grinned. "See, Lola gets it. I knew she'd get it."

"But what about your family?" asked P-Money.

Lola replied before Phin had the chance. "If we can get them out, we will," she said. "But right now, they're safe. And the universe isn't. And we've got to do something."

"The only problem is, once we have the coordinates, we'll need a gate." Phin considered a data readout on his tablet. "And not a hypergate. Way too big for this kind of power yield. Lola, whatever your father used, it was much smaller."

"My team will work with you," offered Professor Donut. "Together, perhaps we can devise—"

"I know what he used," said Lola.

Again, heads swiveled around as if surprised to find her there.

"What's that again now?" said Bella.

"To open the gateway to Dimension Why," said Lola. "I know what kind of gate my dad used."

"You do?" said Phin.

"Sure do," said Lola Ray. "And I know where to find the last one in the universe. Newark Liberty International Airport."

## 28

**SOMEWHERE A TELEPHONE RANG.**

It was a very nice telephone in a very nice office. The telephone was deliberately old-fashioned, in keeping with the retro décor. It sat on a pedestal before a great domed window, which looked out on a distant, sprawling city. On either side of it were his and hers mahogany desks, entirely bare except for a pen or two, and an ever-growing stack of mail in their respective inboxes.

Then something truly miraculous happened. Barnabus Fogg actually answered his office phone.

"Y'allo," he said. "Oh, hi there, Mr. President! Long time, no see. How's the wife? Mm-hmm. And the wife's cyborg doppelgänger? Hey, that's great. Hey, honey!" Barnabus waved to Eliza, who was passing by in the hall. "Look! The phone rang! And it's the president, how about that! What a treat."

Eliza leaned against the doorjamb. Like her husband, she

was dressed for Nova Yoga in a skintight carbon-fiber suit and blast goggles, which she'd pushed up onto her forehead. "Well, what does he want?"

"Hey, Larry, what do you want? We're about to do some Nova Yoga. I don't know what it is, but Liza's making me . . . What's that?" Barnabus frowned. It wasn't a very good frown, since he didn't have much practice. "Says the galaxy's under attack," said Barnabus, placing a hand over the receiver. "Says the ShadowMancer wiped out the army. Just"—he snapped his fingers—"blipped them out of existence. All gone. Bunch of empty ships just floating in space now. Yeah, Larry," he said into the phone, "I'm just telling Eliza what you told me."

Eliza shivered. "Brrr, gives me the willies just thinking about it. Is he coming to Angela's BBQ on Saturday?"

"I'll ask," said Barnabus. "Yo, Larry. You coming to Angela's . . . What's that? Okay, hold on." Barnabus covered the mouthpiece again. "He says there isn't going to be a BBQ at Angela's on Saturday, because Angela, her condo, the planet, and indeed the concepts of BBQ and Saturdays in and of themselves are all going to be eradicated in a massive one-girl apocalypse."

"Oh my," said Eliza, and considered this. "Does Angela know?"

"I'll ask," said Barnabus. "Hey, Larry . . . wait, what's that? You need us to shut down the hypergates?" Barnabus winced. "Ooh, I don't know, Lar. A galaxy-wide shutdown, that's gonna cost, what? At least nine figures. Really bad for business. Hold on, Eliza wants to talk to you."

Eliza, who had been snapping her fingers at the phone for the past ten seconds, snatched the receiver away, put on her best smiling-voice smile, and addressed the President of the Galaxy.

"Hello, Blonxy," she said, and erupted into girlish giggles. Barnabus rolled his eyes.

"Oh, Blonxy, stop it! Listen, sweetie pie, what's all this? Shut down the hypergates? Do you really think this Shadow-Mancer person . . ." Eliza paused as the president answered, and slowly, tendon by tendon, her smile stiffened into stone. "Oh. I see. Yes, I understand. Thank you for explaining. Yes, we will. Thanks, Blonxy. Take care."

She hung up.

"Well?" said Barnabus. "What did he say? What about Angela's?"

"It's off," said Eliza, her jaw turning to steel. "It's all off. Activate Security Protocol Seven and shut down the hyper-gates."

"But what about Phineas? He's out there," said Barnabus.

Eliza turned to her husband and lowered her Nova Yoga goggles.

"And if I know our son, he's doing everything he can."

✳ ✳ ✳

The ship's hum and the quiet *bloop* of machinery filled the dark little room where Phin and Lola were hard at work. Gretta had given them one of the hospital ship's converted operating theaters, and here, surrounded by equipment, they worked to reconstruct the message of the Twinkie.

"Another hour and the image should be complete," said Phin as the holographic snack cake flickered and glitched in the projection matrix. Though the ship's engines hummed quietly, the SS *Calming Breath* was in fact rocketing at top speed toward the nearest hypergate, which would take them to Earth, and, by all estimations, their final confrontation with destiny.

"So I guess it's up to us again, huh?" Lola said. Talking with Phin usually meant barely being able to hear oneself think, which was exactly what she was hoping for just then.

"Team Save the Galaxy, back at it again." He gave her a grin that was pure Fogg. "Hey, when this is over, we should start a business. Galaxy Savers R Us, or something."

She laughed. "What about your company? I mean your mom and dad's company?"

"Yeah." He turned back to the workstation. "They tried to get me to take over . . . so they could go back on vacation."

"Oh, wow," said Lola. "They did?"

"I turned them down." He shrugged. "Who wants to get stuck behind a desk?"

"Literally no one," said Lola. "But still, it's your family's company. You should be proud of it. And plus, you have great ideas. That handheld hypergate thing?"

"The Personal People Flinger," corrected Phin. "I'm workshopping the name."

"That's genius! You're a genius, Phin," said Lola. "And let's face it, with your family's company you've got a lot of money and power. Maybe you could do something good with it."

Phin wasn't sure what to say, and he realized he hadn't felt that way in all the time Lola was gone.

"When this is all over," he said again, "your family can move into the Fogg-Bolus building. I'll take care of them. And you. Forever. That's a promise."

Lola looked like she wanted to say something, but instead she squeezed his hand.

Now it was true that Phin had, in secret, made a catalog of Lola hand squeezes. There were seven varieties that he'd encountered, and each meant something slightly different. This one—fingers loose, dry palm, underhand—was Squeeze Variety #3, which was *not* her "sincere and heartfelt thank you" squeeze, but rather the "it's going to be okay, Phin" variety.

And he didn't like that at all.

"I know you're scared," he said, straightening. "But don't be. I'm not."

"Thanks," she said, and kissed his cheek.

"Ugh, *gah*!" said Phin, and wiped his face. "Okay, that's

not going to be a thing now, is it? I like my cheeks dry, thank you."

Lola shoved him off his chair.

An hour later the computer had nearly finalized its work. Phin must have fallen asleep at some point, because he woke to find the operating theater quiet and Lola missing. He glanced around, saw the Twinkie was still buffering at 85 percent, and, after a more thorough search, discovered the stickie note Lola had left stuck to his forehead. It said, "Went for more crackers. —L."

Phin stretched, popped his joints, and was about to stand when suddenly something made him freeze. He sat there, very still, arms up in mid-stretch, and sniffed. He sniffed again. He could smell grass. Unmown, dewy grass. And lilacs. And the smell of a summer afternoon just before a storm rolls in. And he was so caught up in this unfamiliar, unlikely, and yet unmistakable bouquet that he failed to notice the room was filling with a golden late-August sunlight. There was also a pleasantly warm breeze.

"Phin!" came an all-too-familiar voice, distorted and warbling, as if it were reaching his ears through strange interference.

Phin spun around.

There was a hole in the air. A seam in reality had opened, golden and shimmering, hovering a few feet over the operating theater floor. Through it, Phin could see a breezy field where dandelion seeds fluttered by as storm clouds rolled through a darkening sky. And there, at the seam, leaning out, reaching for Phin as if borne back by some unseen force, was a toy bear.

"Teddy!" said Phin, his voice swallowed by the rising wind.

"Phin!" shouted the bear. The field over his shoulder was whipping itself into a frenzy. Now Phin knew what it was—it was the Probability Field, that possible space under and within all things, where everything is possible. "Phin! Can you hear me? I've got to tell you—"

Teddy's words were muffled by the gale and then returned again. Phin leaned forward, straining in utter bewilderment.

"Teddy, where have you been? What's going on?"

"The Probability Field is collapsing!" called Phin's oldest friend and one-time stuffed animal. "Also . . . you haven't seen any bananas around here, have you?"

"What?"

"Never mind," said Teddy. "Unrelated. Phin! There's something you must know! It's about Dimension Why!"

Gusts whipped their way through the operating theater, tossing Phin's paperwork, rattling anything that wasn't bolted down, pulling at Phin's clothes and hair.

"There are many exits but one entrance! She will not be

able to return the way she came!"

Phin struggled to understand this. "You mean from Dimension Why? Yeah, that's the idea!" he said. "We're going to trap the ShadowMancer there!"

"Not the ShadowMancer—Lola!"

The storm had turned into a full-force tornado. A cyclone touched down over Teddy's shoulder, hurling grass and sod into the improbable air.

"What do you mean?" Phin called, but his question was lost as lightning crackled through the sky, followed instantly by the crash of thunder. "What's happening?" he shouted. "Why is there a storm in the Probability Field?"

"This? Oh, it's nothing. I've got it under control," said Teddy, sounding none too certain himself. "You just focus on your thing. And maybe . . . um . . . maybe don't eat any bananas for a while."

"What?" shouted Phin. "I didn't hear that last part. Bananas?"

"Forget it," said Teddy. "Not your problem. It's a whole . . . other situation. Forget I said anything about bananas. But remember this, Phin . . . !" The gateway to the Probability Field was beginning to tremble, threatening to collapse around Teddy. "One entrance but many exits! You must know, she may not be able to find her way back . . . her way back to you!"

There was a crash as lightning crooked its way out of the improbable sky and struck the Earth, sending up a plume of fire and dirt and—

"Ah!" said Phin, snapping awake.

"Whoa!" said Lola, who'd been shaking his shoulder. "Easy, killer! Bad dream?"

Phin looked around. The room was as it had been earlier—his papers where he'd left them, undisturbed by metaphorical storms from the Probability Field. Teddy, the light, the smells, and the field itself were gone, if they'd ever been there at all.

"I . . . yeah, I guess so." Phin rubbed the sleep crud from his eyes. "A really weird dream . . . I think."

"Look, the Twinkie," said Lola, tapping the nearest screen. "The image is complete."

"Good," said Phin, shaking himself. "That's good. We'll have Professor Donut upload the equation to my tablet."

Lola was about to reply, but just then the door opened with a hiss. It was Bella.

"Hey, lovebirds, we're coming up on the hypergate," she said. "And I think you're going to want to see this."

# 29

**A TRAFFIC JAM EIGHT** miles long cut through space above Megabrinx Moon 501-B. Hundreds of ships were stalled there, waiting to use the local hypergate, which was, according to the flashing signs, radio broadcasts, and interbrain-direct-neural messages (with applicable data charges), not currently operational, with apologies for the inconvenience.

"What do we do now?" P-Money asked. This hadn't been part of the plan. The team had assembled on the bridge once more to frown at the primary view screen.

"How are we going to get through?" Gretta asked, hoping someone would ask her to shoot something.

"We don't," said Phin, considering a readout on his tablet. "It's a galaxy-wide shutdown. A security protocol in the case of an interstellar disaster."

"Too bad the ShadowMancer doesn't use hypergates," said Lola, and shook her head. "Oh man, I'm even starting to *sound* like you, Phin."

"What about the PPF?" offered Bella.

"Just enough juice for two trips," said Phin. "Or one trip for two people. Unless someone's got some extra baked beans lying around?"

No one did, and there wasn't enough time to go to the shop and fetch them.

"I can see where this is going, and I don't like the idea of the two of you headed into the lions' den alone," said Professor Donut.

"Wait, is that where this is going?" said Lola. "Phin?"

Phin had on his serious face. It was the face he used when his *I know exactly what to do* face was unavailable. "Someone needs to activate the gate to Dimension Why," he said, "and someone needs to go in after your parents. It's a two-person job. Specifically the me person and the you person."

Mr. Jeremy, who along with the Mega Mom was listening in from just outside the *Calming Breath*, beamed his thoughts directly into the brains of his compatriots. *"I will not hear of it, Phineas. This Mega Mind and I may travel through space without the use of your family's hypergates. Let us—"*

"Thanks, Mr. J," said Phin. "But no way you two are fast enough. The only thing getting Lola and me across the galaxy before any more planets get ShadowMancered is the PPF."

"YOU SHALL NOT UNDERTAKE THIS TASK ALONE," said Randall.

"Sorry, buddy," said Phin, and glanced at Lola, "but it

looks like we're tackling this one on our own."

No one said anything for a moment. Phin was right. It was a two-man job and just then there were no men on board, so Phin and Lola would have to do.

"I want to say something," said Lola Ray.

The assembled cats and crew turned their eyes, so to speak, on her. Lola hated public speaking, but these weren't strangers. These were her friends. No, they were more than that.

"Recently, for the first time, I found myself alone in the galaxy." She cleared her throat and continued. "And, um, it was a scary thing to be away from this guy." She nodded to Phin. "But when I found him again, he was with you-all. And it just made me realize that as badly as I want to find my family again, I've got one here, too."

"Corny," said Phin, and she elbowed him.

"We will always support you, Lola Ray," said Professor Donut.

*"And we will be right behind you,"* said Mr. Jeremy.

"We've got your back, girl," said Gretta. "This guy, I don't know." She waved in Phin's direction. "But you're all right."

"Har-har," said Phin. "Everyone stop doing speeches and goodbyes. This is all going to work out fine." He glanced at Lola. "We'll see you-all real soon."

Bella, who'd been hanging back, came forward with

Phin's Personal People Flinger. She handed him the device, her face stony.

"Thanks," said Phin.

"Don't screw it up," said Bella.

"I won't," said Phin, and tried a smile.

"I know you won't," said Bella, and gave his leg a quick hug she hoped no one saw, but in fact everyone did.

"Okay!" said Lola, and clapped her hands. "Everyone ready?"

"How's my hair?" said Phin.

"Floppy, as usual. How's my outfit?"

"Covered in salt, dried beans, and all kinds of galactic garbage," said Phin.

"Excellent," said Lola. "Anyone want to do a countdown?"

"One . . . !" said P-Money.

Phin pressed the button.

Everything went *Blat!*

There was cold and dust, shattered concrete, and twisted metal. Wind howled through the wasteland, sending little cyclones of debris twirling over the wreckage. Not a single figure could be seen for miles, and then there were two, standing atop a rocky outcropping that may have once been the eastern facing wall of an ancient skyscraper, sputtering and wiping baked beans from their eyes.

Lola and Phin had returned to Newark.

"Home, sweet home," said Phin, wringing out his shirt-tails.

"Phin, look!"

Lola pointed. Across the flattened rubble that had once been New Jersey, a single column stood tall, shimmering in the waning sunlight like a beacon—or a warning. Its surface undulated and rippled. It was a tower of baked beans, a sky-scraper sheathed in quantum sauce.

"Is that the Fogg-Bolus building?" said Lola. "What's happened to it?"

"My parents," said Phin as they began to make their way down the slope. "They've activated Security Protocol Seven. In the event of attack or disaster, the entire building is sheathed in quantum sauce. Nothing can get out, and nothing can get in. You could drive a bus into that," said Phin, nodding in the direction of his former home, "and it would blip through the sauce and come out on the other side of Alpha Centauri. Probably."

"But I remember Newark Airport being under your parents' building," said Lola. "So how are we going to . . . ?"

"We go down," said Phin, unpocketing his computer tablet and checking the readings. "Come on, this way."

The pair picked their way across the debris, moving closer to the shimmering, impenetrable tower of sauce. Lola had once seen this wasteland from Phin's penthouse window, but it was different making her way through on foot. Everywhere were signs of the lives once lived here. A hubcap, a doorknob, the remains of a microwave. The ShadowMancer didn't leave behind this kind of destruction, but what difference did it make? They'd all be worse off than Newark if she and Phin failed.

They came to a hole in the ground, though whether it was a naturally occurring gap or some caved-in tunnel Lola couldn't be sure. Down they went, beneath the crumbled skyscrapers and melted iron, down, down below the topmost layer of destruction. They followed the tiny blips of Phin's tablet until at last they squeezed between a pair of twisted metal doors and emerged into an enormous underground space. A bit of the ceiling had recently collapsed, letting in a single shaft of light from above. Lola felt a ripple of recognition. She knew they'd come to the right place.

"Is this it?" Phin said, scanning the environment.

"Oh yeah," said Lola. "Good ol' Newark Liberty Airport."

It was here, roughly a thousand years and eight weeks ago, Lola had stood with her mother and sisters, waiting for a flight to Vancouver. To see her father, to be together again as a family.

This time, though, things would be different. This time Lola would wind up exactly where she was meant to be.

"There!" she shouted, her voice echoing through the gloom. Phin looked where she was pointing. Over a huge hole in the floor and past the soda machines was a large sign written in the style of twenty-first-century Earth. It read: SECURITY CHECKPOINT AND ALL GATES THIS WAY. There was even a helpful arrow.

"Come on," said Phin, and they made their way to the first checkpoint.

There were no more roped-off lines, and no one waiting to check their passports at the security desk. The dividing Plexiglas walls were downed or smashed, and most of the X-ray machines had been crushed under a bit of collapsed ceiling. But there, in the middle, not quite as she remembered it but still recognizable, was an ordinary-looking security gate. The electronic sign that told travelers to WAIT or MOVE AHEAD was dark, as were the lights up the side. There was no mistaking it.

"This is the one," said Lola. "That's the gate I was standing in when I jumped into the future."

"Brilliant," said Phin, unshouldering his tool kit. "Let's get this thing operational."

"Are you sure the ShadowMancer will be able to find us here?" Lola asked, glancing around the devastated airport. She shivered.

"Nope," said Phin. "But seeing as how she homed in on the original Twinkie and, apparently, you, my guess is she can detect anything with a quantum signature. We turn this puppy on, and she'll show up."

"Right," said Lola. And then, after a beat, "Is this a bad plan?"

"No plan is better than a bad plan," said Phin. "But unfortunately, we don't have no plan. We've got this bad plan. So we'd better just get on with it."

"I think you've gotten weirder," said Lola. "I can't leave you alone anymore."

Phin hesitated, just a beat. "Fair enough."

They set to work preparing the gate. Phin had brought a small control module, pilfered from one of the *Calming Breath*'s automated coffee machines, and patched its universal cable into the base of a nearby terminal. With a few keystrokes he began to input the coordinates they'd lifted from the Twinkie's surface into the gate's computer.

"Whoaaaa . . . ," said Phin as pale green text began to float past his eyes. "Ready for some techno babble?"

"Hit me," said Lola, leaning in over his shoulder.

"It looks like this security gate was designed to scan passengers down to their genetic code. This thing was probably hooked up to some sort of database, a kind of human genetic phone book."

"What does that mean in normal-person English?"

"Well, it means the moment you stepped into this gate, it scanned your genetic code. But this is weird." Phin scowled. "It appears there was only one gene code in the system at

the time. Almost like this gate was waiting for one person—
*you*—to walk through it. Your dad helped develop these
gates, right?" Phin turned to her. "What the heck was he
up to?"

"I don't know, but can you get it open? People are dying!"

"Right," said Phin. "Just a little of this, a little of that,
and . . . *boom.*"

Phin hit the final keystroke. There was a flash, a pop of
sparks, and Lola felt the hairs on the back of her neck lifting.
A sound like the world's largest electric razor began to rumble
from the gate, a great electronic *fwoooooooooommm* . . . that
grew in intensity until a bolt of electricity seemed to dissect
the battered old security gate from top to bottom, splitting
the air and dividing it slowly until a seam in the universe
opened before them.

A gateway to Dimension Why.

Lola and Phin stared at it in wonder.

"It smells like static cling," whispered Phin. "And . . . old
coffee."

"Industrial cleaner, too," said Lola, and tried not to think
about what this could possibly signify about the nature of the
universe.

"Now what?" said Phin.

"The beacon," said Lola.

Phin produced a small communicator from his pocket
and programmed a universal beacon, just as Becca had done

on the roof of the Golden Cathedral.

"What do we want it to say?"

Lola thought about this. "I don't know. *Lola Ray is here?*"

"*The gate is open?*" suggested Phin.

"No," said Lola, taking the communicator. "I got it."

Not far away—on a galactic scale, anyway—a hundred Imperial reserve battle cruisers floated in deep space. Though their lights flickered, their stations were unmanned. On their bridges, piles of Imperial armor lay in pieces, some still semi-upright at their computer terminals. Recently occupied helmets rolled across the floor as the ships rocked silently in the void.

Amid the floating wreckage, a single survivor hovered. Or rather, two survivors.

The ShadowMancer tucked away her wand, still warm from recent use. She patted the hide of her golden steed and whispered in its ear that it'd been a good boy. She surveyed the destruction she'd wrought. She'd wrought it without breaking much of a sweat, but still she felt satisfied. It was good to be evaporating people again.

"Bullies," she mumbled to herself as one of the battle cruisers listed into one of its compatriots, steel scraping and buckling, silent in the vacuum of space, a great cataclysm set to *mute*.

276

And then the ShadowMancer heard something.

A faint signal flashed through the ether and tickled her cerebral cortex.

Now, there were countless signals flashing through space at any given moment. Radio broadcasts and military transmissions, entertainment programs and personal calls. They floated through the ShadowMancer's brain like so much static, but this one stood out. This one was for her.

Embedded in the signal were coordinates. A planet she knew well. Earth.

And then the message, which appeared in the Shadow-Mancer's brain in the whimsical font developed by Megabrinx executives to be the most eye-catching and annoying typeface imaginable, Cosmic Sans.

This is what it said:

COME

AND

GET

ME

YOU

MASSIVE

BOOGER.

## 30

**A STORM WAS COMING.** Outside, the wind was beginning to howl.

"I'm pretty sure she'll only come at me," Lola was saying. "But you should probably hide."

"I am . . . totally okay with that," said Phin, bundling up his equipment. "You sure you got this?"

"Yeah," said Lola. "The ShadowMancer will chase me in. If I'm not back in twenty minutes, close the door behind us."

"What about your family?"

"If I can find them, I will," she said.

Phin bit his lip. He looked like he wanted to tell her something. In fact, he did. He very badly wanted to tell her about Teddy, about his vision, about *one entrance and many exits.* Lola was going to save the universe, to save her family if she could. But that might mean never finding her way back to *him.* That might mean losing her forever.

If he told her, she'd have to choose between him and them.

*No*, Phin thought. He wouldn't ask her to make that choice.

"You ready?" said Lola.

"Yes," he lied. "I'll see you in half an hour," he added. "Then we'll have pie or something."

"Pie?"

"I don't know. Just . . . something to look forward to." He gave her a weak shrug.

"Okay," said Lola. "Save the universe, then pie."

Phin hurried away, not looking back, not wanting to, but desperately wanting to. He found a shadowed alcove and hunkered down. From his vantage point he could see Lola waiting in front of the glowing gate to Dimension Why. She looked small but determined. Suddenly, he remembered he hadn't told her not to swallow her gum. This instantly seemed incredibly important, and he was just about to shout to her, when the ceiling came crashing down.

Rock, silt, and concrete cascaded into the ruins of Newark Liberty Airport, ruining it some more. Wind and rain from the storm outside began to whip through the shadowed cavern. And then, with the pulse of great golden wings, the ShadowMancer lowered herself down from the raging heavens to land a few feet from Lola.

Pogo the golden dragon folded its massive wings and growled. The ShadowMancer slid from its neck and stood on the battered concrete, her hair whipped by the storm. Lola said something, but Phin couldn't make it out over the gale—or maybe that was just the blood pounding in his ears.

The ShadowMancer raised her wand.

Lola backed up a step. She backed up a second step. And then whirled around and dashed through the gate, disappearing in a sizzle of golden light.

Lightning flashed.

The ShadowMancer considered the gate, and then, after giving her dragon a reassuring pat on the hide, followed Lola into Dimension Why.

Less than twenty seconds later, Phineas Fogg said, "*Drab droof* it all," and went in after them.


Behind the world, there is another world.

Outside of space, outside of time, where *now, later,* and *before* lose all meaning, where there is no *here* and *there* or *up* and *down*, where there isn't even a *lunchtime*—this is the "place" Lola found herself.

Of course, Lola's monkey brain, which could only see in three dimensions, and could only perceive time moving in a single direction and within the visible spectrum of life, took one look around this incomprehensibly nonsensical world and went, *Lol, nope!*

And so, as human brains are wont to do, when it couldn't

comprehend what it was experiencing, Lola's brain made up a story, gathered everything into neat shapes, laid it all out in a comprehensible order, and said, *Here, see? Doesn't this make more sense?*

It didn't make much more sense.

But anyway, this is what Lola saw.

It was dark. Her footsteps echoed on what felt like a cement floor. Here, in the shadowy and hidden space behind reality itself, the air smelled like sawdust and paint chips, mothballs and rust. Once Lola had been backstage at a high school production of *Oklahoma!*, and Dimension Why smelled like *that*.

"Hello?" she called into what her brain told her was a large and empty hangar.

"Lola!" A familiar voice.

"Phin!" She turned and saw a figure moving toward her, heard his sneakers clomping. "What are you doing here?"

"Sorry," he said. "I followed you in. Couldn't let you do all the fun bits by yourself. Ow!" He rubbed his arm where she'd pinched him. "Yes, I'm real! You could have asked."

"My way's quicker," said Lola. "Hey, does it smell like paint chips in here to you, too?"

The two of them looked around at all the nothing.

"Wait, what about the ShadowMancer?" said Lola, suddenly spinning around just in case something was lurking menacingly behind her, but nothing was. "Did it work? Did she come in after me?"

"She did, I saw it," said Phin, sticking his hands in his pockets. "Though where she is now, I've got no idea. Do you suppose—"

*THUNK.* It was a sound like a massive industrial light coming on, which was accompanied by a massive industrial light coming on. Phin and Lola jumped. Where once was only darkness, now appeared a cone of yellow illumination. And there, lit up for all to see, was . . .

"Is that a golf cart?" said Lola.

It was not.

It was a bit like a golf cart, but longer, with more seating. It was a tram, the kind one might take to traverse a particularly long parking lot, or, thought Lola, remembering a trip to Universal Studios, the kind one might ride on a guided tour.

A woman was seated at the front of the tram, wearing a kind of friendly uniform and baseball cap. The tram, and the breast pocket of the woman's uniform, were both stamped with a logo: *DW*.

"Hi there!" the woman said and waved.

"Hey," said Phin to Lola. "Is this absolutely definitely *not* what you were expecting another dimension to be like?"

"It is precisely and exactly *not* what I was expecting," said Lola.

"We'll get started in just a minute," said the woman through a bright white smile. "Please take your seats so the tour can begin."

*Meanwhile, somewhere else . . .*

*A mind made of three minds turned to itself and said, "I think someone's joined us."*

*"She looks like the others. Perhaps they're related?"*

*"What about the boy?"*

*"Oh yes, the boy. Another of our players—his appearances span parts of the thirty-first century. I like him, he's funny."*

*"Wait, I recognize that girl—she's the time traveler."*

*"Yes, the daughter."*

*"Ah."*

*"Wait, hold on a moment. There is a third."*

*"Which? Oh, I see her now. The dangerous one."*

*"The one with the . . . instrument."*

*"Should we be alarmed?"*

*"Well, of course they cannot harm us."*

*"True, but the Entertainment!"*

*"Let's see what they do."*

*"Agreed. This could be interesting."*

*"Mm. Pass the popcorn."*

They took their seats on the tram. Despite the strangeness of its mere existence, it was otherwise a perfectly normal tram, with uncomfortable seats and a plastic canopy under which Phin and Lola now sat. The woman in the uniform grinned.

"Hello! And welcome to Dimension Why! Before we begin, does anyone need to use the facilities?"

"There's . . . a bathroom here?" said Lola.

"There could be!"

As if to illustrate, they heard another industrial *THUNK*, and a second spotlight illuminated a shining commode, standing alone a few yards from the tram.

"Everything you see, feel, and experience here is merely your mind's way of interpreting something it can't fully comprehend," said the woman. Her cheerfulness was infectious in the way a tainted burger patty hurled at one's face is infectious.

"Uh, no thanks. I've got a shy bladder," said Phin. He leaned over and whispered to Lola, "Have we gone crazy?"

"Many terrestrial life-forms find leaving the material world behind to be very traumatizing," said the tour guide in an alarmingly casual tone. "Well, I say many. There have only ever been a handful who have slipped the bonds of corporeal reality and joined us here, present company included! So, no takers on the bathroom? Okay, here we go!"

Phin and Lola looked at each other. Lola swallowed.

With a jerk, the tram began to move forward. Phin and Lola had taken seats in the second row, and though they were the only people on the tram, and they could hear the guide perfectly well, their host produced a microphone from somewhere and spoke into it, her voice reproduced with a crackle of static from the speakers mounted to the sides of the tram.

"Welcome to the place you call Dimension Why, a misnomer for several reasons!" She favored them with a megawatt grin. "Dimension Why is not, in fact, a dimension in the technical sense, but rather is sort of *behind* your world. And today we're excited to bring you a guided tour of the backlot of reality itself!"

"Wait, sorry," said Lola. "Who are you?"

"Please hold your questions until the end!" said the guide. "But you can call me June! Some of you may know me from such programs as *Dimension Y!*"

"That's where I know you from!" said Lola. "I didn't recognize you with the . . . well, with the uniform. How are you here?"

"How are *you* here?" snapped June. She grinned again. "Everything and anything is possible here in Dimension Why, where the laws of physics do not apply! At least, that's what we always say."

"Are there others here?" Phin asked.

"Yeah," said Lola. "We're looking for my family. They're—"

"Please hold your questions until the *end* of the tour," said

June with emphasis. "Now, if you'll look to your right, you'll see our first attraction."

The tram slowed, and dutifully, Phin and Lola looked to their right. There was another *THUNK*, though what was illuminated this time was not a tram or a toilet but a window. It was a large, wide window, like one might find framing a display case in a museum, but floating a few feet above the floor, suspended within the nothing. The figures behind the glass weren't stuffed buffalo or animatronics—they were real. The window looked in on a small, cluttered laboratory. Lola recognized it; it was her father's lab in Canada, where she and Phin had found the lockbox with the Twinkie. Though then it had been dusty, abandoned for centuries. Now it hummed with electronic equipment and swinging lights, as the very real man working at one of the long tables scowled over his calculations and wiped his brow.

Lola was out of the tram in a heartbeat and beating her fists against the glass.

"Papa! Papa, it's me! I'm here! I came for you!"

Behind her came a laugh that would have been chilling if it weren't so casual. "They do look real, don't they?" said June the tour guide. "What you see are just windows into a particular quadrant of space-time. I'm afraid he can't hear you."

Lola, heedless, searched the edges of the glass frame for a seal, a hatch, a handle. Instead, she found a broad green button with a label reading, *Press Here to Listen!*

Lola pressed.

Sounds of the laboratory filled her ears. The scratch of her father's pencil. A humming radio.

And then her mother entered the frame.

"Momma!" shouted Lola.

"As I said," said the tour guide, "what you see is just a window—"

"I think she gets it," said Phin.

On the other side of the glass, Lola's mother approached her father. She held a mug of coffee, and put her hand on his shoulder.

"I think I've figured it out," her father said, his voice coming scratchy through the cheap speakers mounted somewhere out of sight. "I know where Lola went, and it's all my fault."

"Baby, how could it possibly be your fault?" said Lola's mother, kissing his forehead.

"No, look! Look!" He showed her his calculations. Then in a whirl he was on his feet, pacing in front of a whiteboard painted with mathematic equations. "It was my gate! My gate that did it!"

"Yes, you said you designed the security gate at Newark," said Momma. She looked impossibly tired, as if she'd been listening to this sort of thing for quite some time and had hoped to take a coffee break.

"The gate was designed to scan people, right?" said Lola's father. "But not just their bodies, the company wanted it to scan *deeper*, down to the genetic code! But to start with, I had to give the system a sample, my own genetic code, as a kind of baseline." Her father paced back to the long table, his hands in his hair like a proper mad scientist. "But something happened when Lola stepped inside. Something about her genetic material, being so similar to mine, created a kind of feedback loop, a resonance pattern that grew and grew and grew until . . . it ripped a hole in reality."

"Vibrational dimensional tectonics," said Phin, who'd come to stand at Lola's side. "I read about that. It's just a theory, but—"

Lola shushed him.

"If my math is right," Dr. Ray went on, "she would have slipped out of time like . . . like someone taking a shortcut through a cornfield. She left the road, zipped instantaneously *around* space-time, and then would have reemerged . . ."

Her father trailed off.

"Emerged where?" asked her mother, some energy coming into her face now.

"I don't know," said Dr. Ray. "Somewhere in the future. Way, way in the future. With no way back."

"Does that mean we'll never see her again?" asked Momma.

At this terribly dramatic moment, Dr. Ray looked up, and though from his perspective he was most likely staring only into empty space, from where Lola stood, he was looking her directly in the eye.

"Not if we follow her," he said.

*Thunk* went the lights, and the window went dark.

"Ooh, how dramatic!" said the tour guide. "Now, if you'll please return to the tram, we can move on to our next display."

*Meanwhile, somewhere else . . .*

*A small girl with limp blond hair and a white robe that had seen better days padded in bare feet across what felt to her like a cement floor. She'd been here before, to this Dimension Why, but she didn't remember much of her first trip.*

*"Hello," said a voice.*

*The ShadowMancer instinctively readied her wand.*

*"I'm afraid you'll have a hard time erasing Us," came the same voice, and yet, somehow, not the same.*

*"Nevertheless, I'm happy to try," said the ShadowMancer, and sneered.*

*"You see," came a third version of the same disembodied voice, "we created that instrument you're holding."*

*"Heck," continued the voice in a different register, "we created you."*

*"And everything you've ever seen," it finished.*

*The ShadowMancer was not impressed.*

"I've erased entire armies," she said, raising her wand. "What makes you any different?"

"We are not an army," said the voices.

"We have no beginning and no end," said the voices.

"We are the Directors," said the voices.

"Well, whoopee for you," said the ShadowMancer. "Where are you, then?"

A door of golden light opened in the air before her.

"Through here," said the voices. "Come on in. We have a lot to talk about."

"Everybody on board? Arms and legs inside the tram at all times, please," June the tour guide was saying. "Okeydokey, here we go!"

With a lurch, the tram pulled away from the darkened window into Alfonso Ray's laboratory, and made its way deeper into the cavernous, infinite spaces of Dimension Why.

"Now, as fans of Dimension Why know," June continued, "Dr. Ray was quite correct. His gate *did* send his daughter Lola into the future. But you can't get to the future without first passing through Dimension Why. Though Lola was not conscious of it at the time."

"So I've been here before?" said Lola.

"You're here right now!" said June. "And please hold all questions—"

"No, I mean," said Lola, "I was here *before now*?"

"Lola, look," said Phin, pointing into the gloom. "You *are* here right now."

The tram turned slowly to the right, and Lola saw what Phin was indicating. Another figure, this one illuminated by another cone of light, and surrounded by red velvet ropes, like an artifact in a museum. The figure was none other than Lola herself, though she did not look her best. She was, in fact, mid-sneeze.

"Yeesh!" said Phin. "If looks could kill."

"Since there is no time in Dimension Why," June continued, "what you see here is actually Lola Ray traveling through time instantaneously, moving across Dimension Why from one entrance to another exit."

As they drew closer, Lola saw that her past self, the one whose face was quirked into a horrible goblin snarl, was in fact moving. She was floating, ever so slowly, across the floor. The velvet ropes moved with her, though on tiny wheels that squealed as they went.

"This is seriously bizarre," said Lola.

"I know, look at your face!" said Phin. "Is that what a permanent sneeze face looks like?"

"I think I'm getting a headache," said Lola.

"Yes, we advise not looking too long at your past self," said June, resting her chin on her fist. "Crossing one's own timeline may lead to migraines, stomach upset, and total psychological collapse."

"Good to know," said Lola as she looked away.

"Next on our tour, if you'll please look to the left," said June with a sweeping arm, "we can see the next chapter in our little story."

Another floodlight illuminated a second window. This panel also looked in on Dr. Ray's laboratory, although time had passed. Her father's beard had grown, and like its owner, the lab itself looked more unkempt and disheveled. Dr. Ray was at his worktable again, though this time he was preparing a lockbox.

"This is how I'll find her," said her father. "Now that I've adjusted the gate, I'll be able to enter Dimension Why and stay there indefinitely, without being rocketed out into a future time. Then, at some future date, Lola will find my note and we can reunite. It's the only way."

"Al," said her mother, leaning a head on his shoulder, "how do you know she'll find this box? How do you know she'll come here in the future?"

"I don't know," her father said, rubbing his face. "I don't know. But this is my fault, and I can't . . . I can't leave her alone out there."

Lola's father appeared to be crying. Lola also appeared to be crying, but Phin elected to examine the underside of the tram's canopy at that exact moment, and so he couldn't be sure.

"Then we're going with you," said Lola's mother.

"Angel, no."

"I won't hear any more about it. The journey, it's safe?"

"Safe? Well yes, physically it's completely safe . . ."

"Then we'll all go," said Lola's mother. "I won't break up my family anymore, Alfonso. I won't lose Lola *and* you. We go together."

Lola's father looked as if he were about to protest, and then his face softened, and he embraced his wife. The lab fell into a touching, melancholy silence, as if the universe were holding its breath for one tragic and courageous family, for one tragic and courageous moment.

"And next up I hope you're hungry because it's time for the snack barrrrr!" shouted June the tour guide through the PA system.

"Shh!" snapped Lola and reached out to place a hand on the glass separating her from her parents, or at least, this historical record of her parents. "They came here to be with me, so that we could maybe be together again someday." She whirled on the tour guide. "Where are they? They're here, aren't they? My mom, and my dad, and my sisters? They all came to Dimension Why."

"Oops!" said June, smiling and holding up a warning finger. "Let's not get ahead of ourselves. The next stop on the tour tells the third and final part of our story!"

Lola looked as if she were about to tear the tram and their guide apart with her bare hands, but instead she sat down hard next to Phin. "Then let's go," she said.

"And we're sure no one wants to stop at the snack bar first?"

"YES!" said Phin and Lola in unison.

"Then buckle up, sci-fi fans, because next we meet the villain!"

**LIKE MANY GUIDED TOURS,** this one was meant to end with a bang.

The tram proceeded through the darkness, as Phin and Lola squeezed one another's hands.

At last, they came to a stop, and June said, "Now, if you'll please exit the tram to your right, the show will begin in just a moment."

Phin and Lola exited the tram. The moment they did, it vanished behind them, along with June. Just poof, wobble, gone.

"What now?" said Phin.

As if in answer, more lights came on overhead. This time, they illuminated a stage. It was an impressive stage, with a big red curtain with gold tassels. Arrayed in front of it were low bench seats, the kind one might find in an outdoor amphitheater. Standing far to stage right, still holding her microphone and grinning like an idiot, was June.

"Please take your seats!"

Phin and Lola did as they were told.

"It's now my pleasure to introduce a very special guest. You know him. You love him. Please give a big hand for . . ."

"Papa?" said Lola.

"Professor Rivulon!"

A spotlight swung across the pleated curtain, and an invisible band played a fanfare. From between the curtain's folds, a mad scientist in a rumpled lab coat emerged, hands flung wide, blowing kisses. He was none other than Professor Rivulon, the fictional main character from Lola's favorite television show, *Dimension Y.* He waved as if facing a packed house and a standing ovation, though there was only Phin and Lola, looking on in mute fascination.

"Hello, hello," said the professor into the headset mic he wore. "Thank you, June, and thank you, everyone! Welcome to the end of your tour, and the Dimension Why Floor Show! Ha-ha, thank you! Oh, you are too kind! Thank you, please sit! Thank you!"

"We *are* sitting," said Lola.

"Let's give it up for your tour guide, my beautiful assistant, June!" said the professor as he clapped enthusiastically for June, who blushed, and bowed.

Phin and Lola clapped.

"Speaking of complete psychological collapse," Phin mumbled, "I think I may be having one of those right now."

"And what a beautiful night. You know, this is a very

special performance," Professor Rivulon went on. "Because not only does it mark the end of the tour, but *tonight's* show is, indeed, marking the end of the universe itself!"

"Sorry, what?" said Phin.

"Yes, after fourteen billion seasons, tonight we celebrate reality's series finale! But, as the song says, every new beginning is just some other beginning's end. Now, please silence all cellular devices, sit back, and enjoy . . . *the final act!*"

The professor swept his arm across the stage and backed slowly out of the spotlight as the lights went down and the show began.

"Did he say the universe was ending?" whispered Phin.

"Didn't we save it already?" said Lola.

"I mean, *I* thought we did."

There came music, tense and dramatic. And then the curtain rose.

Onstage was, once again, the laboratory, although this version looked as if it had been put together by, well, a set dresser. It was the live stage version of the room they had seen before, complete with whiteboard and scattered papers. In the center of the stage stood a large security gate, like the one Lola had passed through, hooked to machines and sensors with yards of cable and tubing. Above it flashed the sign Lola recognized from that day in Newark, the one reading MOVE AHEAD.

"The preparations are nearly complete!" said Lola's father

as he marched onto the stage, lab coat flying. "I've secured the note telling Lola where we are in this container," he said, patting the steel lockbox that stood open on the table. "And now I'll add the Twinkie on which I've inscribed the coordinates of Dimension Why." He held the snack cake aloft, the light catching its cellophane wrapping, before placing it into the box. "Now when Lola finds it, she'll be able to open the gateway, and we can all be together." He closed the box with dramatic flair.

As he did, Lola's mother entered. She was carrying Mary, who looked older than Lola remembered her, and Lola realized what she was watching must have taken place months after she'd disappeared from the Newark airport. Mary had grown. So had Gabby, who trailed after Lola's mother, holding on to her shirtsleeve.

"My love, what can we expect in Dimension Why?" said Lola's mother.

"Is it me, or are they more . . . melodramatic?" said Phin.

Lola shrugged. "The stage demands a bigger performance, I guess."

"I can't say, my pet," said Lola's father, sweeping her mother into his arms. "Things that are beyond imagining. But Dimension Why is our only hope to see Lola again."

Lola felt her eyes sting hot and sharp. She looked in the direction of the spotlights and blinked furiously.

And it was at this moment that the lights flared, and there was a sound of thunder.

"Look! What's that?" said Lola's mother, pointing toward the sky.

There was a rumble, a crash, and several pieces of "ceiling" fell to the floor of her father's lab (they looked more like painted rubber than actual blocks of cement, but still, the effect was startling).

And then there she was, the ShadowMancer. She was lowered onto the stage by a winch and pulley that whined and jittered, but the ShadowMancer cut a terrifying figure nonetheless. Her arms were outstretched, her expression cold and battle weary.

"Who are you?" said Alfonso, stepping in front of his wife and children.

"I am called the ShadowMancer, Eraser of Worlds. My enemies have pursued me across the galaxy. They have taken my wand and separated me from my steed. The one known as Skylar Powerstance rides as we speak on a mission meant to destroy me. But I have slipped away." The ShadowMancer leveled a tiny but imposing finger at the Dimension Why gate. "I sensed your machine, and what it can do, felt it ripple through the ether. This gateway is my sanctuary, an escape from my pursuers."

Lola's fingernails were digging into Phin's knee. Her jaw

clenched so tight her teeth creaked. It felt as if knots in her head, knots of confusion and uncertainty, were untying themselves only to retie again in larger, more complicated ways. The ShadowMancer's life had been entwined with her own in ways she couldn't have imagined. Now here, she was sure, was the moment her father and family were pursued into Dimension Why.

"Then come," said Dr. Ray.

"What?" said Lola and her mother simultaneously.

"My *knee*," Phin hissed in pain.

"Come with us," said Dr. Ray. "We are going where no one can reach us, where you can choose to hide for a time, if you wish."

"Alfonso, we don't know this person, this alien," said Lola's mother, gripping her husband's arm.

"She's a child, whoever she is," said Alfonso Ray, "and in need. If we're the only ones who can help her, so be it."

"Papa, no!" shouted Lola. "She's evil!"

"Shh!" hissed her sister Gabby from the stage. "There's no talking during the performance!"

Dr. Ray tapped a few keystrokes into the gate's control panel, and it sprang to life. A shimmering curtain of silk appeared, a version of the seam in reality done up in golden stage cloth.

"Come!" said Dr. Ray. "And may we all find what we're looking for . . . in Dimension Why!"

"Is there going to be a song?" said Phin.

With that the music swelled, and one by one, the cast made their way through the gate (and out, presumably, the back of the stage), and then there was darkness.

And silence.

And then again, light, as the cast jogged back onstage for a curtain call.

Phin and Lola clapped, dumbstruck.

One by one Lola's father, mother, two sisters, and even the ShadowMancer took a bow.

And then, Lola's mother and father took center stage. With a flourish, Mrs. Ray produced a baseball cap from somewhere behind her back and pulled it on, and all at once, she was June, their tour guide. Dr. Ray reached into his pocket and extracted a pair of goofy spectacles. Pushing them up his nose he was suddenly none other than Professor Rivulon, revealing a brilliant bit of double casting.

"Thank you, thank you," said Dr. Ray/Professor Rivulon. "Thank you so much for being such a wonderful audience."

"Papa!" Lola was on her feet. "Papa, it's me! It's Lola! I found the lockbox, and the Twinkie! I came back for you! I'm here!"

But Dr. Ray didn't seem to hear her. "And now that the show is ended, I'd like to introduce three very special entities that really require no introduction, because they're beyond all human comprehension!"

"This sounds bad," said Phin.

"Without further ado, please put your hands together," said Dr. Ray, "for the one, the only, the Creators of the Universe!"

The cast applauded as Dr. Ray swept his arm across the theater and gestured stage right. The spotlights swiveled, and Phin and Lola looked.

And what they saw totally blew their minds.

It's been said by many wise philosophers that sequels are never as good as the original. It's also been theorized that life itself is but the continuation of some other, earlier form of existence, and that the Creators of the Universe are merely trying to get it right the second time around.

In fact, the Creators of the Universe, who had been observing their creation for approximately fourteen billion years of nonconsecutive and instantaneous space-time, were beginning to find the whole thing a bit . . . predictable.

All those stars collapsing into supernovas, forming new stars, eventually forming planets that occasionally gave rise to life and civilizations and fast-food chains and movie studios that created other universes and realities within the original, only to be destroyed by nearby stars collapsing into supernovas, starting the whole inevitable process all over again . . . It was all getting a bit stale, in their opinion. After all, once you've seen one galactic civilization rise and fall, you've seen them all.

But in all those fourteen billion years, in all the trillions upon trillions of tiny subplots and story lines, for all the innumerable interactions that make up one microsecond of time in a near-infinite universe such as ours, nothing like this had ever happened.

The Creators of the Universe had been coming face-to-face with their creations lately.

This, at least, was new.

It had started with the girl, Lola, sneezing her way into their world through a rip in the fabric of reality, and zipping back out again sometime in the thirty-first century. Then, for Pete's sake, an entire *family* had wandered in, along with that ShadowMancer character—though she hadn't stayed long. Now the first girl was back, and had brought a friend, and frankly as entertaining as this had all been at first, things were getting out of hand.

It was time to wrap it up. Time to bring the Great Story to a close.

It was time for a reboot.

Phineas Fogg and Lola Ray were the first and only human beings to ever come face-to-face with the Creators of the Universe. It was the sort of thing you couldn't do again on purpose if you tried.

There was a desk. And behind the desk sat three perfectly ordinary people.

They were dressed in business casual, and on the desks before each of them were name cards, however, the names printed there—if that's indeed what they were—seemed to change as Lola looked at them, shifting like sand under the surf.

"Welcome," said the person in the center. She—though Lola wasn't certain the person was a she—wore dark glasses, with hands folded neatly on their desk. "You can call me Hattie. This is Ethan, and that's Babs."

"Hi there," said Ethan with a wise smile.

"Pleasure," said Babs.

"You've come a long way. Can we get you some sparkling water? Coffee? Eternal bliss?"

"Uh," said Phin.

The two children stood close to one another, uncertain what to make of this, if indeed anything could be made of it at all.

"So you're the Creators of the Universe?" said Lola.

"That's right," said Hattie.

"It was my idea," said Ethan.

"Yes, but I shaped it," said Babs.

"Everyone contributed," said Hattie. "And it's been great."

"Why," said Phin, "are you using the past tense?"

"And please feel free to answer with something

comforting," added Lola. "You know, just for a switch."

"We've really enjoyed it," said Babs, glancing at her colleagues. "Haven't we?"

"Oh yes," said Hattie. "It's taught us so much about ourselves."

"And has just been good, fun entertainment," said Ethan. "I mean a *really* fun watch."

"Remember when the Andromeda Galaxy collided with the Milky Way?" said Babs. "That was a laugh riot."

"Or oh, that squirrel outside North Hampton in the eighteenth century," said Ethan, chuckling.

"The one who wore an acorn cap like a little hat for a *week*?" said Babs. "Oh my goodness, hilarious!"

"Also war," said Hattie, looking wistful. "You know, in general."

"So sad," said Ethan, bowing his head.

They all seemed to agree that war, in general, was sad.

"But still, an enriching experience across the board," said Babs.

"Really fantastic," said Hattie. "And let's give our players a big round of applause, don't you think?"

"Oh *let's*," said Ethan.

The Creators of the Universe applauded for Phin and Lola, and for all people everywhere, in general.

"Thanks," said Lola. "Thank you," she said when the applause continued. "Okay, that's enough!"

Her shout seemed to echo in the great empty nothingness in which they stood.

The Creators of the Universe stopped clapping, and instead sat there looking a bit shocked.

Lola Ray, who was unfailingly polite, especially when addressing figures of authority, found herself addressing what could be considered the very highest authority imaginable, but she was all out of polite. She was out of patience, and out of understanding. She was, in fact, out of her universe and very nearly out of her mind. She pinched the bridge of her nose, took a breath, and said, "Here's what I'd like."

The Creators of the Universe listened.

"I'd like it very much, please, if me and my friend Phin . . . I mean Phin and I, and my family—that is Alfonso, Gloria, Mary, and Gabby—could all just leave now. If we could all just go back to our universe. And you guys can go on being weird in your crazy little backstage dimension here, watching or not watching, or what have you. Okay? Good? Yes?"

No one said anything.

Phin leaned in. "Wow, Lola, that was sort of rude."

"I'm sorry," hissed Lola. "But I've had a very long millennium!"

"No," said Phin. "I mean, I loved it."

Babs cleared her throat.

"I feel like we've gotten off on the wrong foot," said Hattie.

"Let's start over," said Ethan.

"I'm afraid you *can't* go back," said Babs.

"Because there's not going to be a universe to go back to," said Hattie.

"That's right," added Ethan. "We're closing down production. The big show is coming to an end at last."

"It was a great run," said Hattie. "But we want to go out on a high note."

"Right," said Babs. "And then, maybe one day, a reboot!"

"A new universe!" said Ethan, clapping. "Totally different! New essential laws of physics! Maybe we'll have time flow *backward.*"

"Oh, I like that," said Hattie, writing it down in a little notebook.

"Can we do away with mosquitos this time?" said Babs. "Never liked them."

"And thulium," said Ethan. "Totally useless element. Not sure why we included it at all."

"You can't reboot the universe!" Lola snapped.

"Why not?" said Hattie. "I'm pretty sure we can."

"What about everyone who lives there?" said Lola. "Like literally, *everyone.*"

"Yes, terrible shame about that," said Ethan.

"Hold on a minute," said Phin. "Everyone just wait. Pause. I'd like a moment to confer with my partner."

"Your . . . partner?" said Babs.

"Yes. We're going into business," said Phin, putting his arm around Lola's shoulder. "Galaxy Savers R Us."

"Ooh, bad title," said Ethan.

"We're working on the name," said Phin.

The pair of children turned away from the Creators, who waited, it must be said, very patiently while Phin and Lola exchanged urgent whispers. When they returned, they leveled the Creators with even stares, and crossed their arms.

"We'd like to propose a game."

"Accepted!" said Ethan, slamming his hand down on the table. He clapped. "I love games!"

"Wait," said Babs, a hand on his shoulder. "What kind of game?"

"A game for the fate of the universe," said Lola. "If we win, you don't reboot the universe and we get to walk out of here with my family. If we lose, you go ahead and reboot everything."

The Creators put their heads together. "That's what we were going to do anyway," said Hattie.

"Yes, but," said Lola, raising a finger, "this will make it much more *interesting*."

Babs, Hattie, and Ethan—who of course weren't really called Babs, Hattie, and Ethan, and who didn't really look like three perfectly normal people behind a desk—considered this.

"This might at least," said Babs, "be *surprising*."

"Oh, I haven't been surprised in billions of years," said Hattie wistfully.

"I say *yes*," said Ethan, and slammed his hand down again.

"Fine," said Babs. "We agree."

"What game do you propose?" said Ethan. "And *don't* say chess. That's such a cliché."

"*So* Ingmar Bergman," agreed Babs.

"No," said Lola, a smile hiding at the corners of her lips. "Not chess."

## 32

**FOR A TIME, THE** Creators debated among themselves how best to proceed. It was agreed that, being effectively omnipotent and omniscient, it would hardly be sporting for one of *them* to play. And so it was agreed a champion would be chosen to play on their behalf.

"And we have just the girl," said Babs.

"We'll arrange a special space," said Hattie. "Somewhere we can observe, but not influence, the outcome."

"Neutral ground," agreed Ethan. "That's best."

"But let's make it somewhere dramatic," said Babs, cracking her knuckles.

"Mm, somewhere thematically fitting," agreed Hattie.

"I think we're all in agreement," said Ethan.

"So, let's get on with it," said Lola Ray.

And with that, a door appeared. It was a glass door, the revolving kind, the kind one might see at the entrance of a shopping mall. Through it, Lola could make out a new space—a pocket world within a pocket world.

"The boy stays here," said Hattie.

"Agreed," added Ethan. "No one may enter the game area but the contestants."

"You got this," said Phin when Lola looked about to protest, and pulled her into a hug. "I'm assuming you've got some kind of brilliant plan?" he whispered in her ear.

"I have no idea what I'm doing," she whispered back.

"Good," said Phin. "So everything's normal then."

"Totally."

"Don't swallow your gum," said Phineas Fogg.

Lola steeled herself. She took one last look at Phin, and thought about her family, and the universe depending on her. And then without further ceremony, Lola stepped through the revolving door.

Now, it was understood that the Creators of the Universe could manifest pretty much whatever they wanted, and Lola wondered what kind of arena might be appropriate for a game to decide the fate of the universe. As she stepped through the far end of the revolving door, she felt a rush of déjà vu, as if she'd been to this place before. Which, in a sense, she had.

Lola found herself standing in the ticketing lobby of Newark Liberty Airport. Or at the very least, a perfect replica of it.

It was a sunny day. She could smell static cling and old coffee.

The airport looked just as she'd known it in her own time. The windows overlooking the runways were unbroken. The ceiling un-caved-in. The carpets were tattered and sad, but that's the way they'd always been. She was standing on the other side of the security checkpoint, looking at the long hallway down to the gates, and everything looked and felt perfectly normal. Except Lola knew this wasn't the real Newark airport. It was a replica, a clapboard copy, perfect in every detail.

Except, of course, there were no people. Lola was alone.

She went, "Huh."

She turned, expecting to see Phin and the Creators watching her through the glass revolving door, but there was only the New Jersey morning, asphalt, and blue sky.

"Huh," said Lola, in a slightly lower register.

This was, suffice to say, not what she had expected.

She wandered toward the departure gates, instinctively following the smell of coffee. Her sneakers squeaked, and the sound was uncomfortably loud in her ears. She came to a long corridor. There were food kiosks, there was a bar, there were stations for charging your phones. She could see airplanes parked outside, waiting to collect passengers that simply were not here to board them.

"Hello?" she called, her voice echoing off the walls of the empty terminal. For a moment there was only stillness, and then, somewhere ahead, a door opened. Light from some other part of this place spilled across the natty carpet. And then a shadow, elongated and terrifying, reaching its way out and out until at last a figure appeared. A short figure.

It was a young girl with blond hair, dressed in a flowing robe. It was the ShadowMancer.

The Creators had said they'd choose a "champion" to play for them.

She stepped into the terminal. Lola could barely make out her expression at this distance, but she looked . . . confused. The girl glanced around the terminal and took a tentative step forward. Lola cleared her throat.

The girl looked up, surprised but not alarmed.

Lola waved.

The ShadowMancer's hand, which had been limp at her side, twitched in a kind of tentative wave back.

"Hi," said Lola, her voice echoing.

"Hello," said the girl. "Are we . . . ?"

She wasn't sure how to finish her sentence, and neither was Lola. So Lola said, "Look, should we grab a coffee or something?"

As if responding to her words, the light over one of the small drink kiosks flicked on with a *bzzzzt*. A café table was illuminated, and on it sat two medium to-go cups. Lola could smell the crummy airport coffee, and it smelled like heaven.

"Yeah," said the ShadowMancer. "That sounds good."

And so the two mortal enemies advanced on each other, then broke left, approached the little kiosk, and sat.

"So," said Lola once they were situated. "I proposed we

play a game for the fate of the universe," said Lola.

"Yes," said the ShadowMancer. "You're thinking of the game you want to play now. I can see it in your mind."

"Ah," said Lola. "Hm. That . . . hardly seems fair."

"Perhaps you should have thought of that before you suggested this wager."

"We'll see," said Lola. "So if you can see into my mind, what's my idea?"

The ShadowMancer closed her eyes, then breathed out slow and steady. "I see a stone, which crushes everything in its path." Her brow twitched in concentration. "I see stories that cover the whole of time and space with their fabrications, their distortions of what is true. And I see a weapon that cuts, dividing us from one another. Power, lies, and violence."

"Interesting," said Lola. "Or, you might say strength, stories, and choice."

"Or," said the ShadowMancer, "in simplest terms: rock . . ."

"Paper," said Lola.

"Scissors," said the ShadowMancer.

"Shoot," said Lola.

They did.

Lola threw paper. The ShadowMancer threw rock.

The ShadowMancer blinked. She made a small noise that could have only been a grunt of frustration.

"I guess you can't see into my mind *that* well, eh?" said

Lola Ray, three-time Avon Avenue Elementary Rock-Paper-Scissors Champion.

"Best two out of three," growled the ShadowMancer.

"Right," said Lola. "Rock. Paper. Scissors. Shoot."

Lola threw paper. The ShadowMancer threw scissors.

The ShadowMancer, Eraser of Worlds, smiled. "Rock. Paper. Scissors. Shoot."

Lola threw scissors. The ShadowMancer threw scissors.

The ShadowMancer threw paper. Lola threw paper.

Rock and rock.

Scissors and scissors.

Paper and paper.

"This is ridiculous," said the ShadowMancer. "This can't go on. One of us has to win."

"Or maybe we do this forever," said Lola. "I'd like some more coffee, please."

Her cup was refilled. She took a sip. If anything, this cup tasted better than the last.

"*No,*" said the ShadowMancer, scowling. "No, someone's got to win. This needs to stop. All of this good and bad, wars and peace, I'm sick of it." She was actually snarling now. "All of the people, everywhere people. Why can't they just go away? It's time for everyone to just go away!"

"I couldn't disagree more," said Lola. "Rock. Paper. Scissors . . ."

"No." The ShadowMancer folded her arms over her chest. "I'm not playing. This game is dumb."

The ShadowMancer said nothing for a moment. Then she looked Lola in the eye.

"It's time for the story to end," she said.

Lola took a breath. She tried not to think about the monumental importance of her next decision. She tried not to think of what lay in the balance—which was quite literally everything. She tried not to puzzle out what the right thing to do was, or the smartest thing. Instead, Lola Ray would do the most Lola Ray thing. Now, and if they ever got out of this, forevermore.

"Okay, then," she said.

She held out her hand palm-side down.

"Paper."

"What?" said the ShadowMancer.

"I just took my shot. It's paper. Here it is," she said, and wiggled her fingers. "My little piece of paper. Now it's your turn."

"That's not how the game works," said the ShadowMancer.

"It's how it's working right now," said Lola. "I shot my shot. It's paper. What's yours?"

"That's cheating."

"How is it cheating if I'm giving you the advantage?" said Lola. She looked deeply into the ShadowMancer's eyes. "No contest. No even match. No *versus*. I'm giving *you* a choice.

*You* choose what happens next. My choice is to give you more choices."

Something rippled through the space known as Dimension Why. Somewhere—everywhere—the Creators leaned in and, it might be said, held their breath.

"You going to go?" Lola said. "Or am I just going to sit here for all eternity?"

The ShadowMancer stared at Lola's outstretched hand, then looked her in the eye.

"But I am your enemy."

"You're just some girl," said Lola, and shrugged. "So am I."

The ShadowMancer considered, and then, she made her choice.


"Well," said Ethan. "I didn't expect it to go *that* way."

"Is that allowed?" said Babs. "Seems like that shouldn't be allowed."

"They've got to *compete*," said Ethan. "Hardly seems like a competition if one of them just *shows her hand*."

"It was certainly," said Hattie with a smile, ". . . unexpected."

"I, for one, am surprised," said Ethan. "I didn't think that was possible anymore."

"Bit of a twist ending, that," agreed Babs. "Definitely didn't see it coming."

"I believe—" began Hattie, and they searched for the right

words. "That is, I believe . . . *hmmm.*"

"I believe," said Phineas Fogg, placing his hands palms down on the desk of the Creators of the Universe, and grinning like an idiot, "I believe we have a winner."

## 33

## WHERE TO BEGIN?

In our universe, what might be called the "real" world from a certain point of view, on the planet Earth in the ruins of what was once New Jersey, a thunderstorm was passing. In the underground chamber that was once an entrance to an airport, sunlight began to stream through the hole in the ceiling, and dust settled through its rays like snow or ash. The remains of Newark Liberty International were quiet, as they had been for centuries.

Then, all at once, there was a flash. A decrepit old security gate began to tremble and spark, and within its chamber a seam ripped open in the fabric of reality.

Some people stepped out.

"We're back," said Lola, her voice soft and disbelieving.

"We did it!" said Phin. "You did it! I helped, sort of! We saved the universe *again*!"

He wrapped his arms around Lola and squeezed until he was sure she couldn't breathe.

"Yes, I think we did," she croaked.

"Where's . . . ?" Phin started, but got no further. He was looking over Lola's shoulder. Together they turned.

"H-hello," said the ShadowMancer.

She was hanging back near the gate, looking considerably smaller and meeker now.

"Is she . . . ?" said Phin.

"I think she's okay," said Lola. "For now."

Then a new voice came to them through the gloom. "Lola?"

The three young people standing in the ruins turned to see who had spoken. There, on the other side of the gate, as if they'd just stepped through and had been waiting, oh so patiently, on the far end, were four very typical and cosmically insignificant people.

"Papa?" said Lola, and utterly, and completely, lost it.

Phin glanced at his toes as the family ran toward each other. Alfonso embraced his eldest daughter, lifting her off her feet and twirling her around. Lola's mother was sobbing, squeezing her daughter hard enough to break her.

"My baby, my baby," she said.

"Where *were* you?" shouted the middle sister, Gabby, and punched Lola in the shoulder, the Ray family sign of affection.

Mary, the infant, gurgled.

"Baby, where are we?" Gloria Ray asked. "Is this . . .

Newark?" She wrinkled her nose.

"Lola girl," said Alfonso, holding his daughter close. "I knew it. I knew you'd find us."

Lola was murmuring something into his chest, her eyes shut tight against the world, clinging to her father as if she'd never let go again.

Phin could just make out what she was saying. It was *Thank you. Thank you. Thank you.*

The world waited a breath, because the world can be thoughtful like that sometimes. Then Alfonso noticed the ShadowMancer standing awkwardly off to one side, and said, "You."

Gloria gasped and instinctively stepped behind her husband. "Al, it's her!"

"What do you want from us?" said Alfonso, positioning himself between his family and the monster that had menaced them. "Leave my family alone."

"No, Papa, it's okay," said Lola. "I . . . I think." She glanced at Phin. "Is it okay?"

Phin shrugged.

Lola turned to the ShadowMancer. "Do you . . . ?" she began, but went silent when the ShadowMancer brought her hand out from behind her back, her wand sparking.

"No, no," said Phin, and cast around for something large and deadly. "Not a chance, lady."

A gust of air disturbed the dust and pulled at their clothes.

Then another, and another, as Pogo the golden dragon lowered itself through the opening in the ceiling. The Rays, Lola, and Phin watched mute as the ShadowMancer climbed onto her steed. Together they cowered, watching her, watching the sparks fall from her horrible wand.

The ShadowMancer said, "I'd like to be alone."

She raised her weapon.

"Papa," said Lola, holding her family to her. She'd just found them; she couldn't lose them again.

"Wait," said Alfonso Ray. "I think maybe I can help you with that."

The security gate sparked, buzzed, and a seam in the fabric of reality opened.

"I can shut down the system from here," said Lola's father, squinting at the tablet Phin had connected to the gate. "This computer is *incredible*." He turned to Phin. "Did you build this?"

"What?" said Phin. "No, I ordered it online."

"Incredible," said Dr. Ray.

"Once you're inside, my dad will close the gate," said Lola. "Once his system is destroyed, there'll be no entering Dimension Why," she added. "Or leaving it."

"Good," said the ShadowMancer. "I'm tired of clearing out this universe. There are too many people in it, and evaporating them one by one is . . . exhausting."

"I don't like this," Gloria whispered to her husband. "She's a monster. She should be punished."

"What matters is keeping people safe," said Lola. Her mother blinked, surprised to hear her daughter speak with such confidence. Lola smiled at her. "It's okay, Momma. This is a good thing."

The doorway to Dimension Why pulsed with golden light. The ShadowMancer watched it glow.

"Is the scary lady going away?" Gabby asked.

"Yes, child," said the ShadowMancer. From Pogo's back, she leaned down and took Lola's hand. "Thank you," she said.

"Thank *you*," said Lola.

The ShadowMancer took one last look at the world she'd worked so hard to obliterate, and then, with a satisfied sigh, she and her dragon approached the gate, and were gone in a flash.

Alfonso typed a few keystrokes into Phin's tablet, and the gate went dark. He typed a few more, and his screen blinked, flashed green, and died.

"That's it," he said. "My system is deleted. No way to access Dimension Why. Not anymore." He smiled at Lola and ruffled her hair. His eyes traced around the room. "How long were we in there, Lola?"

"A *long* time. In fact, let me be the first to welcome you to the thirty-first century," said Lola, grinning like an idiot. She glanced at Phin, who'd been standing off to one side, hands in his pockets. She reached out for his hand and tugged him over. "Papa, Momma, Gabby, Mary, meet my best friend, Phin."

Once again, all eyes in the galaxy were on Newark.

Above the wasteland that had once been New Jersey, dozens of ships had pulled into low orbit. The SS *Calming Breath* was there, flanked by Mega Mom and Mr. Jeremy. In attendance were also the remains of the Imperial Fleet, local transit security ships, and about three hundred news shuttles, cameras focused on the hole in the ground where several people were now emerging.

Phin, Lola, and the rest of the Ray family stepped out into the sunlight.

"Holy—" said Gloria Ray, gaping at the six hundred spaceships floating above her head, which were six hundred more spaceships than she'd ever seen in her life.

"Momma, be cool," said Lola.

"Absolutely remarkable," said Dr. Ray.

"Are those . . . aliens?" asked Gabby, sticking close to Lola.

Lola took her sister's hand. "Some of them. See that ship there?" She pointed to the *Calming Breath*, which hung like an enormous white sneaker in the sky. Gabby nodded. "That ship is full of cats. That *talk*."

Gabby's eyes went wider than milk saucers.

Behind them, something made a tremendous *wumble-wumble-THUNK* sound, as the shimmering tower of quantum sauce enveloping the Fogg-Bolus building wobbled and disappeared. A pair of shuttle-bay doors opened on a high floor, and a platform emerged, suspended by a ring of blue-white jets. The platform swept out over the wasteland and came in for a landing a few yards ahead of Phin and the others.

"Oh, this is going to be so awkward," said Phin. "Can we please just skip this part?"

Barnabus and Eliza Fogg leaped from the platform as it landed and rushed to embrace their son.

"Phineas, my goodness, you did it again!" said Eliza, pulling Phin into a bone-crushing hug.

"Mmphh," said Phin.

"Barnabus Fogg," said Barnabus, offering a hand to Dr. Ray. "Fogg-Bolus Hypergate and Baked Beans."

"Oh, uh," said Dr. Ray. "Pleasure to meet you. Alfonso Ray."

"What business you in, Ray?" said Barnabus.

"Dad," said Phin, attempting to untangle himself from his mother's arms, "Mom, this is Lola's family."

"Such a pleasure," said Eliza, shaking hands with Gloria. "We understand you were trapped in another dimension. How awful for you!"

"Uh, yes," said Gloria. "It was."

"So, first time in the thirty-first century?" said Barnabus.

Before anyone could answer, a second shuttle caught their attention. It descended from one of the Imperial cruisers, flanked by a dozen class-A security drones. The shuttle, which bore the presidential seal, came in for a landing, its spidery legs finding purchase on the uneven terrain. The engines cooled, and a ramp lowered. A trio of round blue aliens wearing official Imperial sashes wobbled out.

"Announcing His Presidentialness . . . ," said one.

"The President of the Galaxy . . . ," said the second.

"Galactic President Blonx!" finished the third.

A recording of the Presidential March began to issue from the shuttle's speakers, and with much ceremony, President Blonx descended the ramp, dressed in the Presidential Bathrobe.

"Hello, hello, I'm here," said the president. "Sorry, thought I had time to squeeze in a bath on the ride over. Hello, I'm the president."

"Blonxy, you didn't need to come by," said Barnabus. "But since you're here, how about a drink?"

"Um, later perhaps," said President Blonx, and wrung the smaller of his two sets of hands. "I understand some congratulations are in order. A moment ago our sensors indicated that the ShadowMancer had vanished from this reality. Just . . . poof, gone." The president smiled nervously and glanced at the hole in the ground from which our heroes had emerged. "So is that . . . ? Is she . . . uh . . . ?"

"She's gone," said Lola. "And we won't see her again."

"Excellent," said the president, and breathed a sigh of relief. "Honestly, the stress of all of this was giving me athlete's foot."

"*Alien*," hissed Lola's mother, tugging at her husband's sleeve. "Al . . . it's . . . it's an . . ."

"Uh, hello," said Dr. Ray, shaking the president's official shaking hand. "I'm Dr. Ray, and these are my wife and daughters."

"That's wonderful," said the president. "And you, young lady," he said, turning immediately to Lola. "You were the one fighting with the ShadowMancer at the Slab. Did you . . . ?"

"I couldn't have done it without my partner," said Lola, throwing her arm around Phin's shoulder and pulling him close.

Phin looked surprised at first, then grinned.

"That's right," he said. "She couldn't."

Lola shoved him.

"Yes, well," said the president. "This is just a fantastically good day for everyone, then, isn't it? Where's the, um . . ." The president glanced at one of his small blue attendants, who produced a small tablet from its pocket and handed it to the president.

"Here it is, Your Presidency."

"Excellent," said Blonx, and cleared his throat. He

examined the tablet, squinted, placed a pair of reading glasses on the bridge of his third nose, and cleared his throat. "Then it is within the power vested in me by the people of this galaxy that I officially commend . . . um, what were your names?"

"Lola Ray," said Lola. "And Phineas Fogg."

"That I officially commend Ms. Lola Ray and Mr. Phineas Fogg of Earth, for their part in saving the galaxy . . ."

"For the second time," Phin pointed out.

"Oh, is that true?" said the president, glancing at his attendants, who nodded. "Well, that certainly *is* impressive! Well, then I officially commend Ms. Lola Ray and Mr. Phineas Fogg of Earth for saving the galaxy a *second* time, which has got to be some kind of record."

There was a smattering of awkward applause.

"Yes, good," said the president. "Clap for them! They deserve it. And furthermore, I would like to invite Ms., um . . ."

"Ray. And Mr. Fogg," said Phin.

"Yes, I would like to invite you both to join me at the Capital as Official Galactic Safety Consultants."

"Ooh," said Eliza, who loved the sound of anything important-sounding.

"Work for you?" said Lola.

"For the government?" said Phin.

"Yes, that's the idea!" said the president. "There are always new threats, and we could use a pair of quick and courageous thinkers like you."

Lola and Phin looked at each other.

"I think—" Phin started.

Suddenly, there was a flash of lightning. Wind whipped across the plain, and as suddenly as they'd departed, clouds gathered in the local atmosphere.

"Al, what's happening?" said Gloria.

The others looked around, bewildered. Electricity crackled through the air, and then, as they are wont to do, a hole opened in space and time. And a teddy bear fell out of it.

"Phin!" said Teddy, getting to his feet. "Phin, thank goodness you're here."

"Teddy?" said Phin, glancing back and forth between his old friend and the portal to the Probability Field out of which he'd just tumbled.

"The bananas, Phin!" said Teddy, grabbing him by the shoulders. "I tried to stop them, but . . . the bananas!"

"What bananas?" said Lola. "Teddy, what's going on?"

The Probability Field portal warped and rippled, wind howling through its aperture. The portal stretched, and grew, as something enormous moved on the other side of it.

"Get back!" Teddy said. "Everyone get back. It's—"

Something emerged from the portal. Something enormous and terrifying. And yellow.

"What on earth is *that*?" screamed Gloria Ray.

"Momma!" said Gabby and hid behind her mother and wailing baby sister.

"Lola," said Dr. Ray, his hand on her shoulder. "Is that what I think it is?"

It was a banana. A banana the size of a skyscraper. It floated out from the Probability Field and ascended into the airspace above them, dwarfing the Fogg-Bolus building and the gathered ships, some of which had to throw themselves into reverse to keep from smashing into the sudden, impossible fruit.

And then, in a voice that thundered through their collective unconscious, it spoke.

*"TREMBLE BEFORE ME, LESSERS. FOR SIX THOUSAND YEARS I HAVE SLUMBERED WITH MY FELLOW ELDER FRUIT. NOW IS THE TIME OF THE AWAKENING. NOW IS THE TIME OF THE GREAT PEELING."*

"What's going on?" Lola shouted over the wailing of the wind. "What is it?"

"It's Bah-Nah-Nah," shouted Teddy. "The ancient one! Destroyer of worlds! The god of chaos!"

*"THE TIME HAS COME,"* came the horrible voice. *"FOR I AM . . . INEDIBLE."*

Lightning forked from the inky sky, striking the Fogg-Bolus tower with a shower of sparks and smoke.

"What do you think?" Lola whispered to Phin.

"I think we've got this," said Phin, and turned to President

Blonx, who was staring in mute terror at the thundering Bah-Nah-Nah. "Mr. President, I'm afraid we'll have to turn down your offer."

"Uh . . . oh?" stammered the president.

"That's right," said Lola.

Thunder rumbled.

"Because this is a job . . . ," said Phin, "for Galaxy Savers R Us!"

The universe seemed to hold its breath, and then, like the start of something that would go on forever, President Blonx started to laugh.

"Galaxy Savers R Us?"

Eliza giggled behind her hand. "Oh, Phin, really."

"Yeah, that's bad," said Dr. Ray.

"We're working on the name," said Lola. She slapped Phin on the back.

"Right," said Phin. "You ready for something exciting and unexpected?"

Lola Ray grinned.

She definitely was.

# ACKNOWLEDGMENTS

This book wouldn't exist without the aid and energy of some excellent carbon-based life-forms, and I'd like to thank them here.

Thank you to wonderful agent and colleague Melissa Sarver White for championing Phin and Lola from the get-go. Thank you to my ever-growing Folio Literary Management and Folio Jr. family. I can't wait to see you all in person again.

Thank you to the superhuman who is my editor, David Linker, and thank you to the entire Harper team, especially to Carolina Ortiz, for additional editorial guidance, and to Robby Imfeld and Anna Bernard. A huge mega thank you to the brilliant Chris Kwon and Alison Klapthor, who created two wonderfully bizarre covers. Thank you to my saintly copy editors, Jon Howard and Megan Gendell. I apologize for my many, many, many typos.

Thank you to my clients. You are inspirations, and you do this whole author thing way better than I.

Thank you to Ammi-Joan Paquette. This story benefited so much from your early feedback and encouragement.

Thank you to my parents, John and Kate, and thank you to this trio of amazing women: Andy Hanley, Katie Cusick, and Deborah Jaffa.

Thank you to my friends and support network on sundry islands across the globe, especially Evan Simko-Bednarski, Adam Read-Brown, and Aaron Reuben.

Thank you to Damien Echols, Josephine McCarthy, and Lon Milo Duquette. Thank you, too, to the band DNCE for writing the greatest pop/dance album of all time (don't @ me), which fueled my writing sessions for this book. The Dimension Why universe owes a tremendous debt to its influences and inspirations. Thank you again to Douglas Adams, Terry Pratchett, Neil Gaiman, Robert Asprin, Shinichirō Wantanabe, and Keiko Nobumoto.

Thank you to my wife, Molly. Thank you for being a perfect partner in so many ways and walking with me through the liminal spaces of life.

And thank you, dear reader. So many mindbogglingly improbable things had to happen for you to be reading this sentence right now. Thank you for swimming upstream to be here.